LUNA GAMBIT

THE WILD NINES
BOOK 6

A.R. KNIGHT

CHAPTER 1
LUNAR STANDOFF

ollow the light. Easy enough.

Davin tracked the cherry glow with both hands, cupping the dot as it drifted up and down, left and right. Curls and sudden dips, the captain had'em all. At least until a long descent had Davin flipping over himself, floating as he was in the *Jumper*'s middle bay.

A modded out old freighter with its share of stories, the *Jumper* provided an even-keeled float from Jupiter's red-gold domination to where they were now, somewhere about interstellar kissing distance from Luna, from Earth.

Its hero would look a little different this time.

Davin completed the flip, did a mock bow to his physical therapist, a black-and-silver orb named Puk. The bot, not much larger than a basketball, blinked the red light off.

"You're progressing," Puk said, injecting some of that AI cheer. "I estimate you're at—"

"No estimates," Davin said, lunging for one of the handles spaced throughout the ship. The *Jumper*'s greasy gray-and-green panels embraced the function over form argument, as should anything built for space travel. "I'll be good enough."

"Good enough for what?" Phyla, the *Jumper*'s primary

pilot and Davin's squeeziest of squeezes—a term, if he said it aloud in her presence, would earn him a hard slap.

"Adventure," Davin said, kicking off the wall to head towards Phyla.

The kick came with a new sensation, a buckle and extra press as the leg braces boosted him along. The jolt came as a disconcerting reminder. Davin had, over the several weeks' travel time from Jupiter to Earth, come to ignore his braces. Their constant pressure no longer threw him off, instead adding mass to his movement, helping his fried and fractured muscles jump, kick, and hold form like they used to.

"Forever?" Davin had asked Riley when the mechanic first slapped them on. "I gotta wear these things all my life?"

"Don't know, Davin," Riley replied. The guy still sent his eyes everywhere, bumped into things as he learned how to roll with zero-G. "I'm not a doctor."

"But you built these?"

"Because Fournine said we should," Riley put up his hands as a frown slid over Davin's face. "Look, the AI's right. It's what all the videos say to do when you're recovering from hits like the ones you took."

The argument had about as much spice as the nutrient goop wallowing in the Jumper's freezers, but Davin accepted it for one reason: Phyla told him to stop being a baby.

Less easy to get over were the hardened patches along his chest and side. Seals slowly repairing laser and shrapnel marred skin from the last awful hours on Ganymede. Those bandages would eventually turn green and pop off.

Until then, anyone lucky enough to get a look at Davin naked would see a patchwork man.

Thankfully, the only person with that kinda luck stood right before him, reaching out to catch his floating approach.

"I think we should try again," Phyla said when their hands gripped. She stood as much as anyone could without gravity, on the walkway as Davin hovered over space.

"Getting a little old for kids, Phy."

She sighed, but smiled in that special way she saved for Davin.

"Alyssa." Phyla dropped the delight. "Eden's all over Earth. I don't want to stay here a second longer than we have to."

"You're just nervous," Davin said. "Once I flash this smile, the whole planet's going to be begging for my time."

"Says the man currently marked as the top terrorist in the solar system."

Davin whistled. "The top spot's mine?"

"Since they took Alyssa off it, yeah."

Now there was a question. No big broadcast the Nines had caught during their trek mentioned Alyssa's capture, death, or other horrible fate. She'd simply disappeared from the list, a broadcast blasted along standard comm frequencies every time a ranking changed. The only explanation Davin had found was, well, that she hadn't done anything awful for a while and Eden had bigger priorities.

Because Eden controlled almost everything now. Not all that long ago, the company had just been large. A mega-corp doing its part to own humanity. Now, with its grip over military, space, and most colonies off Earth itself, Eden was the de facto ruler of modern civilization.

Which made 'em, naturally, the bad guys.

Not everyone met the big expansion with flowers and kisses. Alyssa Reinhart, already a plucky fighter for the outer colonies, swept up the discontent and morphed it into actual resistance. Armed pushback against Eden's grasping hands.

David and Goliath stories tend not to work out the way the first one did. Alyssa's people had pluck, hell, she had a few Nines working for her, but moxie couldn't shoot lasers, couldn't build battleships. Outclassed, outgunned, and tricked—Davin liked to forget the part he'd played in all that—Alyssa's rebellion found itself blown apart.

And Alyssa herself? The shining star meant to guide billions to freedom from corporate crap? She'd gone ghost, even while her lieutenants adopted guerrilla tactics and made Eden's life miserable.

So miserable the big boy wanted to talk truce.

But Alyssa still didn't show. Eden wouldn't accept anyone else's signature on the proverbial dotted line, leading to a slow slide back into the knife fights on moons around Jupiter and Saturn.

And, eventually, Davin's crew was stuck with the task of finding the missing leader. Find her, get her to sign the peace agreement, return things to sanity. A cakewalk job for a bunch of mercenaries turned cargo haulers turned, now, branded criminals.

They had, at least, proved Alyssa still lived. Talked to her, even, before they'd blasted away from Jupiter. There, after performing some skullduggery on Alyssa's behalf, the Nines used their good graces to extract a promise: get to Earth and Alyssa would meet with them, explain the whole song and dance.

Except Earth wasn't, you know, an exact address. The planet crawled with cities, and those cities with people. Davin wasn't about to bop from one creaky mall to the next hoping to spot Alyssa standing in line for coffee.

But if she didn't reply, what other options did they have?

"You can't bail," Phyla said as the pair floated into the Jumper's four-seater cockpit. The two-by-two affair had that lived-in coziness, padded seats soaked in sweat, stress, and a few celebrations. "Opal would shoot you."

The old-school sniper might just do that. Opal packed more baggage than Davin in this fight, having done some devious death-dealing back in her Eden employ. She'd leapt at a leadership role in Alyssa's rebellion, only to find her ships shot out from under her. Hard to roll with a bad turn like that, but Opal feasted on vengeance like Davin feasted on scrambled eggs. She'd be fine so long as Davin helped get some Eden goons in her crosshairs.

The easiest way to do that would be getting Alyssa on the comm. Wherever she was, Eden's flunkies would be too.

A call out the cockpit brought back the same nothing as before. A static hiss. Davin and Phyla stared at the console, willing it to change. Beyond, out the sloping glass shield, Earth's blue shape spun, thumb-sized. At the moment, the Sun lay off to the left, its blasting light a constant annoyance going in this direction.

Like trying to fly with a flashlight pointed at your pupils.

"If she doesn't answer, what do we do?" Phyla asked. "With your friend chasing us, turning around won't be easy."

"We could duck him."

Captain Heath Swane, an android apologist and Eden scuzzball. Despite getting turfed to tacky assignments after Davin and the Nines proved androids were more dangerous to keep around than dump on the scrap heap, Swane nursed a grudge into a retread. When they'd met outside Jupiter, Swane sought to use Davin's execution-by-new-android as a PR stunt, to rescue his own career and rid his nightmares— Davin assumed, anyway—of the Nines captain in a single shot.

Things hadn't quite gone Swane's way, and now he trundled after the Nines at busted-old-frigate speed.

"I didn't get back into this life to be hunted again," Phyla replied. "If Alyssa can't give us a way to stop Swane, I say we take it into our own hands."

"I love it when you get aggressive."

"And I love it when you keep it together, because we'll need your best, hotshot, if we're going toe-to-toe with an Eden frigate."

A suicide mission, that, and they both knew it, barring a little cheat code in the cargo bay. The Nines had one functioning version of Viola's secret toy on board, a ship-disabling miracle device with a simple counter. If Swane didn't know the dodge, the Nines might be able to score a sneaky victory.

If the Eden captain read his mail, though, the Nines would be toast.

"Team meeting," Davin said. "We get the group together, like we always have, and pick a path."

"This was easier when it was just you and me."

"Yeah, but our decisions generally concerned which nutrient goop packets to eat."

"There wasn't a good choice then, either."

Davin made the call and a full seven, eight with Puk and nine if you counted Fournine, the *Jumper*'s converted android AI, meandered into the ship's middle. Like Davin, Viola—Vi—floated in tentatively, her torso and left arm still wrapped up in heavy, ointment-soaked bandages. Her eyes wore the puffy smear that came from pain-killing drugs.

Riley wasn't much better. Both had been lit up by lasers—much like Davin—during the raid on Vi's homestead. Riley at least kept the wounds to his extremities, and the legs at that, two of a human's least important bits in zero-G. If Vi could barely carry herself, Riley lugged a toolbox with him, as if this explained his place in the crew.

Merc and Opal drifted down together from the mess, where they'd been enjoying a meal nobody envied. The two had fast-tracked their romance, dialed it up thanks to constant near-death days. Davin respected their back-and-forth dialog, and the way both could turn an enemy to ash and laugh about it later.

Relationship goals.

Mox had already been in the center when Davin called the meeting, working out his exoskeleton's joints. All the carbon fiber woven into his muscles looked cool until you realized how much work it required to keep functioning.

A greasy hinge was one thing, an arm that wouldn't move was quite another.

"That's the situation," Phyla concluded, holding serve with Davin's lungs still raw. "We give Eden the business, or we go hunting for Alyssa."

"Do we have any leads?" Riley asked. "Back on Ganymede, we'd get big ideas all the time and realize we had no idea where to start."

"The frequency. We can track where we hooked into it last. It's not exact, and Alyssa might've moved in the, oh, three weeks since we spoke last. But that's what we've got."

"I'm all for knocking out some Eden teeth," Merc said, ditching an Opal handhold to scratch the back of his head, "but even I think we're going to die fast running up against Swane's ship."

"Seconded," Opal added. "You're saying he runs a ragged shop, but he'll have us outgunned twenty to one. You fly back at him, you drop us first."

A harsh start, but that's why the team meetings existed. Davin didn't run a dictatorship. The Nines had always been come and go as you please and as you profit.

"That leaves Earth, then," Phyla said. "We try to get to the ground where Swane can't find us, then dig up Alyssa's last known location."

"And pray," Mox grumbled.

"And pray," Phyla agreed.

Vi coughed, winced. "Do we know she's still alive?"

Silence. Eyes meeting each other, surfing the floor. Davin tried to think of something inspirational to say, but nothing bloomed. He blamed his own painkillers.

"Don't be dumb." Fournine's voice came from everywhere, lancing out from the Jumper's loudspeakers with a sardonic slant only a body-less robot could provide. "Your odds against Eden's frigate are basically zero. Your odds of finding Alyssa, while not much higher, are not zero. The answer is obvious. But perhaps not to humans, who seem so incapable of smart decisions."

Davin pointed a single finger up towards the ceiling. "You heard the android. Objections?"

"I'm here to end this war," Mox said. "Getting killed by an Eden ship isn't going to do that."

Nods, murmured agreements followed.

"Done," Phyla said. "I'll try to get us to Earth. You all think of back-up plans in case that doesn't work."

It didn't work. Back in the cockpit with Phyla, Davin watched as she beamed out a permission request. Earth's flight control rejected it immediately, beaming back that the *Jumper* and her crew were wanted for all manner of nefarious crap and they should turn themselves in at the nearest Eden station.

Phyla had Fournine draw up a digital middle finger and send it back.

Throttling down the *Jumper*, really just flipping the ship around so its engines would slow their arrival, Phyla put her hands behind her head and looked Davin's way.

"Told you," she said.

"So the obvious is out," Davin replied. "We can be clever."

"If *clever* means flying through Earth's defense force, then I think you're using the wrong definition."

"I think there's more than one way to get down there, is what I'm saying."

Back when Davin had first met Mox, the hulk had only just acquired his metal machination. Spurred on by vengeance, Mox had broken the rules and made some risky moves, ones Davin took as a sign that Mox matched the Nines' temperament. Part of the deal to bring Mox into the fold, though, meant realizing that revenge.

And the target had snuck onto the Moon through some more subtle channels.

"Not going to work," Mox said, still in the *Jumper*'s center, still greasing up his rig.

Phyla elected to hang in the cockpit, keeping an eye out

for any harassing patrols. Since contacting Earth, the local space would likely know sooner rather than later the *Jumper* and her wanted crew were around. The need to jet off or fight back might be imminent.

"You're about to tell me the Moon's tweaked their procedures, right?" Davin asked. He lay on his back, floating about a meter off the ground. Almost like laying in his bed. "That they're so good at monitoring traffic now, any sneaky play is foolish."

"Right."

"So foolish a Centurion couldn't get us through?"

Mox threw a narrowed glare Davin's way. "I want a life to go back to, Davin. Not sacrificing that."

"If you don't, then we have to dive down Earth-side. You know those odds aren't good."

"You're pinning me."

"It's what I do best."

Mox grumbled. Squeezed some oil onto a cloth and rubbed it along his left leg.

"Lucky you have friends like me," Mox said as he finished.

"Luck, or design?"

"I'm gonna design a new shape for your bones if you don't float your ass away."

"Appreciate you, Mox."

Luna's foremost former Centurion came through with a series of tight-band calls to the Moon. Thankfully, if there was one thing Lunar folks despised more than anything else, it was Eden. The company had ravaged the lunar economy, removing its gray plains as the kick-start to space travel by building orbital stations everywhere.

All because Luna wouldn't allow Eden to buy up vast swaths of its dusty regolith.

Mox took the conversations private, refusing to deliver names and details to anyone. Phyla and Davin waited outside the cockpit, sliding door shut, for Mox to appear with coordinates, docking codes, and a new name.

"*Stardust Swill*," Mox said. "That's what we're calling the *Jumper* while we're on Luna."

"Not much of a change," Phyla replied.

"It'll be enough," Mox said. "We land, we leave, they'll keep her sealed off."

Phyla issued one of her patented suspicious stares. "Sealed off how?"

"Evidence," Mox said, a slow grin. "We're criminals, right? Luna's gonna keep our stuff locked away until we get caught or turn up for a trial."

"And if we want to leave?"

"We gotta clear our names first. That's our ticket in, and out," Mox replied. "Either that, or give Eden enough trouble Luna thinks we've earned it."

"Phyla," Davin whispered, "this is the only deal we've got. We take it."

"You're telling me to leave my ship. I'd better get it back."

The pilot's words took on a sharper edge when she repeated them two days later, when Phyla and Davin were the last two hopping down the *Jumper*'s ramp into a dusty, near-abandoned docking bay on the Moon's dark side.

A motley bot collection waited to greet them, a remote-monitored skeleton crew meant to keep the two berths available for emergency landings. Tight ovals hollowed out in the gray sand, the berths lit themselves up in orange for the *Jumper*'s approach, and now shifted their spectrum to a pleasant blue-white as the Nines moved into the bay proper.

Davin told the crew to pack light—as if anyone on board had enough stuff to do otherwise—and the shambling collection looked more like wayward tourists than a hardened mercenary company.

At least if you ignored the hidden holsters, the long back-packs just large enough to store a rifle or, in Davin's case, a particular energy-blasting shotgun.

Mox's Centurion subterfuge served not only to get the Nines onto Luna, but also to secure them transport. The enclosed rover would be picking them up shortly, then would ferry the Nines to one of Luna's couple cities. From there, find a way to forge some IDs and sneak onto Earth.

Simple.

So simple, Davin actually napped while they waited in the bay's small terminal. The vending machines here, so isolated, held only water and, yes, nutrient goop. A disappointment so profound Davin could do nothing else save find one of the soft plastic benches and spread out. The rest seemed more interested in stretching muscles gone so long without even a hint of gravity.

To each their own.

Phyla's hand squeezing his shoulder pulled Davin back from oblivion. It'd been a nice oblivion too, free from worry, pain, dreams, anything. The look on Phyla's face said there'd be plenty of stress, at least, in the waking world.

"Our ride's close," Phyla said as Davin blinked sleep from his eyes. "They brought friends."

When Davin was the one making snap changes to plans, things were good. When someone else did it, well, Davin snapped open his bag and hauled out Melody.

"Any coffee in this place?" Davin asked as Phyla checked her rifle's power pack.

"Powdered," Phyla replied.

"I'll take it."

"Then get it yourself, captain." Phyla nodded back towards the doors to the *Jumper*'s bay. "I'm getting back on board to get her ready. Have a feeling we might need a quick exit."

The other Nines had themselves hustling too, gearing up

for a fight that hopefully wouldn't be necessary. Then again, Davin's history tended to be filled with unnecessary fights.

This one turned a whole lot worse when, powered coffee in hand, Davin saw Phyla stalk back from the Jumper's bay, raw anger etching lines across her face.

Davin called the Nines together with a whistle and Phyla gave the unfortunate update: the docking bay doors were shut, the *Jumper* sealed in.

"Can't blow our way through?" Merc said.

"These aren't thin," Phyla shook her head. "We'd need artillery."

"Then we're assuming those speeders coming in aren't friendly?" Opal asked, her look angling towards Mox. "Thought these were your people?"

"They are my people," Mox replied. "They're also Luna's people."

"They're cowards then," Riley said. "The only people after us are Eden, which means they're rolling over for—"

"For their lives and everyone on the Moon," Davin finished, putting a hand on Riley's shoulder to quiet the kid. "It's a bad call, but I get why they might be making it." His crew leaned in a bit to hear the whispered words, prompting Davin to clear his throat before he started in again.

This was supposed to be inspirational, and a captain gasping his way through a pep talk wasn't exactly that.

"We set it up right," Davin said. "Positions. Make sure these Centurions know a fight's going to cost them, and while they're thinking about it, I hit 'em where it hurts."

"You will not shoot them," Mox said, the tone brooking no argument.

"Don't worry, big guy," Davin replied. "Shooting's not what I have in mind."

The Centurions swept in on their speeders, encircling the docking bay. The Moon skiffs all had a couple flimsy turrets on the top, enough capacity for five and a pilot. Twenty

Centurions in all piled out, suited up for vacuum, their crimson capes drifting down as they came through the facility's lone airlock.

Standing there, looking decidedly less flashy in his burned out coat, wraps and patchy, torched hair, was Davin. Mox stood alongside him, law-breaking exoskeleton on full display. Sure, the Centurions had granted Mox an exemption back when he played for their team, but now?

A full ten fanned out before Davin and Mox, the other half taking the speeders to positions around the facility. Davin only knew this because Vi fed the details into his ear. With Mox's door-busting help, the engineer had the base's sole office and its attendant systems at her fingertips, including area scanners.

Truly a blessing to have a technical wizard on the team.

The lead Centurion, denoted by gold fringes on her cape and around her crimson uniform, strode forward. Rifles hung on one side, short spears on the other. A striking look, though a bit grand.

Not that Davin would ever say such a thing out loud.

The Centurion touched the side of her helmet with black-gloved fingers, the visor whisking away to reveal the serious face so often worn by people who valued duty over everything else.

Davin wanted to ask if she woke up every morning believing the fate of the universe was at stake, but held his tongue.

Authority figures liked opening things up their way.

"Davin Masters," the Centurion spoke with bold certainty, a judge delivering a verdict, "you are under arrest, as a—"

Davin sighed, loud. "I'm gonna stop you there. Can we do some intros? Feel like it's not fair, you knowing me, me not knowing you?"

The Centurion's eyes flicked to Mox, her mouth tightening. Her hand went towards the spear, which, Davin noticed, included a power pack built into its handle. The thing could probably send him into shock at a touch.

So Davin waved a hand.

A tiny blue dot appeared on the Centurion's forehead.

"Let's keep it friendly, shall we?" Davin asked.

The Centurion noticed the dot, or rather, the rifle creating it, and moved her hand away from her weapons. The other nine, thankfully, followed suit. Davin could feel their glares, could imagine the curses, the plans whistling through their comms.

"My name," the Centurion said, "is Commander Ferra Latrice, and you are making the biggest mistake of your life."

CHAPTER 2
MEDICAL MENACE

Not even Mox could keep his composure at that threat. The man laughed, a low roll that echoed around the otherwise quiet facility.

"Commander Latrice," Mox said, "do you know who you're talking to? This man has made more devastating mistakes than anyone I've ever known."

"He's not wrong," Davin took the wheel back. The bluster was starting to take a toll on his lungs, so he'd have to end the party here. "My deal's a simple one, makes us all look good. You give us one of your speeders, we take off. You get to claim you found this place empty, but you scored our ship."

Did it hurt to give up the *Jumper*? Always and deeply, but Davin couldn't see the Centurions stripping it for parts. Mox always claimed the Lunar police were reputable, honorable. A helluva thing to trust with the ship that'd been his home for decades.

But life kept pushing him into these decisions.

Latrice glared Davin's way, her fire giving a clue she wouldn't impinge her honor by making deals with wanted men.

Thankfully, Opal wasn't some novice who needed permission to take a shot. Latrice went for the draw, a light flashed, and the Centurion leader found her pistol missing the bottom half of its barrel, a dark line running along her leg where the laser scorched the uniform.

"Nobody needs to die, commander," Mox said after looking at Davin and seeing the captain's finger pointing at his throat. "This is an easy out."

Latrice fished her broken pistol from its holster, ditched it on the ground like a dead thing. She turned back to her Centurions and for a long breath no sound made its way to Davin. An earpiece aficionado himself, Davin figured there were hot takes spitting back and forth among the red capes.

Time to nudge them a bit further.

"Latrice," Davin said, mustering past the pain, "The *Jumper*'s AI will detonate the ship if you shoot us. It'll blow the building apart, taking you and your team with it."

Latrice held up a single finger, turning back Davin's way.

"You say you're here to hurt Eden?" Latrice asked.

"Definitely."

"And you won't tie what you're doing to Luna?"

"Not planning on it."

Latrice searched Davin's eyes for lies. There were none to be found.

The Lunar surface looked much like Ganymede's, all crater-pocked. Unlike Ganymede, though, the first half of their journey across the regolith zipped by in darkness. Davin, resting in a chair behind Phyla's helm, admired the view through the bubble glass.

"You get this in the *Jumper* all the time," Riley said, next to Davin. "Why is this so much better?"

"Not better," Mox answered, watching the stars like his captain. "Different."

"Something beautiful seen from a different side's still beautiful," Merc added.

The fighter pilot and Mox held down the speeder's middle, while Opal kept her eyes out the back. The sniper's rifle hadn't left her hands for more than a few seconds, but now she sensed Merc looking at her and threw him a grin.

"Usually she's watching me," Merc said with a happy shrug.

Vi sat on Riley's other side, already asleep. An easy move given the soft, bouncing ride as the speeder's microjets kept them aloft. It'd be an hours-long journey too: while Latrice and her group came from a closer domed town, Mox wanted to make for the capital directly.

More contacts, more options.

"And better doctors," Mox argued. "Eden will find us. You need to be ready."

"Vi too," Riley added, ever protective.

The crew had kept watch, but so far there was no evidence Vi had anything other than friendly affections for the man. Riley followed the fairy tale playbook, seemingly smitten with the childhood crush now returned to his life. Vi seemed happier to have back-up scrubbing out the *Jumper*'s air filters.

For his part, aside from amusement on a long, dull trek from Jupiter to Earth, Davin didn't give two craps. What people did, who they loved, wasn't his concern unless and until it messed with his crew's performance.

Thus far, Riley hadn't let the love blind him to the daily drudgery, so Davin let it lie, closed his eyes, and let the speeder's gentle recyclers soothe him to sleep.

You want a picture of life off Earth? Think small corridors. Simple white lights. Cramped boxes made for efficiency and little else. Nutrient goop by the liquid ton. Constant vibrations and thrums rolling off devices keeping you alive.

Luna defied all that. Or, at least, tried its damndest to make it look good. Flush with cash from mining and space operations, Luna's modest beginnings died as its population grew, throwing curling majesties up before Davin's eyes. Domes many times higher than the squat functionaries on Ganymede spiked towards Earth. Speeders, courier bots, people in their masses shuffled between destinations interlaid with hardened trees, grasses, bone-white tile. Musicians busked, fresh-made food wafted by, and confidence suffused it all.

These weren't scared, desperate scrappers on humanity's edge but ordinary civilians. People who expected their lives to go on without gunfights, catching asteroids, or catastrophic failures.

"Always found it boring," Merc said as they disembarked the Centurion shuttle. The fighter pilot helped Davin out into the crowded bay where, already, docking officials were throwing them expectant looks.

Speeders needed to be in and out here, not sitting in slots. At least Latrice had held true to her bargain: she'd given them a Centurian pass, allowed them several extra hours to get away before she'd report the speeder stolen.

"If," Mox had said during the ride. "If it gets reported stolen. No Centurion wants that on their record."

"Yeah, except she had a bunch of witnesses," Riley said.

"Not a one will rat her out. They all want to see Eden hurt."

Given Riley's stunned look, Sandeer must've not had that loyalty in his fly-by-night operation. The Ganymede bartender had roped in a motley fool collection, tasking them with sabotaging Eden's gradual control in small ways. Not too hard to imagine someone in that group, with little back-up and a lot to lose, folding under Eden interrogation.

Davin, for once, kept that opinion to himself. Riley hadn't ever been off Ganymede. No sense calling the kid out. Davin suffered his own hard education when he'd left Vagrant's Hollow, trading picking pockets on Miner Prime for running cargo and contraband across the solar system with crews ranging from slapdash to straight up murderous. You learned a lot leaving the nest, best let Riley figure it out himself.

The Nines split off from the speeder. Phyla, Opal, Riley and Merc hauled belongings—one thing made much easier in low-G—off to find somewhere to stay. A hotel that didn't ask too many questions, below the Eden pay grade.

Mox, meanwhile, would escort Davin and Vi somewhere for real medical attention. Or, at least, as real as they could get without identity verification.

If the Luna surface sparkled with refracted rainbows, artificial weather, and the promise of interstellar utopia, its undercity told the steel truth. Davin, Mox, and Vi headed down on a wide escalator, past the tram level and deeper into the tunnels.

"Feels like home," Davin said as they stepped away from the churning blue-metal steps and out into a greasy, steamy square.

People, always people, sprawled around them. At first glance, a mistake Davin saw so many make when entering Vagrant's Hollow, you could believe they were being lazier than their upper level counterparts. Some appeared to be lounging, others walking slow from spot to spot. Look closer, though, and you'd realize they were all hustling harder than their buddies up top, and for less reward.

"Eden sent me to Luna plenty of times," Vi said as Mox led them off a tunnel to the left, past a loan outlet and a cheap lab-spun kebab joint. "Not once did I come down here."

"We hide it," Mox said, not shading the words with any shame. Luna needed tourism to survive, the undercity didn't boost it. Them's the breaks. "We need it, but we don't like to admit we do."

"I tell that to Phyla all the time," Davin added.

"No wonder she's constantly pissed, you ass," Vi replied.

Puk, drifting behind them, let out a low beep. "You never say you need me, Vi."

The engineer rolled her eyes, leaned a little more on Mox's helping arms. "Help, I have a robot with self-esteem issues."

"You're a good bot, Puk," Mox said.

On the right, in a scattershot sparking glow, Mox's destination came into view. A red cross, that symbol of health and help, undermined somewhat by the signs hanging in the front windows advertising all sorts of questionable treatments for all sorts of questionable prices.

"Where the hell are you taking us?" Vi asked.

"You need something done without anyone knowing, you come here," Mox said. "We've let them operate for years, because it's better than having criminals die in the streets."

"I've seen worse," Davin said, pressing the call button next to the locked doors. "This place, on Io? Literally carved out of a wrecked ship. Used the old reactor for its power. Flip the wrong switch and everyone would go boom."

Instead, a charming robotic voice greeted them, said there were openings, and asked the trio to leave their weapons outside in the lockers provided. Once the three did so, the doors unlocked, swung open, and the nose-killing scent of formaldehyde and rubbing alcohol welcomed them in.

No lobby, just a double-wide corridor heading straight to a T intersection and a large screen. Price-grabbing posters dominated the walls on either side, screaming for this or that drug, this or that procedure: new limbs, nuclear anti-depressants, memory killers to keep nostalgia from gripping you too hard.

Not a single one bothered with disclaimers, with legalese. This, too, felt like home. Where everything was a risk, the only question was how much you could take.

"What a lovely place," Vi said as they walked, Davin leading and Mox bringing up the back. "How many organs will I be donating today, I wonder?"

"If they take any, I'll destroy them," Mox said.

"Your angry vengeance makes me so happy." Vi topped off the words with an eye roll.

"As happy as the prices?" Davin said, reading the screen. "I think we can actually afford these."

Not that Davin, if he really thought about it, was poor. Years working mercenary jobs, hauling cargo, and that blissful hero-of-Earth sponsorship cash infusion made sure his accounts were buttery smooth. That said, medical care had a tendency to torch even the healthiest accounts, which was why the Nines used to employ a doctor.

Getting patched up on the run was so, so much cheaper than a hospital visit.

"They skimp enough on the decor to cut costs somewhere," Vi said. "Which option are we taking, and can we pick it soon? The painkillers are getting soft."

Of the offerings, the comprehensive review and repair offering seemed to fit the bill. Davin double-tapped it, let the computer scan his restored wristlet from the *Jumper*'s stock, and the screen chirped an affirmative when the payment was accepted.

"I'll be back," Mox said, turning to leave. "Have some people I should see while I'm here."

"Leaving two wounded warriors behind, eh?" Davin asked, but before Mox could follow up, a hand tapped Davin's shoulder.

Going by the horrified look on Vi's face, Davin squared up his stomach for the turnaround. Goggled yellow eyes looked back at him, the apparatus bleeding back into a three-spike red hairdo and down into an outfit looking more at home at a butcher's shop than a clinic. The man had a wristlet in one hand and a syringe, loaded, in the other.

"Hello, hello," the man said, his voice as sing-song as decades sucking smoke could make it. Various addictions made their presence known on the man's visible skin, trails and bruises, yellowed patches. "Welcome to the best clinic this side of the shade." The man peered past Davin, clocking Viola and her expression. "Oh, don't worry. Looks aren't everything, especially down here. I find it's helpful, as a physician, to try everything my patients do. Helps me empathize. Bedside manner. You understand."

"Do I?" Davin asked.

"Well, you will." The man stood aside, waved them through behind him. "The name's Jarris Posey, and you're in the best hands Luna has to offer."

"Davin," Vi said, "we really doing this?"

Ignoring Jarris's goggled grin, Davin held out a hand to Vi. A braced hand, one whose every move crackled inexpert stitching, tugged at burned blisters still rippling over his body.

"We're already wrecked, Vi," Davin said. "It can't get much worse."

"A great mindset to have, my friend." Jarris nodded. "Never fear, though. Our treatments are second to, well, many, but none nearby!"

Davin and Vi followed Jarris into the clinic's bowels, which catered to the privacy offered by the front. Every room in the gridded out place had slate glass coating the entrance, blacking out the insides. Patient details, all anonymized, splayed across the glass. Things like heart rate, temperature, ordered drugs and scheduled procedures listed out in ways clear enough to suggest some skill was, in fact, at hand here.

Vi's breathing slowed and her snide comments disappeared.

"I know, the front is deceptive," Jarris said, "but we keep it that way for a reason. Our patients expect privacy, skill, and reasonable costs. We deliver all, as you'll see."

See, they did. Jarris dumped Davin and Vi into neighboring rooms, and within moments a combination of bots and masked personnel went in and out. Davin, lumped onto his bed, had his clothes tossed off in favor of a cream gown. The half-assed stitches were ripped away, replaced with strong salves. They stuck oxygen onto his face, had him breath deep while a whirling, blinding bot sliced and diced into his lungs. Torched tissue was scraped away, blisters were popped and repaired, and even older injuries, like a lingering bone bruise in Davin's left knee, had their causes removed.

And how long did this take? Davin couldn't tell. It all passed by in a fog, a bedazzling drug cocktail that had him swirling through past, present, and various futures without ever setting foot in any of them.

If there was a constant impression in that mental miasma, Jarris was it. The man kept poking in, those yellow eyes snapping Davin's slapdash senses back to the present. Jarris would lean in close, as if counting Davin's nose hairs, then pull back and nod. After this happened several times, with the nod growing more vigorous, more excited each instance, Davin saw Jarris again with shadows. The blurred forms didn't come close enough to take shape, but hung in the doorway.

When Davin finally gathered enough consciousness to wiggle his toes and feel his fingers, neither Jarris nor the shadows were there. Only a single, forlorn medical bot.

"Feeling well?" the bot asked as Davin blinked at its corroded gray, spindly form. An oval approximation of a face had been staked, like a scarecrow, at the top of the spindle, and it stared down at Davin with a fixed smile. "Your vitals are good."

As if vitals were the only thing that mattered.

But, Davin was almost ashamed to say, he was feeling better. His lungs didn't rasp with every breath, though they felt sore in a good way, like an overworked muscle. Looking down at himself, Davin saw healthy, fresh skin where blisters once marred, clear lines free from stitches. Some new scars, yes, but those were inevitable.

The medical bot kept talking, running down the list of treatments, procedures, and, as Davin sat up, recommended therapies.

"How much?" Davin asked as the bot finally came to a close. "No way what we paid covered all this."

The bot had Davin hold that thought till it could summon Jarris, who confirmed that all the treatment fell under what Mox paid for.

"A ridiculous deal, I know," Jarris said, giving Davin an apologetic shrug. "A smart man would adjust the terms, but I am only an honorable one. Nothing to do except get you and your friend back on the streets."

"S'pose not," Davin replied, and with nary a handshake and a hustle, he and Vi were escorted out the clinic's side door.

Melody and Vi's pistol waited for them, overseen by a pleasant bot in the narrow alley otherwise occupied by trash bins and a weak orange light.

"Better?" Davin asked Vi.

"Like a new woman," Vi replied, though she scrunched up her face as she said it. "I don't really know what they did, or how, but it worked?"

"If we didn't have Mox's guarantee, I'd bet on it all falling apart in a day." Davin slung Melody over his shoulder, checked his wristlet and confirmed the team's chosen hotel. "As it is, I'm sure we're full of illegal juice now."

"Just what I always wanted."

Davin threw her a sidelong glance as they left the alley, headed back towards the escalators. The team had found a place up on the surface, near an Earth shuttle port. Not a far walk, though Davin figured the hop-steps would be good for his lazy muscles.

"You've bounced around a bit now, Vi," Davin said, the Luna street around them busy in the early morning. Shop-keepers, deliveries getting ready for the day. "Done the daughter duty, the corporate gig, and played mercenary for a while. You have a favorite?"

"Guess which of those didn't involve getting shot?"

Davin threw a dart. "Being the daughter?"

"You'd think so, but I shot myself plenty with my experiments. Not with full strength lasers or anything, but you know how it goes."

"Again, do I?"

As they crossed the courtyard, both stumbling here and there while they reacquainted themselves with bodies not riddled with damage, busted tendons, or broken minds, Vi rattled on about her projects. Perhaps it was a childhood growing up in a similar sketchy place, but Davin picked out the trio fast. They lingered near the boxed-in entry to the escalators, sucking on jolt sticks. Their eyes were up, watching, not like the ground-bound glares from the working class shuffling through. The real people down here, they'd be busy keeping themselves clear of trash, would be walking a route memorized by days doing nothing but. These three? These three were hunting.

"—then I tried spooling up the battery to two hundred percent, and you should've heard my father when I blew out our entire circuit board," Vi was saying when Davin held out his arm to catch her latest hop.

"Let's go right," Davin said. "The next escalator's not far, and it's closer to the hotel."

"But it's so grim down here."

"Then treat it as an education in class capitalism."

"Okay, dad."

They swapped directions, cutting between a donut'n'-coffee spot and a scrap dealer. Luna, playing to the day-night cycle, had its lamps shading blue-gold for the dawn. Someone in the donut shop played news radio loud enough for the voice to spill into the street: Eden's stock shook up thanks to conflicts with Galaxy Forge.

Good.

Less good was that damn trio. Davin caught their reflection in the donut shop's glass windows, their shadows glaring off as they left their post and bounce-walked in Davin's direction.

"You're being so quiet," Vi asked, "what's up?"

"Do me a favor," Davin said, "keep talking like you were. Don't stop moving."

The three tailed them with purpose, but not urgency. When Davin and Vi left the courtyard, hit the side-street proper with its packed capsule housing burrowed into the sloping sides, the followers didn't speed up.

And if you weren't worried about catching your prey, it meant you already had'em trapped.

Vi's story cadence went erratic after Davin's ask, the tales veering into nonsense, cutting off and starting up again without connection. She could fight under pressure, could repair a ship as the enemy blew it apart, but Vi was no spy.

Oh well. Neither was Davin, and in another minute, it'd be time to blow this charade.

While they walked, Davin's fingers played on his wristlet, pinging the team their location, the situation. Replies were fast, with Phyla chipping in that she'd like to lay someone out after the frustrating flight from Ganymede.

"Davin?" Vi said, finally taking a look at her wristlet. "What's happening?"

"Another day in our storied lives, that's what," Davin replied. "Keep your hand near the pistol."

Up ahead, the street and its houses bent to the left, curling along with the moon's surface. Around that bend came a quartet matching the first three in slick gray-black outfits. The tones unremarkable, the clear eyes and bulges where weapons would be very much the opposite.

In seconds, Davin and Vi would be surrounded. By whom, he didn't know, but he could guess why.

Before they'd hit the Moon, Phyla had joked about Davin's bounty, about how much Eden would pay for the Nines captain alive.

"More than we ever made taking contracts," Phyla said. "How about that, hotshot?"

"Can I turn myself in to collect?"

"No, but I'm thinking about it," Phyla said, throwing a look around their quarters on the *Jumper*. "Could get this place a facelift."

To his left, some poor sap opened his capsule, heading out to work, to live.

"Sorry, buddy," Davin muttered. "Vi, follow me fast."

Davin bounded towards the door in a sharp hop, nearly colliding with the dude, whose face was buried in his own wristlet.

The sap, a squat sort with struggling reaction time, barely managed a yelp before Davin pushed him back inside the capsule, Vi following behind. The engineer knew enough to shut the door without Davin asking.

"Who are you and what do you want?" the man asked as Davin unlimbered Melody and pointed the weapon in the guy's face. "I'm not rich."

"You have a basement?" Davin asked, looking out the front window as the seven goobers assembled in the street.

"Yeah?"

"Get down there and don't come up till we're gone," Davin said.

When the man tried to protest, Vi added her pistol to the mix. "Now's not the time for questions. Do what he's asking, please."

Something in Vi's tone, something that didn't sound so cynical, so dried, tried, and dead, convinced the man to stop the blubbering and vanish down the capsule's stairs.

Otherwise the capsule held true to its name, a narrow single room holding the kitchen, the couple meters dedicated to a screen and a chair. Steps going up to the lone bedroom and a lavatory stuck in between.

And people thought living on a ship was bad.

"What're we going to do?" Vi asked as Davin confirmed no back door, no alternate entries.

"Ever been in a siege before?"

"No?"

Davin double-checked Melody's power pack, nodded out the window. "They're gonna come to us, and we're going to make them regret it."

CHAPTER 3
BOARDING: DEAD OR ALIVE

Davin's shoulders about spanned the width between the capsule's circular door and its front window. Vi stood to his right, one foot having drifted upon the upward stair's first step, retreat already on the mind as she typed on her wristlet.

The small living room showcased its owner's spare life: a single chair, cushions malformed and splotched. A screen too small for the plain white wall it hung upon. The heart, though, lay on those walls, which were bedecked with pictures framed one atop another, as though the house was built by those deep wood rectangles rather than the mortar, the regolith, the chemical bonds that'd thrown up this entire tunnel who knew how many years ago. The family in those pictures, going by the quiet, clean house, was long gone.

Wandering impressions tended to swallow Davin when his life stood at a precipice. Surprise him and he'd fall into the action without a thought, a whirling verb until the enemies lay dead, his team alive, the danger dealt with.

But the seven outside decided to take things slow. Gave the captain a chance at introspection, a chance taken because Davin felt pretty damn good for the first time in far too long.

He'd just acquired health and now, here, these jerks wanted to tear it away again.

"They're coming," Vi said, and Davin snuck a glance out the window, expecting to see the gang approaching. Instead they stood, the gray-white goons conferring among themselves. "I mean ours. Mox, Merc, you know."

Vi would be in Davin's same spot. Rejuvenated. So might the photographer cowering in his own basement. Davin would bet his hefty account the group outside was trying to decide how much ruin they could endure to score Davin's head—it had to be Davin's head, had to be that Eden bounty. If they went too far, Luna's Centurions would rip them apart.

"What's the strategy?" Vi asked. "We wait for them to kick in the door?"

Hell, if the Nines came here in force and threw down, the Centurions would come and take everyone away. Davin's team couldn't afford a street brawl. They needed a way out, one that'd erase the gang without implicating the Nines.

"New thought," Davin said. "How do we scare them away?"

Vi squinted at him. "Scare them away? What?"

Davin looked out again. Did a double-take. Only three enemies stood in the street, these all holding more conventional arms of thuggery: a bat, brass knuckles, and, of all things, a crowbar.

Where were the other four?

"Publicity," Davin said. "Luna's all about image. We get out that there's a gang terrorizing down here, the Centurions will respond fast."

"I can call the emergency, but you're a criminal, so . . ."

"He's not," Davin nodded at the photographs. A crack, a glassy crinkle came from above. "Get down there, get him calling for help in the most public way you can find. But don't put yourself on camera."

"What about you?" Vi said as she stood, looked up the stairs. "They're coming in."

"I'll do what I do best," Davin said. "Charm."

Vi shook her head, threw a look Davin's way as she hit the basement stair. "Don't die on me."

"They won't kill their treasure, don't worry."

They might beat him up, but he could take a punch or two.

Curling to the door, ignoring the stairs behind him and the morons definitely about to descend, Davin opened the spiral portal. Strode out into the street with Melody in his hands. The three goons eyed the weapon, didn't make a move.

"Gentlemen," Davin announced, loving the way the Moon's gravity let his coat, frayed and fraught, swish around him, "I get the feeling you're looking for me?"

The middle man stepped forward, bouncing his bat off a hand like some cliched movie cutout. His defining characteristic seemed to be his hair, which sprawled up and out in every direction like a spaghetti Afro. A silver crescent tattoo curled beneath his left eye. Tight-fitting clothes, snazzy shoes meant more for clubbing than the muck.

"Davin Masters?" the man asked, his voice glitching at the end of each word, a sign he'd had some implants put in.

Kids these days, nobody liked it natural anymore.

"Guilty," Davin said, savoring the word and spreading it out with a smile. Every second counted. "Who do I have the dubious honor of addressing?"

"Ecco," the man replied. "And you can take that dubious honor and shove it."

"Done and done."

Ecco jerked his head to the right, down the street. Behind him, Davin heard the clacks as Ecco's fellow henchmen descended from the rooftops.

"We're going this way," Ecco said.

"Have a nice walk," Davin replied, sticking right where he was.

Ecco laughed. "You're a cocky one, eh?"

The voice implant slid Ecco's accent around like a hockey puck, matching tones and places to make Ecco's history impossible to trace. Didn't matter.

"Look," Davin said, sweeping his eyes across the three in front then sidestepping to put the oncoming four, also wielding a mugger's medley, into view. "We all know where this is going, so let's make it sporting."

"This ain't about sport," Ecco said.

"It's about looking good, I know. So how about I give you the chance to show off before your buddies? A little one-on-one throw down with Earth's greatest hero ought to do wonders for your street cred."

Ecco laughed again, the noise bouncing up and down the near-empty street. The few passersby took note of Ecco's group and scurried the other way. A known crap quantity, this guy.

"Let's do it then, hero," Ecco said, and he went from bat-patting to bat-hefting. No ceremony, just a duel. "Right now."

Davin swept his left leg around, considered angling Melody up and blasting Ecco to pieces. Would've been satisfying, not sporting, and if Vi was working the plan, there'd already be cameras pointed their way. Davin, though, had his own reputation to consider, so he dropped the gun. Put up his own calloused, gnarled hands. His cocky grin slipped a bit as he caught his own skin, the wrinkles, the thinning lines.

When had he become so old?

Ecco gave Davin the courtesy of calling his own shot, stepping into a go-for-glory swing angled at Davin's head. The dude was still at distance though, so Davin did a little back step and watched the faux-wood, a light cherry mix, swish right before his eyes.

And caught the real play in Ecco's own. The spiker hadn't

been going for a decapitation, but a setup. Ecco's irises angled over Davin's left shoulder, giving the mercenary captain a split second's clue to prep a sharp elbow.

A heavy hand landed on Davin's jacket, and Davin drove his pointed left end to meet its owner. The blow stuffed its way into someone's gut, a grunted gasp all the evidence Davin needed. The hand lifted off his shoulder, freeing Davin for a sudden dash right at Ecco and his bat.

People that dressed and moved like Ecco tended to be actors. Players putting appearance before results, giving a lot of bark and ignoring the bite because it might get their clothes messy. Davin hoped Ecco went the same way, that he'd fold over after a couple jabs and call off the others.

Turned out, Ecco had earned his bizarre outfit.

Davin's lunge made it inside Ecco's reach, making the bat an awkward tool, but Ecco made the savvy play, angling the wooden haft in front of himself like a shield, catching Davin's first swing, a right-handed kidney shot, on the bat's fat end.

And ouch. Damn.

Ecco pushed back as Davin cursed, driving forward into the captain as a whistling told Davin something else swung at his back.

Thankfully, gravity gave Davin an assist. Pushing off with his right foot, Davin fell left. The pipe, corroded and red-orange, whisked over his shoulder, forcing Ecco back. The Moon's lighter tug gave Davin enough time to get his feet under him, a dancing move that must've looked ridiculous to anyone watching. That nonetheless bought Davin—

Two more thugs hit Davin from either side, the crowbar dude and another from behind with those grasping, leather-gloved hands. Gravity rescinded its help, leaving Davin stuck in a sort-of-slow motion, the crowbar crashing into his left shoulder, letting those hands get a stronger grip on Davin's waist, wrapping up for a tackle.

Before Davin could throw another elbow, the grabby one

planted him on the ground, face down in the stones. A soft buzzing filled the air as Ecco told someone to knock Davin out. Stun batons. Great.

The scum who threw Davin on the ground tried to plant a foot on the captain's back, to pin him. A neat move if perfectly done, but Davin's ratty coat and tilted body meant the step didn't stick. Davin rolled with the contact, sliding the foot off him and turning face up. The stomper slipped, giving Davin a clear view of the new guy with the glowing stun baton. This dude looked all business, shoving aside his bumbling pal and jabbing his glow stick right at Davin.

Davin leaned on his left arm, kicked up with his right foot and smacked the offender's wrist, throwing the baton jab into the street instead of Davin's chest. Planting his left palm on the ground, Davin pushed himself up and into baton man.

"Little unsporting, don't you think?" Davin huffed, trying to keep the sparking weapon away from his body.

At least the baton, and its propensity for numbing, kept Ecco's other goons at bay. Oh, they angled for a strike at Davin's back, but the captain kept his feet moving while he held his opponent's weapon away.

The world's dumbest, most necessary dance right here, folks.

"Give up already, man," Ecco said as the struggle went his way. "This is embarrassing."

"Maybe for you," Davin replied, while his partner-in-baton cursed him out. "I've got no pride to lose."

Ecco must've found some courage in that response, because he came in with that bat again when Davin turned his back. The man seemed to know what he was doing, but boy did Ecco make himself predictable.

Davin heard the step, saw the look in the faces surrounding him, and dropped the grip war for the baton, falling away as Ecco swung the bat in an overhead crunch.

Ecco made the adjustment—Davin's dive a hair early—

and clipped Davin's shoulder, throwing the captain again into the dirt.

But the spark. The flash. The bum with the baton thought he had victory in his grasp, lunged the freed weapon right where Davin would've, should've, been, and caught Ecco in the thigh instead.

With a yelp, Ecco collapsed, dropping the bat and matching Davin on the flagstones. A minor victory, seeing as baton boy, backed up by the others, still loomed.

Then Davin heard another surprised scream, followed by a gray-coated body soaring through the air over his head. The gangsters turned, brought up their weapons, and another went flying as he picked himself up. Baton boy noticed, said a real weak *hey* and jabbed towards Davin only to get smacked by the third body of a colleague to go flying in the last few seconds.

Davin could guess at the cause.

"Bit late, yeah?" Davin said as Mox, picking up Ecco's bat and wielding it like a sledgehammer, drove off the gangsters.

Five seconds later, the goons were gone, save a trio, Ecco included, too beat up to run.

"Came as fast as I could," Mox said. "Where's Vi?"

"Inside." Davin pointed to the house as he scooped Melody off the ground. "She'll be out shortly."

"Better be. We're drawing the wrong attention."

With the gray coats' retreat, the street crowded over with curious onlookers. Some stared from a distance, while others edged towards the bodies, eyes on the weapons, the clothes.

The same thing would've happened in Vagrant's Hollow: not only would you lose the fight, you'd lose everything else too.

"The others aren't here?" Davin asked.

"The others are going where we need to be," Mox replied. "There's an earthbound shuttle we can get on, and with this stunt, it's gotta be now."

As if on cue, Vi emerged from the house, tossing back a wave to the photographer guy, who peeked out at them before bringing up his camera for a long shot.

Davin gave the man a grin, held up Melody in an action pose.

"I caught it all live," Vi said as she joined them, with Mox wasting no time heading back towards the square, its escalator. "Said Eden's funding local thugs to attack people it doesn't like."

"Beautiful," Davin said.

"Why?" Mox asked. "I'm risking my reputation to get us cover, and you're blowing it?"

"And I appreciate that, my guy," Davin said. "But here's the thing, Eden's got to play a bigger game than us. They've got investors, a nasty public to keep happy. If we're lucky, Vi's video will help make us untouchable."

Mox grumbled that he didn't get the details, so Vi and Davin took turns rambling off the playbook: Davin was already a local legend, and while Eden had branded the man a criminal, they didn't have a counterweight to Davin's star power. Coupled with their earlier broadcast out beyond Saturn, the Davin Masters as Man of the People project was in full swing.

"They'll see one guy versus seven," Vi finished as they crossed the courtyard, keeping away from a Centurion squad dashing towards the fight scene, red capes flowing. "Davin will get sympathy points. Eden will go on the defensive. They'll have to be more careful."

"Best of all," Davin added, "no snipers."

Any kill shot now would look like Eden playing the wrong game, approving assassinations instead of rolling its wrongdoers through the justice system. Sure, Davin and crew could still be arrested, but outright murder?

"Lucky us," Mox grumbled at the finish.

"Damn right, lucky us," Davin replied. "Can you imagine

getting me in a court room? I'd have Eden arresting themselves before the day was out."

Sure, Mox and Vi rolled their eyes at that, but deep down, Davin knew they agreed.

You don't get to be a celebrity without getting used to watching eyes. As the trio ascended the escalator, Davin's skin crawled with uncounted stares. Some had to be collateral looks, splashing off Mox's imposing shirt-n-metal skeleton combo, but others held to Davin's face, their descending stares matching his stubble, jawline, ragged hair to the latest photos Eden blasted out.

How many did that because they recognized Davin from the news, had a faint recollection of someone important looking like him, and how many held the same gaze wondering about the Eden reward and whether they could collect?

"Jarris is going to receive a visit," Mox growled. "The man knows better."

A younger, more sassy Davin might've gone along with the idea. Jarris had seemingly sold them out, but Davin didn't know the details. Was it all about greed, or did the doctor have other pressures? Regardless, a service had been rendered, a valuable one.

"Don't bother," Davin said. The escalator had them shoving up towards a brighter daylight, morning advancing, and maybe the happy glow smoothed his mood. "Jarris fixed us up good. Eden's the one dropping the bounties, the doc's just trying to survive."

"Vi?" Mox asked. "You with him on this?"

"You think I'm not going to take the nice girl angle for once?" Vi replied. She raised her right hand, waved the wristlet around. "You know what's not pleasant? Sitting in a basement with a scared man wondering if you're about to get the crap kicked out of you again. Screw Jarris. You don't have to kill him, Mox, but if he's promising privacy, he should deliver."

Davin did the ol' double-take, appraised Vi's hard stance in the reflected sunlight as the escalator reached the surface. Traumas added up, and you could never tell which one would break you.

Maybe Ecco and his gray boys had done some real damage there.

The escalator dropped them up on Luna's surface, a broad square offering a traveler's banquet: shops, newsstands, maps, and more. Fresh fried doughnuts and their cinnamon scent wafted by. Above them, the escalator's grind was matched by air taxi terminals, the speeders whisking in and out with manmade efficiency.

Amid all that, Davin counted five separate groups keeping tabs on them. Several had hands inside coats as they lingered near benches, in the spaces between stores.

"Did that Eden bounty say alive only?" Davin asked.

"They'll take your corpse too," Mox replied. "The killer'd lose a bit on the deal, but they'd still be richer than you ever were, boss."

"Maybe I should pull the trigger," Vi mused as they took a hard right, cutting across the square. "Eden would never see that coming."

"They might even offer you your old job back," Davin said, trying to put his eyes everywhere at once.

Straight up murdering someone in the open seemed a risk not worth taking: you couldn't exactly collect a bounty on Davin without proving you'd killed him, which could land you inside a Centurion prison. Most of these seemed content to wait till Davin went somewhere less crowded, less watched.

"We're never getting on that shuttle," Davin said as they neared a cross-dome walkway. For anyone too cheap to pay an air taxi, the long, wide tubes shuffled people on moving pads between domes. Transportation for the common man.

"Why're you saying that?" Mox asked.

"You're not picking up all the people suddenly interested in where we're going?"

"We're walking with a celebrity, aren't we?" Vi said.

"One they'd like to knock out," Davin replied. "Mox, can we stay in the open the whole way there?"

"Not in the bays."

Luna and Earth sent an absurd amount of people and cargo back and forth. Given the gravity advantages, most everything routed through Luna first, the big boats docking off the Moon and shuttling containers onto Earth-bound hopper craft. Svelte little teardrops, the shuttles popped off bandoleer-like strands, entering into a declining orbit at precise points to end up at their preferred Earth spaceport. The buggers would suck up some fuel, reload on crowds and crap before sprinting skyward again.

The bandoleer nearest them, like every one on Luna, swapped beauty for bustle. No fancy domes, just circular launch bays lined up one after another. The entry, a squat and wide line-up, had consoles with a destination array, launch times, and remaining seats. According to some digging done while Davin and Vi were in recovery, the starting point for Alyssa's whereabouts was a city Davin had never heard of, definitely never been to.

"Quito?" Davin asked as Mox punched in the tickets.

On their left, the exit spewed forth travelers, many stumbling over themselves as they traded Earth's gravity for Luna's lack thereof. Not too long ago, during the cargo running days, Davin and Mox would grab lunch at a nearby cafe and chuckle at the rubes finding their footing.

Would probably be a while before they could do that again.

"You'll have to ask Alyssa," Mox said. "Opal used some of her old contacts to get the idea."

While Opal had gone diving for Alyssa's whereabouts, Mox had used his own Centurion network to conjure up some new IDs for the Nines. Phyla, Opal, Merc, and Riley were already beyond the gates waiting for the shuttle, and Mox scanned Davin and Vi through with him.

"What names didja give us?" Davin asked as they went through into the building, a not inconspicuous lineup following them to the consoles, no doubt buying the cheapest ticket to get through.

The fun, if any fun was to be had, would start not all that far ahead. Though it'd be an interesting sort: the bays had warnings plastered all over that weapons were forbidden past the cargo checkpoint. Mox scanned the wristlet again at one of several different screens, each scan spitting out a tag to slap onto whatever the Nines members wanted to send with their shuttle.

Davin pulled out Melody, gave her the new white patch, and sent her sliding along. Vi eyed her pistol, as if wondering whether the small gun was even worth it, but shrugged, stamped on the tag, and dropped it after Melody.

Mox took nothing, his big cannon left on the *Jumper*.

After the conveyor belt was a wide blue-black line. Warnings posted before the two-meter thick strip insisted anyone dumb enough to try crossing with a weapon would simply be warned to turn back, and, if they kept moving, would be shot immediately.

On the other side of the line, three automated turrets, each two meters high and glaring with red lights near their barrels, made the threat more than idle.

"Guess what?" Davin said as the trio took their first steps onto the black line. "Past here, it's all fists and feet."

"Or, you, know, we could try not getting in a fight for once?" Vi suggested.

The black line made Davin's body vibrate, an unnatural massage coupled with a faint burning sensation as lights and lasers beamed his body and declared it safe. Mox and Vi, too, were given clean bills.

Past the turrets, the warnings disappeared and the berth bandoleer put on a pleasant face, with restaurants, bars, and shops offering respite to anyone needing a pre-Earth pick-me-up.

"Where are they at?" Davin said. "We have a couple hours, right?"

Quito, not being a high-profile destination, only ran a single shuttle a day. Thankfully, that shuttle left in the mid-afternoon, perfect for a bite and a beer before departure. One Davin, at least, could use.

"You have a wristlet, you know," Vi said.

"Sure, but I'm trying to see who's going to kill us first."

The shifty scumbags who'd been eyeing Davin the whole time had followed them across the blue-black scanners. The bounty chasers took Davin and co's loitering and disguised themselves in dumb ways, like vanishing behind a store's clothing racks or ordering an ice water at the bar.

Mox, giving Davin a sigh, said, "They're all at the gate already. Phyla says we should hurry."

"She say why?"

"Yeah," Vi replied as Mox started off, Davin and the engineer padding after. "The pilot doesn't want to fly with our wanted butts onboard."

CHAPTER 4
IN THE SIGHTS

What's a wanted man to do?

Feeling rather infamous, with a gaggle of bounty chasers continuing to pursue, Davin joined his team at the shuttle to Quito. Looking rather drab, any futuristic mystique died at the hands of straightforward gate efficiency: a large screen against the musty steel back wall declared this was, indeed, the Quito shuttle. Next to it, a slim portal led to a docked shuttle unseen behind the walls. Chairs, flimsy and padded with only the cheapest plastics, sat in rigid rows.

Their occupants? Phyla, Merc, Opal, and Riley. Not another soul dared fill them, though that hadn't always been the case.

"We have a reputation now," Phyla said as Davin, Mox, and Viola approached—Davin slurping a scrumptious mango-banana smoothie. "Your video from this morning riled people up. Someone recognized me, tied me to you, announced it to the people here, and they all vanished."

Davin shrugged. "More room for us?"

"Yeah, except the pilot's refusing to fly," Phyla continued. Merc wore a small grin and sat next to Opal, whose eyes were shut. Only Riley looked the least bit worried; he'd noticed how many people trailed Davin's trio.

"Tell him we'll fly the shuttle down," Davin said.

"Like that's allowed."

"Phyla," Davin turned to the side, waved at the bounty chasers. One, a young kid, was so brazen as to wave back. "In case you haven't noticed, we're criminals. Why not live up to our name."

"Stealing a shuttle?" Vi asked. "Davin, that's—"

"Borrowing," Davin replied, using the age-old movie logic. "In fact, I'd say it's better than borrowing. We're going to Quito, we've paid for the trip. There's no argument against it."

"I can think of several," Phyla started, but Mox grumbled. Not words, specifically, but a deep noise meant to cut off conversation.

And cut it off Mox did.

"We can't stay here," Mox said. "There's too many after us."

"You could scramble them like so many eggs if they tried," Vi noted.

"Unlike you, I would prefer my job back when this is done. Where is the pilot?"

"How is it that all our adventures turn into disasters?" Phyla asked.

"I'd say bad luck," Davin replied. "But I think we just like'em more this way."

Davin's stride towards the shuttle was cut short by an accusing shout, beginning and ending with choice curses and Davin's name between. Hard not to turn around at something like that.

"You can't just leave!" called the same kid who'd given him away. "It's not fair!"

Shooing Mox and Phyla on towards the shuttle—the craft needed to be ready for an evac—Davin folded his arms as Vi,

Merc, Opal, Riley and, floating in forgotten from the ceiling, Vi's bot Puk formed up around him.

"What's not fair?" Davin called back, the crowd building. At least fifteen now, ranging from old to young, couples to trios to quartets. Most had hands in pockets, nobody openly brandishing anything yet. "What're you all looking for?"

The rabble had, in their haste to pursue Davin's golden goose, forgotten to elect a leader. That's what thinking only about yourselves would get you. Davin's cocked eyebrow climbed higher and higher with every tick of the moment's metronome, looks thrown around the place like darts. None struck home.

"You!" the same kid, finding some courage in desperation, called out as Davin started to turn his back on the bunch. "We're after you."

Clarity in purpose restored, the mob seemed to find their courage, edging forward around the chairs, across the hall—much to the confusion of poor ordinary tourists—and towards the gate.

"Davin, hate to be a downer," Merc said, "but I'm not feeling like brawling with all these people."

"I'd feel bad shooting them too," Opal added. "Did enough of that before."

Fair points both. Davin felt the pressure on his shoulders, the slight weight coming down whenever he had to make a captain's decision. Embrace the mantle, make the call.

So he whistled.

The noise, high and sharp, cut through the growing mob momentum. The closest two, a pair looked cut from a greasy cloth, their uniforms still on, came to a sudden halt. Had Davin just unleashed some rabid hounds or summoned Centurions to arrest them all?

Eden had built up his legend, marked him as their number one target, so who knew what Davin was capable of?

"Run," Davin whispered.

Genius came and went in many forms, and Davin chose to exercise his in fleeting footsteps, trailing Opal and Merc, with Puk buzzing along above, down the boarding ramp. The crowd, confused for a critical moment, found their voice and roared.

Getting a coordinated stampede takes time and effort, practiced soldiers marching in concert. Davin only had to listen to confirm the bounty chasers at his back were not such an illustrious bunch.

The curses, the shouts, the bangs, the frustration came pouring after Davin, and not a single enemy soul reached his back foot before it crossed the shuttle's threshold.

"Shut the damn door and get us going," Davin hollered, though he didn't need to: Mox draped the entry, slammed the thick hatch as soon as Davin flew by.

The shuttle lurched a half-second later, Phyla at the controls. The others scrambled to their seats, the design the same, if a smaller size, than the Galaxy Song's escape option. After a quick confirmation that nobody had suffered a stubbed toe or a surprise shanking, Davin joined Phyla up front in time to see the crowd's foremost fighters throwing up some pointed gestures their way.

Davin laughed, expecting Phyla to do the same, but all she had on was a frown while her hands danced across the shuttle's controls.

"To them you'd mean everything," Phyla said when Davin asked her why. "That bounty would change their lives forever."

"You trying to make me feel bad about running?" Davin asked. "Should I have held a contest, see who most deserved to drag me into Eden's arms?"

"If anyone deserves that bounty, it's me."

She turned the shuttle left, its microjets lifting it off the smooth rock. They would taxi away from the berth, out through a magnetic shield and into pure vacuum. The shuttle's AI would guide them to the take-off point, where Phyla would aim the ship right at Quito and cast off.

"Only if we split it," Davin said, but Phyla spoke up again before he could lace in another joke.

"We've got to find Alyssa," Phyla said, back in mission mode. "Eden's scared of her. She's the only chance we've got to make this change. Break their hold."

"And we know for sure she's in Quito?"

"It's what we've got," Phyla said. "And frankly, Davin, don't know if you've noticed, but we don't have many options at this point."

"Then I say we go for this one with all the speed we can."

"Doing and done."

The shuttle glided free from the docking bay's dome, angled upward from the Moon, and rattled as its bigger engines kicked in. Not quite the *Jumper*'s level of killer thrust, but enough to push Davin back in his seat, give him some more weight.

Not a bad thing, seeing as Earth would be the heaviest spot he'd touched in quite a long time. No matter the amount of exercise, no matter the amount of muscle-boosting nutrient goop he drank, returning to one G always felt a bit like getting drunk and gaining a hundred kilos.

Earth itself sat above and to the right, its blue-white wash blocking out the stars before them. A strict green trail blazed out the windshield, angling ahead and to the left. Their path, and one Phyla wouldn't have a chance to alter unless things went wrong.

"You're just an ornament, huh?" Davin asked as the Moon fell away below and behind them.

"Not for long." Phyla pointed at the central console.

Shapes in all colors and sizes splashed across the large screen, a muddled backdrop only intelligible to those who'd been taught. Every shape meant a ship, a space station, or some debris large enough to worry about. Colors indicated speed and proximity: a red diamond showed a ship that might be on an intercept path, while a green circle meant a station on radar's edge moving away.

Phyla pointed to a red diamond trio, a selection moving away from a yellow square, meaning a larger ship.

"Too far away yet to know for sure," Phyla said, "but I'd bet your life that those are Eden interceptors."

"My life?"

"I don't gamble with my own," Phyla winked.

"Says the racer."

Davin reached for the shuttle's comm system to warn the group, then stopped. Captains had to have plans, had to have ways to respond when the mission turned ugly. Just because this one had been ugly for a while now didn't mean Davin had an excuse to squawk scared.

"Can you outfly them?" Davin asked.

"In this boat, I'd be hard pressed to outfly an asteroid."

Phyla, though, didn't have the clenched teeth or the razor eyes she normally showed when pressed into a crap panini. Gears turned beneath that red hair and cranked out an idea.

So Davin asked what the hell had her so calm.

"We're going to use you again," Phyla said. "Earth, too."

"Right," Davin nodded. "But, just so I'm clear, can you explain what you mean by that?"

Phyla tapped the console, zooming in on a cluster hovering near Earth's outer orbit.

"Eden owns a lot, but they don't own Earth or its defense force. In another thirty seconds we'll be in comm range, and that's when you work your magic, Davin."

"By screaming for help?"

"Eden gets to make its bounties, but they don't get to break Earth law. We get inside Earth's jurisdiction, you can plead for a trial. Declare there are innocents on board, like Vi and Mox here. Eden doesn't have them named, not to mention all the Earth property in this shuttle's hold."

"You mean they didn't—"

"Yeah, after the pilot bailed, so did the passengers, but nobody took out their luggage. So we're sitting with all kinds of good reasons not to space us." Phyla pointed at the comm. "Go time, and make it fast. We've got two minutes before those Eden Vipers can blast our asses."

Contrary to the odd souls manning comms in the solar system's outer reaches—you had to be a bit off to clock the phones out by Saturn—Earth gave Davin a straight conversation. They listened, he spoke, they asked questions, Davin gave them the slanted answers they needed. A succinct summary: one of Earth's greatest living heroes was about to be gunned down in cold blood above Earth's own atmosphere, and with a few priceless bits of Earth property to boot.

Earth dispatched fighters, sent a warning to the Eden trio. Phyla sighed, sat back, all relieved. Davin gave into his cocky grin, told Phyla that it was pretty wonderful to be famous.

The red diamonds didn't stop.

"What're they doing?" Davin said, pointing at the shapes, still closing. Less than fifteen seconds to laser range. "Shouldn't they be turning back?"

"Should be," Phyla said. She reached, pressed a different button on the console's screen, wiping away local radar for a visual readout. The shuttle's cameras weren't exactly top tier, but this close, they could snag a solid picture.

A clear enough view of fighters that weren't Vipers, that weren't bulkier spheres, but instead an arrow both pilot and co-pilot recognized.

The same damn drone fighter that'd torched Phyla's shuttle back near Jupiter. Which meant that yellow square had to be the idiotic, the omnipresent, the annoying captain Heath Swane.

"He's ignoring Earth," Phyla said, slapping at buttons and pulling on levers in rapid succession. The shuttle juddered with the presses, the green path blazing out the windshield fading as Phyla pulled the flight into manual. "He'll claim it was a malfunction or something."

"We must've really made him angry."

"No," Davin said, "it's still a PR stunt. He wants to show his fighters can catch and kill anyone, anywhere, and dodge the legal liability."

"Clever bastard."

"Don't give him that credit, he's just a desperate maniac," Davin said, then flipped on the shuttle's internal comm. "Strap in, people. It's about to get interesting."

Phyla, meanwhile, opened a second band to Earth, bumping up the panic. Earth's dispatcher had the grace to get angry, say that Eden's been getting a bit too big for their britches lately.

"Then teach'em a lesson," Phyla said.

As if hearing her directly, the four yellow diamonds showing Earth's fighters kicked up their acceleration, blitzing across the console in a tighter orbit to intercept Eden's trio.

An intercept that'd come well after Eden could nuke the Nines' shuttle.

The first rule to fighting in a new ship was to make that new ship feel as familiar as possible. Davin and Phyla used the last ten seconds to scan every possible button, switch, configuration they could find. That they completed the scan in ten seconds showed how little they had to work with.

Phyla broke their flight path first, burned the shuttle away from the approaching Eden fighters and cranked up the engines, draining batteries not meant to be used until it came time to rocket back off Earth's surface.

So there'd be a bit of a delay on the outbound. Oh well.

Davin shifted the shuttle's shield energy, a paltry amount meant for atmospheric entry and micro-meteor protection, to cover their butts.

The only other option? A single lifeboat, capable of

holding everyone on the shuttle if they mashed themselves in like sardines. The Nines would find it plenty cozy, though.

"At least we can run," Davin said as the Eden androids kicked into their opening salvos.

"We drop out now, they'll blow us before we hit atmosphere," Phyla replied, juking the fat shuttle to port. Declining the orbit bit by bit. "We've gotta get into cover first."

The first hit came as she finished the sentence, the lead drone fighter delivering a searing strike to the shuttle's left rocket. The shields sucked up most of the burn, but a flashing indicator still popped on the console.

Twenty percent of their thrust gone.

"New plan," Phyla said, twisting the shuttle hard as the drones neared. The Eden fighters, racing to close, had to flip, too, and their velocity carried them past the shuttle. Laser fire splashed all around. "We have to protect the engines or we'll fall to the ground like a rock."

On an asteroid, hell, on the Moon that might be fine. On Earth, everyone inside would get pancaked. Real gross.

"Got it," Davin said, feeling a bit useless. There had to be another option. He slid the shields as Phyla continued the turn, burning the engines hard then cutting them as the shuttle's cockpit faced the fighters. "What if we do something different?"

"Different?" Phyla kicked on the shuttle's maneuvering jets. The things were too slow for dog-fighting, but would keep the shuttle from sitting still. With Earth now sitting above them, Phyla shunted the shuttle that way, closing the distance. "What kind of different?"

On Davin's right, four little buttons controlled the shuttle's cargo compartments. Each one could be opened, shut from the front, giving the shuttle more means to control its weight in a catastrophe's event.

He flipped the first one, ejecting who knew what into

space. Melody might've been in the mess, a chance Davin hated, but his beautiful shotgun wouldn't mean anything if its owner became space dust.

"Kick the reverse jets," Davin said as the first lasers came spitting their way.

The blue-white bolts crashed by, one smashing into the shuttle's forward shields and shrinking them by half. Others, though, went wide, went low or high. Erasing, every one, some spare luggage.

"What're they doing?" Phyla asked.

"Trying to kill me," Davin replied. "Heath wants me dead, and my target profile's a lot smaller than the shuttle. They're trying to make sure I'm not skipping ship."

He flicked another lever, dumped cargo hold number two into its sacrificial orbit. The drone fighters took the bait, their angles flitting off to annihilate the disparate debris. Two gave up their attack vectors entirely, looping around to ensure every spare suitcase met with a fiery end.

"Guess they're not all dumb," Phyla said, spinning the shuttle with its microjets to dodge another laser flurry from the lone remaining fighter. "Any other ideas?"

"Yeah," Davin said. "Suits on."

With the Earth fighters still a minute out, Davin broadcast the warning through the shuttle. The Nines scrambled, Mox throwing two suits up their way. The shuttle's shields absorbed another two strikes, crackling and fizzing out, leaving their poor boat undefended as Earth sucked them in.

Davin released the third cargo hold. Melody was now a sure loss, along with their various rifles, pistols, clothes. The drone fighter ignored the clutter, left it to the others.

"Sorry," Phyla said as the drone settled in for another straight strike. "I couldn't do it."

"Not you," Davin replied, his helmet snapping into place, the oxygen levels going good. "It's this crap ship."

"Appreciate that."

The fighter shot. Phyla juked. The laser slammed into the shuttle's front-right corner, blowing off a hole. Vacuum slammed Davin into his seat, the sudden leak throwing the shuttle into a spin. Alarms blared.

"Everyone alive?" Davin called.

The fighter shot again, hit the shuttle in its center as the craft spun. Something exploded behind him. Steam hissed from a busted valve, immediately racing off into the nether. The temperature inside the shuttle plummeted, Davin's seat going brittle.

But the check-ins came. Mox, Vi, Opal, Merc, and Riley all clicking that they'd lived through the volley. That they'd done the sensible thing and found the lifeboat, clambered inside.

"We should be doing that too," Davin said.

"Not yet," Phyla replied. "If it gets another free shot, it'll torch the lifeboat too."

The shuttle's waning batteries responded to Phyla's call, juddering the poor ship into turning one last time. She put the wounded side, the one without the lifeboat on it, towards the fighter, presenting a fat target, putting all the hull she could between the laser and the lifeboat.

"Now we go?" Davin asked, reaching over and unclipping Phyla from her chair. The whole dance to put on uniforms mid-firefight had been bad enough, but fleeing in them? "This isn't going to be easy."

"Since when is anything we do easy?"

She floated free from her seat, Davin kicking up with her. Using the windshield as leverage, he led the way with a kick-off from the cockpit. Phyla grabbed his foot as he went by, keeping his arms up in front to try and ward off disaster.

Shrapnel sucked under all circumstances, but dealing with it suited up in space put a whole other mess on top: the tiniest slice would siphon off their air real quick. Bigger gashes would make'em suffocate and chill them to the absolute bone.

So when Davin took his first good look at the ruined

shuttle behind him, a laser-blasted steel frame cluttered with drifting chairs, wrecked rails, and spinning bits of plastic and metal, he wanted to turn right around and go back into the cockpit.

"It's real ugly," Davin said, navigating to the cockpit's end.

Looking out into the shuttle's body, past all the damage and destruction, Davin spied the lifeboat hatch back and to the right. Shut tight, but still there. His crew waiting.

The floor and ceiling had large patches missing, space's infinite below and above, bracketed by charred frames. Laser flashes mingled with the shuttle's few remaining powered lights, strobing the view.

"Any second, that fighter's going to finish us off," Phyla said, joining Davin at the edge. "Ready?"

"Jumping off into certain death with you by my side?" Davin asked. "Always."

"You're so melodramatic."

"That's why you love me," Davin said, kicking off as he spoke. As they had bantered, Davin had hooked Phyla's suit to his own with a link line, kept it taut so they'd never be separated by more than a meter.

Together, then they launched off, batting away encroaching garbage, debris, death. Davin swatted away a miserable chair cushion, blinked as a cup holder bounced off his helmet. Phyla swore, her leg catching for a moment on a jagged hull piece.

"Only five percent loss," Phyla said a second later as they crossed the shuttle's center. "Should be fine."

A hard white light splashed across the pair. Davin turned, saw the drone fighter coming to a rest near the shuttle. Inspecting, looking for a target. This close, the fighter seemed massive. Earth cut across behind it, a crescent cerulean line. The drone fighter's front flaps were open, its twin cannons pointing right at them.

No chance they'd get away from this one.

"Nice knowing you," Phyla said.

"Nice loving you," Davin replied.

He couldn't help it: immediate death tended to make him a bit emotional.

The drone fighter narrowed the light's beam, centered it on Davin and Phyla as they reached the lifeboat's hatch.

The laser fire burned everything away.

CHAPTER 5
WELCOME TO EARTH

Davin didn't see the laser, only the aftermath. The world went nova orange and white, a splash leaving his eyes spotted even with the helmet's tinted visor. Death should've followed, but instead those spots cleared to show spinning wreckage, the after burn as Earth's fighters blazed past.

"Get in here," Mox said over the near-field comms.

Advice well-taken: the blown drone fighter's bits flung through the shuttle around them, bouncing off hull plates and steel frames. Shrapnel shooting too fast for Davin to see, and nigh invisible in the scattershot light.

Mox, using the hatch door as cover, pulled Davin and Phyla, still linked via the cable between their suits, into the hatch. He closed the circular door and started the small airlock cycling.

The captain took account of himself, of Phyla.

He hadn't felt any scratches, hadn't felt vacuum's pull on his suit, and that relief came through on his cursory inspection. Sure, frayed bits stuck out here and there. His visor held scratches along its faceplate, but no cracks.

"Dammit, Davin," Phyla said, yanking his attention away from himself to her. "One hit me."

The sliver wasn't hard to spot, jutting from Phyla's leg a solid several centimeters. Both Davin and Mox bent to look at it as the airlock finished cycling, the inner hatch popping open.

"We'll treat it inside," Davin replied.

Phyla's skewer looked about the size of a pencil, driven into her front thigh. Not likely mortal, whereas a subsequent assault on their ruined shuttle before the lifeboat launch would be decidedly fatal for everyone.

Merc kicked the lifeboat off as soon as the trio finished climbing inside. The lifeboat held no gravity, but it did have air. The *thunks* and *bonks* receded as the droplet capsule dipped away from its ruined host.

"Follow the flight plan," Davin called to Merc, his visor still up, the suit blasting the words on an open, close-range band. "We're still trying to get to Quito."

"Got it, boss," Merc said. Opal was next to him, working the comm. From the snatches Davin caught, Opal split time between reaming out Earth's slow-ass ships and thanking them for the rescue.

A soft-slip curse drew Davin's attention back to his primary patient. Phyla.

"Vi," Davin said. "Medkit, now. And get your bot over here."

"You can address me by my name," Puk said, floating over and shining a light on Phyla's injury.

Mox and Davin had Phyla laid out across several seats, the placid cushions and crash belts shoved out of the way. Under the flight plan, they had a few minutes to get Phyla stabilized before everyone would have to step in: riding a drop into Earth's atmosphere was not something to do free-handed.

Mox backed away to give the Davin-Vi-Puk trio room to

work, with Vi springing open the lifeboat's medkit and cursing as the contents promptly floated everywhere.

Davin, hooking his knees under the chair lips to keep himself secure, bent down for a closer look at the stabbing. The metal piece, glinting and jagged, looked like it cut clean through the suit's fabric. The suit itself had done what the best suits did, closing as best it could around the tear to minimize oxygen leaks.

"Get it out," Phyla said.

"Not till I see where it's gone in," Davin replied.

Taking off the suit in their current situation—who knew what was going on between Earth and Eden's fighters?—was a risk, one Davin asked Phyla to take.

"Either we leave it in until we land," Davin said. "Or we take it out and patch the suit now."

"Take it out, dammit," Phyla said.

"You heard her," Vi added, the re-packed kit coming back into play. "I'm ready."

"Puk, can you give us a bigger hole?" Davin asked the bot, and the machine complied.

Hovering overhead, Puk's sphere split open a small panel, a micro laser jutting out.

"Don't you dare burn me," Phyla said, glaring her furious green eyes.

"As if I would make a mistake like that," Puk replied, igniting the blue-white laser.

Smoke wafted up from Phyla's suit as the laser, powered precisely to not burn too far through, cut a patch. Davin boosted his opinion of Puk a few bits in that moment, started wondering if he'd been keeping the bot a little too far down the crew's bench.

Maybe Vi could up that laser's charge a bit and Puk could—

"Hold on!" Merc shouted, the shuttle juddering hard as its microjets kicked it into a sudden turn.

The lifeboat had no windows save the cockpit, only thick hull all around. Zero-G boats would give you some nice views, but this one had Earth's atmosphere as its primary objective, so Davin couldn't see what caused the maneuver, but Merc filled him in quick enough.

"Those androids are a damn sight better than the bums Earth's flying with today," Merc said. "They're dodging the Earthlings and coming after us."

"And this stupid lifeboat doesn't have any guns," Opal added.

What lifeboat would? Davin wanted to ask. Regardless, he made a promise to himself: no more missions on toothless ships.

The medical quartet pulled and pushed themselves back into position, Merc calling out a five-minutes-till-atmosphere clock. Phyla's right leg had a nice patch burned off around the skewer, bloody skin bubbling up at the impact point. Davin winced, Vi sucked in her teeth, and Puk offered a straightforward diagnosis.

"It's deep but not mortal," Puk said. "The angle and location suggests it did not pierce an artery."

"So get it out," Phyla replied.

"Get the patch ready," Davin said to Vi. "I'll yank the skewer."

"No," Puk countered. "I will remove the skewer. Your human hands may get cut, and your pull may be imprecise."

"Who the hell are you calling imprecise?" Davin asked.

"Not now," Phyla cut him off. "Do it, Puk."

Vi handed Davin the bandage, keeping the suit patch for herself instead. The little bot lowered a tiny mandible, one Vi must've designed for help building all those horrors she'd left on Ganymede. With its light shining bright, forcing Davin into a squint, Puk drifted down, put a tight clamp on the skewer.

Merc cursed, the lifeboat cracked. A bright line ran across

the lifeboat's ceiling, alarms blaring as the craft rattled. Phyla bounced off the seat as Merc twisted the lifeboat, throwing Davin and Vi away. As Davin bounced towards the cockpit, he saw Mox spring up, grab Phyla.

Phyla's blood flew from her leg, the skewer gone.

"Suit's on!" Merc said, between more curses. "Can we get a patch on that hit?"

"On it," Vi said, kicking herself off the shuttle's floor. As she went, Vi threw a silver square Davin's way, the suit patch for Phyla. "We don't have tons on here, so let's not get hit again."

"Tell that to Earth," Opal said.

Vi, swapping the med kit for the lifeboat's repair box, bounced towards the bright line, where a laser's near hit had thinned out the shuttle's hull. Going into Earth's atmosphere, that'd be a problem, likely turning the lifeboat into an unpleasant pressure cooker.

Wild Nines flambé.

Mox bounced Phyla back to the chairs where Davin and Puk met them. The little bot still held the skewer in its mandible, crimson end sharp and ugly. Its gnarled edges proved damning, tearing a broader gash in Phyla's leg than anyone wanted.

"Swear to God, Davin, you get that bandage on or I'm gonna kill you," Phyla said as Davin, suit patch in one hand, bandage on the other, went to work.

"Don't know if you've noticed, love, but it's a bit crazy in here."

"Not my fault."

Davin placed the bandage, its adhesive sealing fast and tight around the edges when Davin put pressure down. A tiny pod in the bandage's center released nanobot-infused cream, a medical miracle that'd surf through Phyla's wound and rid it of anything nasty.

The suit patch came next. Phyla sighed as Davin put it

over Puk's burned hole. The little bot, ditching the skewer and fishing painkillers from the med kit, offered pills to Phyla, who gulped them down with a helpful, straw-poked water pouch.

"Integrity good?" Davin asked, stepping away.

"Suit's telling me I'm not going to die," Phyla said, her eyes closed. "Leg's telling me I'm going to be limping for a while."

"Could've been worse," Mox said.

Davin, the not-too-long ago detonation outside Heath's frigate replaying in his memory, said nothing, just held her hand while Merc spun the lifeboat through one maneuver after another, dipping down into Earth's atmosphere.

Another wild ride.

Dock on a space station or a moon and your entry would be as quiet as the trip. A drift without air, without much gravity. Burn some microjets and settle in for a gentle landing.

Crashing into Earth on a lifeboat felt like getting the galaxy's worst massage from a mech with iron hands. The ship juddered, rumbled, yanked from side to side as Eden's fighters threw off any easy entry.

Davin and the others had themselves strapped in, an action rendering the experience an inert suffering. Vi, her rapid spray-patch on the weakened ceiling line completed, nonetheless kept her eyes sharp, especially as Earth's heat and drag caused the line and plenty more to grow bright all over again.

The temp inside the lifeboat climbed, and Davin broke out into sweat inside his suit. The droplets collected, ran down into his eyes and mouth as he couldn't move his hands to wipe them away. Phyla, next to him, slept, the painkillers doing their hard work fast.

Puk provided the entertainment, the little bot having nowhere to sit and thus blasting its microjets constantly to keep itself stable, bobbing and bouncing around the lifeboat like a metal balloon.

Merc cheered a few seconds into the crashing entry, Opal clarifying that Earth had managed, at last, to knock out a second Eden fighter. Only one left, as if that wasn't more than enough.

Otherwise, Merc kept the updates streaming along: they were on a general course for Quito, where the spaceport was aware the Nines were crashing down. Of course, as Merc said, he'd given zero evidence only the Nines were on the ship, or even that he, the pilot, was a member of Davin's mercenary band. All Earth knew was that Eden had sent some rogue fighters to attack a shuttle, one potentially packed with civilians.

"Going to keep it that way as long as I can," Merc said.

Not that it seemed to matter. Davin, with his head back against the seat rest, stared ahead towards the cockpit, watching the fire blaze against the windshield. The orange and white disappeared, replaced with a frosted blue, and below that white.

Clouds.

It'd been a long time since Davin had been back to Earth. Cargo running in the *Jumper* tended to be more profitable between Luna and the outer systems. Easier to stuff the ship full when you didn't have to leave Earth's gravity well. So the blue planet's natural wonders did what they tended to: made all the other concerns fall away.

Most spacers Davin met, Sandeer on Ganymede definitely included, took Earth as an unreachable legend. An expensive place to get to, a difficult one to survive. The planet's gravity meant you had to keep yourself in strong shape, suffused with muscle-boosting nutrient goop, or your bones might break just setting foot on the place.

If you managed that, then you'd find a whole different culture. Out among the asteroid belt, the far flung moons, everyone operated with extra caution, the knowledge that death was an atmospheric leak away. That everything necessary for survival came from off-world. Earth had abundance.

The beauty stunned Davin every time. Earth had rebounded from climate crises and industrial pollution to transform itself into something of a paradise, genetic marvels coupling with massive vertical farms to make a planet of plenty.

Earth did, after all, feed the whole damn solar system.

And all the people on the planet seemed to know it, seemed to regard spacers with pity, as if there'd been some sad misfortune forcing Davin and his ilk off into the stars.

In moments like this, with his bones rattling, teeth chattering, the lifeboat veering between hot and cold, Davin could agree. Maybe Erick and Trina had it right, settling down on an island with a big family and watching the sunsets roll on by.

"Hold on," Merc said, a pilot's angry slash in his voice. "I can't move this damn thing in atmosphere."

"The drone's coming in right up our ass," Opal added. "Earth's blowing it."

"Like they do every time," Mox rumbled.

The laser struck the lifeboat's engines, blowing into the rockets as Merc tried to level the craft out. South America, its replenished jungles sprawling out below them, swung into view and out of it again, the lifeboat entering into a tumble as Merc tried to get its microjets working.

Someone screamed. It might've been Davin.

Merc and Opal jabbered at each other, hands flying frantically. The lifeboat lurched. A laser flashed by, then another, beyond the cockpit's windshield.

Davin felt himself letting go. Not an easy thing for the captain, but he wasn't in a spot to change fate. He could do only one thing: trust his crew, and do it without getting in their way.

The lifeboat took another hit and the inside lights went dark. The engine whines ceased, only one sputtering microjet played a pockmark tune. Hull panels rattled. Wind—wind!—howled. The temperature climbed again and the green drew closer.

"Popping the chute," Merc said. "You got a god to pray to, a lucky charm to rub, now's the time!"

The lifeboat lurched again, swinging its nose to the sky as the chute launched from the craft's front. Designed, per some smart person, to have the engines hit first and cushion any impact.

Gave Davin a sublime view of the sky, a sunny day sprinkled with thin cirrus clouds cutting across the blue.

"Looks nice out there," Davin said.

As if hearing him, a narrow arrow, smoke bleeding from one side, swung into the view. The drone fighter, angling for another strike. Two Earth craft, three-pronged ships, angled in behind it, lacing the drone with lasers. The android fighter twitched, its microjets shoving it ever so slightly to one side or another to dodge the lasers.

Merc, utterly unable to do anything, held up double middle fingers towards the drone.

Maybe Heath was watching, maybe the man saw the gesture. Davin would bet anything Heath cared only about the final explosion and what it would mean for his android marketing scheme. His fighters had outflown Earth, had destroyed the Nines.

What more proof did you need to invest?

The drone zipped in closer, adjusting its angle. The lifeboat's chute, expanding, cut off the view. Gave Davin an idea.

"This thing have a backup chute?" Davin asked.

"Hopefully we don't need it," Merc replied.

"We do now," Davin snapped, the moment clearing away

his zoned-out, gonna-die zen. "Cut the main chute, right as it gets in close."

"It?"

"The drone fighter!"

Merc made a delighted noise, connecting on Davin's idea. The man waited another two seconds, saw the drone spit another laser round that miscalculated the lifeboat's descent by a hair, then released the chute. The lifeboat plummeted again, dropping fast towards a destination Davin couldn't see, a fall jolted away as Merc deployed the secondary chute.

The first, its colors a brilliant yellow and blue, sucked right up and wrapped around the drone fighter. For a long few seconds as their second chute deployed, the Nines had a killer view as the drone fighter's engines, its contours, snarled in the chute's wrapping. Now with all the evasive qualities of a plunging whale, the drone finally proved killable for Earth's patrol.

Another benefit of being in atmosphere? The explosions looked really cool.

"The captain comes through," Merc said as the second chute sprawled wide over the sky. "Amazing call."

"Desperate call, more like," Davin said. "How long till impact?"

"Couple minutes. Opal's trying to see about a lift."

"Don't," Mox interjected, his rumbling carrying a more urgent tone. "We can't let them take us."

"What's that?" Vi asked. "We're about to crash into . . . wherever and you don't want help?"

"They will arrest us," Mox said. "We stole a transport shuttle. Earth will take us and hand us to Eden."

Opal, cutting off the comm, clicked into the conversation. "Mox's right. First thing we do after hitting the ground is get as far away from the shuttle as we can."

"If we live," Vi said.

"If we don't, then it's not a problem," Opal replied.

Always cheerful, this crew.

The impact came hard, the lifeboat chewing through trees and vines like they were soft bread and little else. Davin felt every impact in his bones, but the hull plates held. The lifeboat's battery packs, potential bombs waiting for their moment, were wrapped in enough protection to keep a wayward rock from making them all go boom.

About the worst that happened was Puk, bouncing off the shuttle's ceiling as the gnashing crash continued. A little dent pocked its head, an almost charming divot in the otherwise perfect sphere.

Phyla slept through the whole thing.

Getting out of the settled lifeboat, its butt on the ground and the crew in the air, was a patient process. Crash belts were unsnapped, suits were taken off and tossed aside with one hand on the chairs for support.

The air, heavy with a chill humidity, felt delicious in Davin's lungs. This was the pure, good stuff. Not recycled oxygen that'd been filtered endlessly for decades. Scents intermingled, from flowers to ozone from the shuttle's torched electronics. Sounds sparked from the wreckage, metal sighs as the damaged craft leaned into its natural crib.

And what a crib! Climbing from the hatch behind Opal—Mox was coming last, Phyla held over one shoulder—Davin looked into a tree-filled canopy. Clouds stretched above, only the tiniest dying trace remained of the combat. Leaves fluttered, unknown birds squawked questions at the intruding craft. Bugs blitzed, assaulting Davin's exposed skin along with the hot sun.

Davin grinned at it all anyway.

Because that was the thing about Earth. It might be hell to get here, might make his body feel like he was a century old, his muscles already aching with gravity's yank, but damn if it wasn't grand.

"You going to move?" Mox asked from behind him.

"Working on it."

They gathered the lifeboat's emergency rations, the med kit. Given the number of people the craft was supposed to hold, the food was plentiful. Sure, it felt a little bad to snack on nutrient goop as they started off into the jungle, seeing as Earth's abundance was all around them, but Davin figured he could endure the sludge for a little while longer.

They'd survived, they had their feet on the ground. Opal said Earth was sending help, people the Nines didn't want to meet. Instead, Merc pegged Quito as a few days' hike away, a couple dozen kilometers through some valleys, up some hills, and passing by a village or two.

Nothing a crew of hardened mercenaries couldn't handle.

"Right?" Davin asked as they took their first steps along the lush, leaf-and-mud-dominated forest floor. "We got this."

"After what we just went through?" Opal said. "For once, Davin, I agree with you. A nice long walk seems right up our alley."

CHAPTER 6
A NIGHT OUT

The walk was pleasant until the Nines started lifting their legs, planting their feet on the wet ground. Earth's gravity hit them hard, every step an effort. Conversation dipped and died after the opening seconds as everyone concentrated on not falling over.

Mox, the lone competent one, his exoskeleton assisting, picked up Phyla when her wounded leg made progress impossible.

Wrapped as they were in spare clothes, makeshift satchels holding nutrient goop and the med kit, the Nines hardly resembled a dangerous mercenary crew. Dirty, scratched up, smelly, and once again sweating, the lot of them were a mess.

Except Puk. Despite the dent, the little bot zipped around using its microjets, blistering ahead to scout out the way and occasionally blipping back to tell the Nines to lay low: Earth ships, both rescue and otherwise, canvased the area, their lights shining down through the thick canopy.

Puk's directions—straight to Quito, they'd figure things out from there—led them largely uphill, the jungle fading around them and giving way to long wavy grasses, tree clusters, and whipping clouds as the afternoon descended into evening.

"Oxygen's thinner up here," Opal huffed. "Makes me want to put a suit back on."

She, Merc, and Davin formed the front trio, with Mox, Vi, and Riley, along with Phyla over-the-shoulder, in back.

"Suits are heavy," Merc said. "You want to try walking in one after this?"

"At least I could breathe."

Davin could sympathize. His own lungs felt like they were never full, constantly searching with every breath for something more. Tack on the sheer exhaustion from a day that'd begun fighting goons on the Moon, and something had to change.

"Puk," Davin said the next time the little bot came buzzing back, the group now stalking through a wide open ridge. "Get us to the closest hotel you can find."

If Puk had any objections, the bot's logic must've seen the sheer state of the Nines and flipped. Instead, the bot said there was a small town not all that far away, one that'd be a perfect place to drop in for a night.

"Then lead on," Davin said, and Puk bounced away down and to the right, towards a valley nestled between jagged hills.

Larger mountains faded in, the landscape looking much like the ruptured plains of Ganymede or Luna, just covered in plants instead. Spacecraft and various planes flitted across the sky, some circling back towards the crash site. Few bothering to orbit out beyond it.

During a much-needed rest break beneath a craggy outcropping, Davin leaned his head against the gray-white rock and waved at the ships in the distance.

"Thought we were lucky at first," he said to Phyla, set down by Mox so the big man could catch his own breather. "Now I'm starting to think we've got a friend over there."

"Over there? With Earth?"

"We didn't blow the shuttle," Davin said. "Didn't do much to cover our tracks. Any half-assed search should've found our bum selves before we'd gone a kilometer."

"Watch who you're calling a bum," Merc said between sips from a nutrient goop tube.

Beet'n'greens read the flavor label. Merc could have as many of those as the man wanted.

"Another mystery?" Riley asked.

"Welcome to the Nines, kid," Opal replied as Davin shrugged. "It's all questions until someone gets bored and starts blowing things up."

"Usually Davin," Vi said.

"It works, right?" Davin fought through the energy to put on a slacker's grin. "We have a method."

"It's a miracle you're not all dead," Riley shook his head. "You've been doing this for years? Stuff like what just happened?"

"It's a living," Merc replied. "You get used to it."

Puk rescued Riley from reckoning with his choices, the bot hovering in to mention the nearest hamlet with a place to stay was less than a kilometer away, and, crucially, downhill.

With twilight coming on fast, the Nines slumped their way down the hillside. The deep purple sky became a light show, those ever-cruising starships illuminating their pathways one blinking glow at a time.

Would've been beautiful, except odds were every one of those dots wouldn't mind turning Davin in for cash, or killing him for the same.

The hamlet, at least, proved worthy of its name. Straddling a canyon-crossing roadway, the small town glowed with torch-light. Not real torches, mind, but electric versions spitting a safer dancing flame into the air. Music picked up as the Nines neared, carried on the ever-present gusting mountain wind. Happy tunes, guitars and a lone trumpet.

They approached from an unused angle, tramping in through a field and onto a gravel roadway. Fences long rotted away left a few posts, clues about a livestock lifestyle rendered obsolete. Instead, the closer fields looked dominated by luxury food crops, fruits and vegetables that'd sell for a pretty penny to any ship hopping starward.

Earth and its damn soil, such a cheat code.

Modest stucco homes rose up around them, most dark. Many bearing stenciled art across the outside, rainbow banners, local traditions, things Davin could respect even though he didn't know them.

"Looks like a nice place to spend a few days," Vi said as they padded on. Puk placed the local inn in the village center. "Rest up, eat some real food?"

"One, maybe two nights," Davin replied quick, before anyone else hoped on the vacation train. "Remember every day we spend here, people are getting killed out there."

"Feel like that's on Alyssa, not us," Merc said.

"If she's able to make the call," Opal shot back. "We don't even know if she's free. We keep telling ourselves this is some simple meet up, but who the hell knows what's going on?"

"See?" Mox said to Riley. "All questions."

The town didn't do anything to answer them either, save one: where and why the music played. By the time the Nines dragged themselves, under Puk's watchful eye, to the town square, they saw why the houses were dark, why the narrow streets were empty save the occasional wandering dog.

Two people danced in the center, around a statue of someone Davin didn't recognize. Around them, moving to their own beat but giving the middle couple the starring spot, swerved seemingly hundreds. All around the square sat, stood, talked, and chowed hundreds more. Pop up tables held victuals running from meats to fruits to chips to desserts Davin could neither name nor describe.

His mouth, salivating, did its best.

Nobody cared to notice the Nines as they stood beneath one of the torch lamps, watching human life celebrate. Davin didn't quite know how to take it, his muscles spent, his bones aching, his head mashed after the long day. After all they'd gone through in the last few hours, how could something like this be possible?

How could people be so filled with joy?

"Is this a wedding?" Phyla asked.

"Obviously," Riley replied.

"Shove your obvious," Phyla snapped, then softened. Mox still held her on his back, like some small child. "Sorry. Long day."

"We've never been to one," Davin answered Riley's confused look. "Not one like this anyway."

There'd been quiet celebrations in Vagrant's Hollow, but most people were too busy hustling for their next meal, their next chance to get away, to bother with life's fluffy side. At least, that's how it felt back then.

Maybe Davin's parents would've said different, but they'd been gone a long time.

Several numbers came and went, the dancing couples rotating in and out. The middle pair changed up, too, though one of them always seemed to be in the spot, swaying with a brother, sister, father, mother.

"I've found a way around," Puk said as yet another song came to a close. "Unless you want to watch this all night?"

Watch, no, but slinking away faded as an option while Puk spoke. Since the Nines had posted up at their station, they'd drawn glances—particularly Mox—and those glances must've become words, because a ten or so villagers split from the party and made their way over.

Davin expected suspicion, even fear or threats to be thrown their way. It couldn't be all that often a group like them stumbled into town without a vehicle, without bags, wearing a long day and not much else. But the first eyes he saw were kind ones, the first words suggestions to help themselves, to join in, to escape whatever troubles they'd so obviously been through.

Merc, with a grin Opal's way, answered for them all. "Hell yes."

Fruity wines and fruit itself banished the exhaustion, piercing the day's stress with a sweetness. Once welcomed, the town treated the Nines like their own, an arms-wide approach a more sober, less tired Davin would've found suspicious. Instead, he didn't give a damn.

Opal and Merc were the only ones with enough confidence to get out onto the dance floor, where Earth's gravity threw off their steps, had them twisting like mad people, but as various spirits spiked the whole party, the dancing turning into a celebratory mosh. The trumpet wailed, the guitars went wild.

And Davin found a chair with Phyla, food and beverages handy, to watch it all. Mox disappeared with their slapdash satchels to get them rooms, and, with the privacy, handle clearing their names with Luna's Centurions. Vi did the same, promising Puk some repairs.

Riley, at least, summoned up some courage and mingled.

"I kind of like him," Phyla said as they watched, along with the town, Riley try and fail to imitate a particular dance. "He's real green though."

"Like Vi used to be."

"Like we used to be too."

Davin chuckled. "Were we ever? I don't think Vagrant's Hollow gave us that."

"For a little while." Phyla smiled. "We had those adventures, the three of us. Nothing scary."

Sneaking around rubble houses, searching for useful scrap

amid the junk that'd get dumped on Miner Prime's worst level. They'd been kids as long as they were allowed to be.

"You're saying things are scary now?" Davin asked.

Phyla tapped a light finger on her wound, the bandage changed minutes ago. "They hurt a lot more than the skinned knees, at least."

"But this," Davin raised his ruby red drink, "is a lot better coping device."

"You still going to raise one every time I win?"

"Win, lose, I'll be there."

Phyla nodded. The number changed. Riley, Merc, and Opal were pushed in a long line snaking through the tables, the whole village clapping in tune. At some point, a hand reached Davin's way and yanked him up, into the dance.

The captain didn't know what he was doing, could barely lift his legs, but the grin gracing his face was the most genuine one he'd worn in far too long.

The day had long since started by the time Davin had a coffee mug in his hands. The inn had a back porch to dine on, an open-air feast for the eyes. The hillside dwindled away beyond the stone patio, houses fading after not-so-many meters to crop fields and rocky grasses.

Only Vi was out there too, and she looked so buried in her wristlet, a half-eaten pile of huevos and melon on the table, that Davin let her be.

Later, he'd say it was instinct.

The coffee hadn't gone two sips before a slim-fit man in aviator sunglasses pulled out Davin's other chair. Holding nothing, looking dangerous enough anyway, the man slid into the seat. Eyed Davin up and down while Davin raised his mug.

Alarms went off in Davin's head, silenced by grim experience. If the man wanted Davin dead, he could've shot the Nines captain and walked away. Now that he'd made the approach, the Nines would see him, would be put on instant alert.

In other words, this guy was here to talk.

"You're not a quiet man," Sunglasses said. "Even when you ought to be."

"That's one way to say hello," Davin replied.

"Is your whole team here?"

Davin shrugged. "I don't keep them on leashes."

Sunglasses stared. The man's mouth twitched. His skin looked good, moisturized. Haircut neat. Certainly not someone bopping between the planets. The way he'd slid out the chair, sat with the right amount of force, suggested an Earth native. Or someone who'd been here long enough.

"We can keep talking past each other," Sunglasses said, "or I can get to the point."

"Please do." Davin lifted the coffee mug. "I'm a busy man."

"I found you because someone in this town uploaded a video last night. Very festive. Looked like fun." Sunglasses leaned forward. "If you looked hard enough, and trust me when I say Eden's bots are looking hard enough, a few familiar faces stood out."

"Your besties from school?"

Sunglasses snorted, sighed. "I see why Alyssa likes you."

A clue! Saying Alyssa's name so casually, with a tone matching a friendship, marked this dude as an ally. Or at least someone who Davin didn't need Vi to knife in the back.

She'd looked up from her wristlet and noticed a minute ago, had taken Davin's expression to mean something less than nice. Vi'd probably sent a warning to the team, and had edged closer now, a firm grip on her syrupy butter knife.

Puk, a far more effective weapon, hovered at the porch's edge, micro laser out and ready.

"She likes me because I crack jokes?" Davin said.

"Because you're determined and don't blink under pressure," Sunglasses said. "We've had too many walk away lately."

"Maybe because she's doing jack while her team gets slaughtered?"

"Maybe you don't know what you're talking about."

Davin spread his arms. "Feel free to tell me, Mr. Get-to-the-point."

A slight smile. Killed the sunglass badassery, but at least this guy wasn't made of stone.

"I've got a speeder one block over," Sunglasses said. "I'll take you and your team to Alyssa. She'll tell you what you have to do next."

"Hold on. Tell us? We came here because her side didn't know what the hell was happening. We're trying to find her."

"You have." Sunglasses looked down at the empty table, then back up at Davin. "She'll explain the rest."

"You really afraid of eavesdroppers out here?"

"Not at all. But to say anymore would make you privy to certain plans." Sunglasses killed his grin. "Before that happens, Alyssa has to decide whether she wants you dead or not."

"Well, now you've sold me."

"Up to you, Davin Masters. Come with me, or sit here with your coffee until Eden, Earth's defense force, or both descend on these poor people guns blazing. You might even have time to brush your teeth first."

After hiking the hills, riding in a speeder was a blissful experience. Unlike the hardier craft on Ganymede and other moons, this one didn't have a bubble shield. Other than a slight glass bit rising up from the front to keep bugs and crap out of Sunglasses's face—the man had yet to give himself a name—the thing blitzed along in the open air.

Seasons weren't a thing Davin paid particular attention to,

seeing as they were an Earth-only problem, but the pleasant chill prompted Phyla to ask and Sunglasses to confirm: mid-Spring, a great time in this part of the world.

The curving road took them over and around hills, craggy cliffs, and through cloud forest valleys. They passed menageries, from other speeders covering the size and weight gamut to older craft, including, hot damn, actual wheeled cars and trucks.

"If it works, it works," Sunglasses said when Riley kept pointing them out. "You have an older model here, it's not going to kill you if a part fails."

Coupled with the various vehicles and homes—no domes here—came the other Earth-only element: animals. Birds, bugs, bigger beasties like dogs freely roaming around. Not pets or science experiments dumped in private enclosures. Life living its natural life.

Even Mox, the hardy Centurion who made regular Earth-side trips for his police work, seemed overwhelmed. He'd taken the backseat on the speeder, one meant for a full three people, and every time Davin glanced his way, Mox's head seemed to be on a swivel, turning and taking it all in.

Vi wore a permanent smile, her wristlet off and arm over the speeder's side. Phyla sat between her and Riley, leaning back and letting the sun splash on her face. Sure, they'd doused themselves in sunscreen today, courtesy of Sunglasses, after yesterday's trek left rose red burns across their bare skin, but that didn't stop the pilot from soaking up the rays.

"Last time I was here with Alyssa," Davin said, "we hit the jungle too. Deeper in the rainforest then. Have a couple friends that live in the Caribbean."

"The islands are a wonderful place to live if you can handle the water," Sunglasses replied. "Me? I get seasick."

"Must make space travel hard."

Sunglasses laughed. "Never been off my home. God-willing, I never will be."

"You don't want to try it?"

Sunglasses tapped his fingers on the speeder's flight stick, an affectionate pat.

"Why would I ever want to leave perfection?"

That perfection, Sunglasses clarified, didn't extend to everywhere. Quito, a city sprawling over hilltops, blending ancient and modern in a haphazard mix, had its blemishes. Sunglasses only hinted at rougher quarters, though, instead pointing the Nines to happier places like the old cable car climbing up to a beautiful view. Various squares and restaurants with rooftop balconies. The music, the soul in the stone streets so much brighter now that fewer wheels ran over them.

Sunglasses piloted them through newer neighborhoods towards more classic quarters, where age mingled with choice upgrades. Shops within ancient buildings sold new model wristlets, and cafes boasted traditional meals alongside vitamin shakes and, unfortunately, nutrient goop. Even the bars advertised Martian booze.

"You look disappointed," Phyla said as Sunglasses took the speeder down a narrow, descending street.

"Sometimes I'd just like to be somewhere different, is all." Davin shrugged. "For all the work we did to get here, to see nutrient goop again?"

Sunglasses laughed, the speeder slowing down.

"Those signs are for people like you," Sunglasses said. "The tourists who don't know what to do with themselves. Tell you a secret?"

"What?"

"I've never had nutrient goop in my life."

That revelation stunned Davin as Sunglasses stopped the speeder alongside a pastel orange building. Three stories, balconies carved along the top level and scratched-up stone at the base. A flute carried a melody from above, fighting with nothing else in the empty alley. City noise rumbled, a vague honey scent on the chilled air. Sweet enough for Davin's stomach to rumble, but when Sunglasses made for the sole door, a single dark wood piece with a literal handle, Davin figured his hunger wouldn't be addressed anytime soon.

Sunglasses led them inside, Mox taking up the tail, and through a restaurant-grade kitchen. One that looked well-stocked, going by the pans, knives, stuffed fridges.

"Closed today," Sunglasses offered by way of explanation.

"Why?" Vi asked.

"For you," Sunglasses replied, his tone frosting over.

The Nines took note. They didn't have weapons, but they could all throw a punch—and Mox could break a wall—so Davin met a few eyes, caught a couple pointed looks.

Would Sunglasses go through all this trouble just to try and kill them? Seemed unlikely, but—

She sat, alone, at a large cloth-covered table. Set with places for each of them. Alyssa looked up from her wristlet as the Nines left the kitchen, and Davin's first impression was . . . exhaustion.

The rebel leader had gone through a lot, even in the time Davin had known her. First, Davin and Phyla themselves had played a part in Alyssa's sister dying on Europa. Then Alyssa herself had tried a gambit to steal away those damned androids, only to wind up losing most of her core people in the process. Now her forces, the desperate people in the solar system's outer reaches, were getting assimilated by the very company she despised.

A rough go, and one that left deep lines along Alyssa's face. Gray hairs abounded, and the greeting smile Alyssa attempted barely qualified as such.

"I hear you've been looking for me," Alyssa said as Sunglasses bade the group to take their seats. "Sorry it's been so hard, but I have to take precautions."

"Like leaving your own side to die?" Opal said.

A younger Davin, more afraid about securing contracts and keeping everyone happy, might've jumped on the words, asked for an apology or told Opal to keep quiet.

Now? Hell yeah. Tired or no, drained or no, Alyssa's side deserved an explanation.

"If you'd talked to anyone, we wouldn't need to be here," Davin continued while Alyssa waited, like a mom absorbing a tantrum. "Cass told us on Freestar that everyone's waiting for you. Eden even offered peace, but you said nothing."

"You know that was a lie," Alyssa said, mild enough to make Davin's hands itch.

He chose to grab the silverware instead. Sunglasses came back with pitchers filled with glistening water. Another man brought out several bottles of wine—white, red, rosé. Merc, doing what Merc did, started filling glasses.

"Sure, but it might've worked," Phyla said. "We had every eye in the solar system on us. We could've forced Eden to make a play."

"If I'd been there, you would have faced much worse than a strike team or two," Alyssa countered. "Bad publicity doesn't scare Eden. I do."

Mox set both hands on the table, elbows planted. The glassware rattled.

"Then why are you hiding?" The Centurion asked.

"I'm not hiding," Alyssa replied, taking Merc's offered rosé and sipping it. "I'm winning."

Davin wasn't sure he had a more skeptical look to give. His eyebrows hit their height, one eye slid large, and the scoundrel's grin became a loose frown. It'd really be a bad turn if they'd come all this way to find Alyssa delusional.

"And now that you're here, we can start the final piece," Alyssa said.

She raised her wine glass, sent an expectant look around. Merc had finished his pours, everyone had their beverage of choice. Davin didn't know what the hell was going on, but he knew one thing: wine would make this nonsense easier to handle.

"What're we toasting?" Davin asked, raising his own to match.

"The Wild Nines," Alyssa said, eyes sparkling. "Eden's greatest undercover operatives."

CHAPTER 7
PLOTS, PLANS, PAINS

Being the sort of guy that gets around, Davin had met a lot of so-called masterminds, geniuses whose greatest satisfaction came when they laid out their clever plans for Davin and everyone else to see.

Alyssa didn't come off quite that bad, mostly because the seeds of a sneaky stab into Eden's back lay at her idea's core, but she spent the dinner detailing a scheme so convoluted as to be useless. At least, useless to anyone outside of Alyssa herself.

There were scared investors and companies on Earth and Luna, people afraid that Eden would become unstoppable. Moneyed folks who proposed fighting with stocks and supplies over lasers. Alyssa, continuing to down the rosé with gusto, laid out all the acquisitions made in secret, the traps laid through Eden's contractor web that'd make the whole company grind to a halt unless Eden changed its ways.

And the last push to get Eden over the proverbial edge?

Alyssa's very public, very glittery arrest. All those investors would see Eden's last obstacle taken out, would pull the trigger on the purchases they'd been lining up, and

Eden would find itself with Alyssa and nothing to kill her with.

"Except all the stuff they already have," Vi said when Alyssa finished her speech with a flourish. "They can still kick you out of an airlock."

"Not if they don't own the ships anymore," Alyssa replied, holding that wide grin. She'd thought of everything, this one. "Eden's all debt-financed. Growing fast, fighting a war's expensive. My friends will call in those debts, and Eden's going to have to sell."

"You're playing games instead of fighting a war," Mox declared, pushing himself back from the table. "This isn't what I signed up for."

"What did you sign up for, Mox?" Alyssa asked quick, before the metal man could stand. "More bodies in bags? More scars to add to your collection? I'm trying to end this in the least bloody way possible." When Mox opened his mouth, Alyssa slammed it shut with a stamp of her left hand on the cloth. "We cannot win this fight with guns. We have to use the only weapon they care about: money."

Nobody had an immediate counter. Davin used the silence to surf his crew's faces, see what he could pick out. Opal seemed to be nodding along with Alyssa's argument while Merc had his attention on the next wine refill. Vi stared down at the table, brow furrowed in the obsessed look she tended to get whenever a sticky problem found its way to her. Riley? Riley was still a fish very much out of the water.

Phyla, though, gave Alyssa a healthy glare. She caught Davin's eye, grimaced, and broke the silence.

"You say 'they'," Phyla said. "Who is 'they'? Everyone that's bought Eden stock?"

"Not quite," Alyssa replied. "But close. When we cut Eden's legs off, it'll be their employees who do the fighting for us. They won't wage a brutal war in ships that won't fly, with guns that won't shoot. They'll push for change, and the suits at Eden's top won't be able to stop it."

"You're talking like a rebel again," Davin said.

"Never stopped being one. Just got quiet there for a little bit. Had to lower my own temperature to get the meetings I needed."

"Why are they helping you?" Vi asked. "Why risk their biggest business partner?"

"Biggest?" Alyssa scoffed. "Try only. Everyone sees the endgame if this continues. Space will be Eden's and Eden's alone. Make ship parts? Guess who's your only buyer. Thinking about mining that asteroid? Better hope Eden gives you good terms. Eden represented opportunity once. Now it's the toll everyone doesn't want to pay."

His crew asked more questions, threw more barbs Alyssa batted away with rehearsed precision. This wasn't some improvised ask once the Nines happened to land. Alyssa had planned for this, and Davin figured if the Nines hadn't made it, she would've found some other group to do the same.

Always being used, but this time the price would be, should be, freedom for a lot of people Davin cared about.

He called the vote after the meal, a delicious yucca, rice, ceviche and coconut medly far outpacing any flavor nutrient goop could hope to achieve. With Alyssa watching, the Nines came back unanimous to go along with Alyssa's arresting idea. Convoluted, sure, but all the risk, as Davin said before calling for hands, sat with Alyssa herself.

The Nines would get a clean name. No way Eden could press its campaign if Davin's crew turned in their enemy's leader.

With the steps confirmed, Alyssa herself begged off to work on the plan. She wanted to get media lined up, make sure the show would get everywhere human eyes could see it. Her protests would break Eden's rotting enchantment in the public's eye and break economic binds.

"Still think it's stupid," Phyla said as she and Davin walked from the building, Vi and Riley with them.

A soft darkness lay over Quito, charmed by the electric torches and the constant music drifting along the streets. Overhead, spacecraft lights glittered more brightly than any star.

"They tried the shootout," Davin said. "They lost their fleet, most of their fighters."

"What happens when Eden cuts off their cash?" Phyla argued. "All these contractors are just going to take the hit?"

"We have to step up," Riley said, the four of them walking—limping, in Phyla's case—down a broad Quito street. "The outer planets have to play the game. We're trying too hard to support ourselves."

"Bold talk, kid," Davin said.

"He's right," Vi added. "When I worked at Eden, I'd see it all the time. If I needed a new thing made, I'd get bids right away. Everyone's desperate for Eden cash because there's nobody else."

"That why you're heading to the comm center?" Davin asked.

When he and Phyla left dinner saying they had a message to send, Vi and Riley had joined in after sharing one of those meaningful looks.

"We're going to tell Sandeer and my dad," Vi said. "They get enough heads up, they can get in place to take advantage when Eden bites it."

"So you think it'll work?" Davin asked.

"I'm choosing to bet on us," Vi replied.

Davin should've used that phrase. would've, except he still had doubts about this whole enterprise. As it often did running around with rebel plans, a cargo hauler's life looked attractive. So boring, so many less shots to the back.

The comm center came and went without much issue. Using the frequency and encryption Cass gave them, Davin and Phyla tossed a message out to Freestar. Without many specifics—encrypted or no, interested parties could intercept and probably hear the message—Davin emphasized pulling back from the fighting and trying not to die.

"Real inspiring stuff there," Phyla said as they left. Vi and Riley had already gone, Quito's night descended into an urban dark, purple and yellow pools wherever torches shone. The dinner crowd drank their first round, was wandering for their second. The city hummed, and Davin found exactly nothing appealing about going back to Alyssa's dark, brooding haunt.

"Here," Davin said, pulling Phyla into a random bar. Earth sapped their muscles, made pulling the old, red-painted door open harder than it should've been, but the inside was worth the effort.

In space, history was a recent feel. Everything came about within the last couple centuries, rapid advancement coupled with equally rapid destruction as old components collapsed under radiation, micro meteors, poor piloting, or plain old neglect. Anything looking a bit derelict was cause for suspicion.

Here? History reigned.

The patchy bronze and wood inside bustled with more local flavors inlaying the countertops, adorning the walls. Screens abounded, all showing football matches while patrons quaffed pints. Two pool tables lay in the center, coins docking the sides where next-ups staked their place in line. The balls clattered as shots struck, laughter mingled, and the thick, homey air of human camaraderie held sway.

And that history? Davin felt it in the worn tiles beneath his feet. In the old signs on the walls advertising booze and events from years long ago. He used a hand rail to get down a couple steps, not quite trusting his control, and in the refinished wood was the thousand, million nicks of customers past.

Intoxicating.

Though not as much as the cinnamon-spiced rum Phyla and Davin downed seconds later. They found a table against a side wall, forgotten and perfect.

"We could've been doing this for years," Davin said as they sat down, clinked glasses. "Why didn't we?"

"Because we went right from saving Earth to running deliveries," Phyla replied, throwing Davin a shrugging smile. "Quite the comedown."

"We needed a break."

"We took one," Phyla said. "One that lasted a bit too long, went a bit too slow."

One without a plan, too. Once the media circus wrapped up, the two had blundered about in places not too far different than this. Without a mercenary crew, Davin and Phyla couldn't exactly accept contracts, not that people wanted him around: most folks didn't want escorts who'd draw more attention to the job.

The first run came almost as an accident, a chat with a Luna docking official who said a ship had broken down, but a bunch of batteries needed to get out that day. If Davin and Phyla were heading towards Mars, could they carry them along?

"You were so nice," Phyla said. "Whistled your way through, said look at us, helping the common man again."

"And getting paid."

"Money wasn't ever our motivation and you know it."

"Could've fooled me," Davin said, knowing it was a lie even as he spoke the words.

You didn't get to be a captain without loving the crew. The Nines took contracts as much to keep themselves together as to grow their credit accounts. The rambling back and forth through the galaxy, the bar nights and blasting days, all worth way more than any bottom line.

"So we're arresting Alyssa now?" Phyla asked.

"Apparently," Davin replied. "Getting to be Eden's best buddies."

"Just in time for them to fall apart?"

Davin shook his head. "That's what I don't understand. She thinks Eden's going to roll over, I don't buy it. How many times have we cornered someone and had them surrender?"

"Point."

"Bet you Eden shoots back. Tells those suppliers either work with us or we'll blow you to pieces, march in and take you over."

"Earth won't stand for that."

Phyla's words lacked conviction even as she said them, because she knew as well as Davin did Earth had no way to force Eden to do anything.

So Davin laughed.

"You want to change Eden, you either need to smash it to little pieces first, or you need to get someone, maybe several someones, high enough up their food chain to force a change."

"And who's that going to be? Vi's out. We don't know anybody else."

"Admiral Yang seems solid enough," Davin said, referring to the officer who'd drafted Vi back all those years, who'd just toasted the rebel fleet. "Don't get the bloodlust vibes off him."

"And what's your argument, Davin?" Phyla swirled her cinnamon cocktail. "Hey, Yang, how about you and me over-throw this giant company and break it into pieces?"

"Can you imagine me, or you, or any of us in a damn board room?"

"Only if we're holding them all hostage."

They wound up back near Alyssa's place as the hours crept past midnight. Phyla and Davin weren't drunk, exactly, definitely not. They'd had plantains, they'd had fruits and nuts, they'd had lemony sorbet, and all that turned the alcohol from deliciously devastating to delightful.

Alyssa's manor, her estate, whatever you wanted to call it, still seemed too dark despite the time. No lights beckoned through the windows. The fancy carvings on the walls, around the windows hardly showed save for flickered shadows.

Davin and Phyla both sighed as they found the main door, heard not a whisper coming from within.

"Just you and me," Davin said, hand on the door's handle. "Since when did our crew get so lame?"

"Next time, make it mandatory," Phyla replied, eyes glittering just like emeralds in the faux-firelight. "Crew bonding."

"A great idea, pilot."

"Co-captain."

Davin chuckled. "Co-captain."

Pulling the door open, Davin led the way inside. From the street, he could forgive a lack of noise. The rooms had windows, people might be sleeping. Maybe the urban sounds washed everything else out.

From inside? The empty lobby spreading into the table-cluttered, yet abandoned courtyard?

The quiet cut a sober knife through Davin's good times, prompting a halt just inside the door. A reach for a pistol he didn't have. For Melody, lost somewhere in space above Earth. Phyla caught the same pulse, stopped next to Davin, searching the gloom.

"Something seem off to you?" Davin whispered.

"Everything here seems off to me."

Davin cursed his own idiocy: he hadn't asked Alyssa where they kept the weapons. The manse was large enough he and Phyla could dig for a while without finding a pea shooter, and if whatever caused the quiet was still around?

"Run?" Phyla asked.

Dash back out the door, try to disappear into Quito's

streets, and what? They had no ship, had no contacts, no weapons.

"If there's a chance we can save someone, we've gotta take it," Davin said.

"Then go right," Phyla replied. "Now."

The pilot gave the directions, Davin led the way, letting the door shut softly behind. Phyla's course put them from the lobby into a sitting room, one overlaid with floral decor and sporting a fireplace along one wall. Phyla made right for the yawning portal, grabbing a poker from the holder and tossing the iron bar towards Davin. She picked up a second for herself.

Despite the cocktails, despite the laughter they'd been sharing in the hours before, Phyla had on her serious bent. This was the pilot, this was the woman who kept Davin on track, and he felt his own nerves steel themselves up.

Someone might've had the drop on Alyssa and the Nines, but that someone was going to find it hard to close the trap.

"Let's go hunting," Phyla said.

First goal, get up one level. All the bedrooms were on the building's second and third floors. Any Nines still sleeping deserved to be found, added to their retinue.

The building had sweeping stairs up from the central courtyard, but those had about as much cover as waltzing into the open screaming their names. Instead, Davin and Phyla went out of the study through the other door, passing into a dead-end nook with a toilet. On its other side lay a dining room, and beyond that the kitchen with its back stairs for subtle servant movements.

Davin adopted the leader's mantle again, leading the way into the posh dining room. Tables and chairs set perfectly, as if they hadn't been used in years—Davin did find it hard to imagine Alyssa sitting at a spot like this, so formal. Shadows danced through thin pulled curtains, the faux-firelight creating a ghostly ball with the spindly furniture. Big hutches loaded with plates and glasses sat along the walls, leering.

Davin quick-stepped, rolling his feet along the stone-covering rugs. Kept the motion quiet, kept his ears open. Now that they'd ditched the entry's outside clutter behind, nicks and knacks reached their ears. The cracks of an old building, the rush as water went through a pipe somewhere. Someone washing blood off their hands?

Davin felt Phyla's back against his, their feet syncing up. A move they practiced for fun in the *Jumper*'s simulators, playing through games together on the long flights from one planet to the next. Not one you'd expect to use in a galaxy of lasers and long range fire.

But one that proved useful.

As Davin neared the dining room's far exit, the shadows shifted, a dark form moving to stand in their way. Bigger, bulkier, like Mox but with extra padding along the middle and legs.

The form might've been one of Alyssa's dudes, but when it raised the red-glowing rifle barrel, Davin went for self preservation and whipped the poker, a quick flick that would've been useless if they stood much further than a couple meters apart.

"Behind!" Phyla said at the same time.

The crack as Davin's poker whacked his target served as his answer. Davin charged after his throw, the hit forcing the person's rifle out wide enough for Davin to get his shoulder charge in play.

He barreled into the form's chest, bounced off hard armor and fell on his ass. The form didn't grunt, didn't move a millimeter. Davin's eyes narrowed as the rifle's red found him. But the captain's hands found the fallen poker, and again Davin's reflexes proved faster.

Jabbing up with the poker, Davin stabbed through the rifle's center, prompting sparks and ionized gas to blow out in a purplish mist. A jolt ran through the poker, made Davin's hand twitch, but adrenaline kept his grip. A pull down, an aim adjustment to go for the knee, and Davin felt the form's heavy foot crunch into his side.

Davin flew, crashed into a chair, felt the antique wood snap around him as he collapsed to the rug.

Aches bloomed.

So much for feeling good.

"Getting real tired of this," Davin wheezed, the form following up its kick with an awkward step forward.

Bright red flashed behind him, and Davin couldn't resist a check on Phyla. At first he saw nothing more than a second form stitching lasers along the table. Then he noticed Phyla, poker in hand, ducking beneath the heavy furniture.

"It's not going well," Phyla said as Davin backpedaled across the carpet towards her.

"Really? What was the clue?" Davin asked.

The rifle fire that should've killed them both slowed to a stop, only a few bolts burning through the table to scorch the rug. Both attacking figures marched to the room's middle before turning to face the table Davin and Phyla hid beneath.

"Something strike you as unnatural about those two?" Phyla asked.

"Smells like Heath, but these are a bit clunky for androids," Davin answered.

The things stood real rigid, didn't try any conversation. Made no noise when whacked by the fire poker. Davin could've gone on, but he turned his attention to an escape.

"Give up," came the inevitable call, not from either figure but the doorway Davin had been marching towards.

"Dammit," Davin muttered.

The voice belonged to Aya, Heath Swane's chief annoyance officer. The soldier seemed to float through life, only coming awake when she could shoot someone or, in Phyla's case, scan her bits to turn them into an android.

"Come out slow, or I'll have my friends here turn you to molten sludge," Aya said. "Not what Heath wants, but what we're prepared to do."

Davin met Phyla's look, saw her tighten the grip around the fire poker. His left side hurt, not bad, but a reminder of where he'd been not all that long ago, where they'd return to if they tried busting out from here.

"I'm not letting them shoot me again," Phyla whispered.

"Davin?" Aya called. "Ten seconds."

"We don't die for nothing here," Davin replied. "They want us for something, which means we have a chance."

Phyla kept her face set, her grip tight. "You first. If it goes south, I'm not giving in."

Davin pressed his lips together. No good comeback to that, and he could read her muscles. This was the racer committing to a course. She'd been captured, she'd been set up and shot down. Phyla had every right to say she'd rather go out fighting before letting that happen again.

And Davin had every right to keep that from happening.

He swept up from under the table, ignoring the two stomping machines, and went straight to Aya.

"You have the answers to all my questions?" Davin asked as Aya smiled her floaty-ass smile.

He noticed, too, she still had a wrap on her left foot. Coolant burns could take a long time to heal. Good.

"Of course," Aya said. "But first, can I welcome you?"

"Welcome me?"

"Eden's deepest undercover team," Aya said, tilting her head. "Working so hard to bring in our foremost target. Congratulations."

Alyssa, dammit. The arrest play was already on.

Davin ran the reaction through his scoundrel filter, saw the play and made it, dialing up a grin.

"Is that how you surprise us?" Davin asked. "Trying to kill us with those things?"

Aya looked past Davin, shrugged. "Low-cost models. I had them on standby in case any of Alyssa's cronies came back later. An unfortunate accident." Aya gestured at the table. "Phyla can come out now. We won't hurt you."

"We're a little trust deficient at the moment," said Davin.

"Understandable, but Davin, you have to get cleaned up. The cameras will be here soon, and Heath wants you looking your best for the show."

CHAPTER 8
TWO AGAINST THE WORLD

You try spending a night out on the town, ending it in a fight against two monster bots, then looking good for the viewing public at dawn. Davin's odyssey towards that final leg began with a pull, at Aya's lead, pistol out and ready, towards his room in Alyssa's old town mansion. The big bots kept Phyla in the dining room where, according to Aya, she'd be waiting until someone came for her.

"Someone?" Davin asked as they went through the courtyard towards the central staircases.

"We're pulling in more resources," Aya said without looking back, "but even Eden has a hard time getting many people here at this hour."

Davin did, though, catch three more of the big bots and at least a squad of the more organic variety roaming the balconies. Two people with long rifles stood on the roof, too, looking inward more than out.

This wasn't some slapdash raid then. Eden hit hard, in force.

If Alyssa had done the tipping off, she'd really sold it well.

"So why are you here?" Davin asked as they went up the

granite steps. "Didn't think Heath was well liked by the big boys up at Eden HQ?"

"Heath is expendable," Aya replied, as carefree as ever talking about her boss like a toy. "If the tip didn't bear out, then Eden could roast Heath without a problem. If it did, well, Heath and I aren't the only ones interested in androids coming back."

"So everyone in Eden's a scumbag?"

"Unfortunately no," Aya replied. "We still have work to do on that front."

Davin watched for clues as they hit the second level, the other Nines and their rooms now direct eyeshot from where he stood. Scuffles didn't sound, and he didn't spy blast bolts on the walls. No broken doors. The raid would've been fast, then, and efficient.

No way Mox would've gone down quiet.

"What'd you do to my friends?" Davin asked as they walked by a watching guard, hand on his assault rifle.

"We made them a simple offer," Aya said. "Either they surrender or we have one of our agents put a laser into your skull."

"What?"

"Did you enjoy those cocktails?" Aya asked. "We watched you drink every one. We heard your conversations. Very introspective, very sweet." Aya stopped by Davin's room, waved for him to open the door. "We would have left you and Phyla dead if not for your crew's cooperation."

Boiling rage wasn't exactly a distant friend. More like a drinking buddy. Being able to call upon the emotion to have an extra heft in his next punch, to push through yet another body blow . . . that was an asset, once Davin sorely wanted to dig into now.

He measured the distance to Aya's pistol, the odds he could tear it away, roast her and get a good shot off on the other guards. A grim calculus, that, but Davin started a lunge her way anyway.

Beyond everything else, Davin was getting damn tired of being a prisoner.

Aya didn't flinch away, didn't pull the trigger. Instead, she batted away Davin's reach, pushed him back a step.

"If you were sober and rested," Aya said, "I would relish another try at you. But I don't kill for sport."

Davin dished her a curse that didn't feel as good as he wanted, then stuck his wristlet up to the door. With a click, the red-with-ornate-iron flower entry swung open. Aya pushed Davin in with her pistol's barrel.

Close enough he could've spun, stole it from her.

Could've, but what he saw robbed him of the impulse.

Back in orbit around Ganymede, when Heath Swane's damn frigate caught up to the Nines and their disabled ship, Davin had gone from prisoner to rescuer in rapid fashion. A sly search for Phyla brought him to a room, one bright-lit and filled with beds. Rather than sterile hospital cots or military-style bunks you'd expect on an Eden frigate, these looked like torture devices. Metal limbs rising up, a big helmet meant to cloak the victim and subject them to . . .

"Hell no," Davin said, snapping from the thing occupying his room's tight confines. The original bed had been mashed up against a wall, the new monster eating up the space between mattresses end and the wall. "You're not turning me into one of those things."

The puzzle pieces fell into place, as they often did, too late to be of any use. Why pick Heath, the lowly Eden castaway? Because he could do a damn deepfake now.

Androids could always wear masks, but their twitchy programming made convincing mimicry a non-starter. Heath's last creation, good ol' Mecha-Phyla—may her circuits rot in Ganymede's rubble—scored zero points in that area, which meant what?

"I'm not understanding," Davin said as Aya kept pushing him inside.

Two goons waited next to the android-making-machine, their eyes buried in their wristlets, their hands tapping out instructions. Calibrations, coded commands, who knew and who cared.

"Your androids can't dance like me," Davin continued, his knees bumping the bed. "No way your tech's improved that much in a couple months."

"Believe what you want," Aya replied. "Now lay down. Time is running out."

"Yeah, for you," Davin said, wincing at his own crappy comeback.

He turned, bending as if he was going to sit down in the machine. Glancing behind Aya, he saw no secondary fighter, no covering chonker with a beam-spitting rifle. The opening was there.

Throwing a knee, pressing the pistol wide with his left hand, Davin locked Aya against the wall. Heath's chief crony took the hit with unexpected grace, falling back and letting Davin snare the pistol. Not expecting to get the weapon by the barrel, Davin took a half second to register he'd just won the arms race.

A half-second turned out to be enough time for one of the goons to nail Davin's neck with a stunner. The little hand-held taser pushed Davin's nerves to their max, causing a shaky jumble and the pistol to fall to the floor. The other goon reached out, pulled Davin back onto the android cot while the Nines captain tried not to chew through his own tongue.

Success came with experience: Davin had been stunned like this so many times by now the spasms felt almost like home.

Perhaps, just perhaps, a sign he had a problem.

"You waited," Aya said, retrieving the pistol and helping

to strap Davin in. "I expected the attack sooner. You should have been more reckless."

She talked like she knew Davin. Her stare said Davin hadn't played his programmed routine the right way. Her attitude said she needed to get out more, if she thought humans would make the same moves every time.

Not that Davin could give her the advice. The stunning zap was already starting to wane, but they had his hands and feet anchored in now. Had a headrest pushed up against his neck to keep his top half vertical.

Comfy, this was not.

"You'll feel a buzzing as the helmet clicks into place," one goon—Davin, head locked into Aya's sharp gaze, couldn't tell which one—said. "It's expected. Then, follow the prompts."

"If I don't?" Davin said, his words coming out fractured, more noises than anything, but Aya must've understood.

"We'll kill them all, Davin," Aya replied. "Not just your crew here, but everyone you've worked with. Then, and this will be the fun part, we will replace them." She didn't smile. No joy tinted her eyes. The helmet started down, its gears giving a soft hiss. "We won't let the families get close, of course, because that would ruin the illusion. Instead, they'll think the ones they loved abandoned them, and they'll never know why."

"That's comically evil," Davin sputtered.

The helmet closed over his eyes, settled on his shoulders.

"Then don't make us do it, Davin," Aya said, the helmet muffling her words. "It's up to you."

Take a ride in a simulator and you'd feel your whole body pulled along for the fun. Davin would nestle into a pod, hook his arms and legs into the right spots, and suddenly his senses would be transported to an icy moon, a volcanic wasteland, or a crowded city street.

Aya's android machine wasn't so fancy.

Davin heard the noise cancellation click in, the

surrounding sounds from the hotel room vanishing, replaced only with a chilly robotic voice.

"State your name," the voice said. Davin tried to discern a gender, a mood, and failed on both counts. "Please."

To resist or not? Aya's threat, an army of clone machines systematically eliminating Davin's friends, seemed about as cornball as you could get.

But he'd also felt Mecha-Phyla's hands around his throat, saw those glossy green eyes glaring at him just like the real version would. Not an impossible trick to pull from distance, especially if you simply eliminated anyone who caught on.

"Davin Masters," he said, buying himself some time.

Not like stating his name would bring about the end of the universe.

"Repeat each statement," the voice continued. "Dog, cat, Red Voice, murder."

"Two of those sound normal."

"Please repeat the statements exactly as spoken."

"That's the only way I'm getting out of here, isn't it?"

Words began to pour out, five or six at a time in sentences, both questions and statements, that seemed to hold no relation to one another. Davin repeated each one, trying to figure out what the plan was. He caught a few familiar names—Alyssa, for one. Eden and the Wild Nines—but always wrapped in nonsense.

Mecha-Phyla hadn't spoken, other than growls and grumbles. A couple ideas percolated, but the session ended before Davin centered on any one reason.

The helmet went dark, silent. Then, without any warning, a bright light flared on Davin's right. He winced, the light vanished. Something poked his right side and Davin jerked, uttering a curse. A chill ran across his neck where the helmet touched, prompting a shiver. The sensory bombardment continued, Davin wasn't sure for how long, wasn't sure of much in those minutes.

This time, when the helmet fell dark, someone pulled it off, bringing Davin back to the hotel room. Natural light bled through the curtained window, morning on the approach.

"Thank you," said the lone goon in the room, the man decoupling the helmet from the bed and placing it into a solid silver case. "You did very well."

"Great. That mean you're letting me out?"

"Sorry," the goon pointed past Davin's head, to the small TV mounted on the wall. "Aya said you need to watch this. After, I don't know."

The goon clicked on the TV, found the right channel. A breaking news broadcast, dawn's hazy blue glow filling a courtyard. The courtyard, Davin realized, in their building's middle.

Captain Heath Swane stood alongside several other Eden officials, and at least two Earth Defense Force commanders, going by their uniform colors. All looked serious. Less so was the man in the middle.

"Hey," Davin said. "That's me."

The Davin standing center looked, in fact, better than Davin himself. Dressed in Davin's black leather coat, armed with what looked like a darn good Melody replica, the Davin copy threw a wave, a wave just like Davin's own that he'd given to countless crowds on the Galaxy's Song cruise ship, as he stepped up to a hasty, Eden branded podium.

"It's not really you," the goon said.

"I get that," Davin replied. He should've been disgusted, should've been enraged, but with all the pieces clicking into place upon seeing the android, it was hard not to appreciate the effort. "How good is it?"

"Better, after what you just did," the goon said.

Mecha-Davin proved the goon right over the next few minutes, rattling out a speech with words Davin recognized real well. After dishing out a quick thanks to Eden for the opportunity, Mecha-Davin said his highly skilled team infiltrated Alyssa's organization, found their way to her, and called in the cavalry. Now they'd collect their paychecks and, with consciences clear, retire to enjoy their golden years.

"I'd never say any of that," Davin grumbled. Throughout the speech he'd been testing the cot's restraints, found them tight. Something Mox could destroy but not him. The goon, too, kept a stunner in his hand, and not even Davin could dodge that while locked into the bed.

"But you did," the goon replied. "With the helmet. That's why we had—"

"Yeah, I get that. I'm not a moron."

The goon didn't confirm or deny that assertion. Instead, after Mecha-Davin retreated from the podium, they watched some Eden admiral make a new call to the rebels to surrender, that their efforts were in vain, and yada yada yada.

"There'll always be another, you know," Davin said to the goon.

"Another what?"

"Leader. You don't get away with hurting this many people without some rising up against you. Just doesn't happen."

The goon shrugged. "Maybe, but we're getting really good at crushing you now. The old androids could just kill. With these?" The man sounded like he was describing his new favorite toy. "We can turn every revolution against itself."

Aya came back for Davin later that morning, all business. The real Nines were getting shipped out to a particular Eden prison facility. They'd rot in orbit around Venus until their lives gave out.

"But," Aya concluded, "you'll get the best in Eden meditative entertainment all day every day."

Her smile put on a vicious edge. Davin summoned up some saliva, meaning to toss it her way, but Aya had the goon stun him first. Aya put the cuffs on him herself, the two of them pulling Davin out onto the balcony, where his own damn doppelgänger waited. The android threw a hood over Davin's head, blocking out everything.

"Can't have anyone taking an unfortunate picture," Aya said as Davin fought with his own trembling muscles. "The only Davin that matters, after all, is right here."

The hooded march from the building marked the second time that day that Davin had been guided against his will. This time, though, the walk didn't occur in night's near-silence. Instead, voices cracked around him, reporters hollering questions and Eden reps replying back with static answers. Rich coffee clung to the air, along with pastry's tangy sweetness.

Not that Davin could get any. Should he dare to speak up, so Aya said, the Nines would be slaughtered long before reaching their prison. Friends and families too.

Amazing how much the threat of a loved one could paralyze a person.

The hood came off after hands shoved him inside a waiting vehicle. Davin sat on a bench, cuffed hands resting on his legs. A rusty red interior threw up all around him, poor maintenance evidenced in the discolored splotches. No windows. A working air conditioner, thankfully.

"Here I wondered what they were waiting for," Opal said, one of two other persons sharing the space with him. Her hands were cuffed just like Davin's, and it looked like she'd slept as well as he had. "I get stuck with the traitor?"

"Morning to you too, Opal," Davin said, trying to free his mind from exhaustion's mushiness only for hunger, thirst to take its place. "Why am I a traitor again?"

As he spoke, Davin took note of the third person, the only one standing. Wearing Eden's green fatigues, a full face mask, and a rifle in both hands, the guard said nothing. At first, Davin wondered if the man was another android, had a fearful moment wondering how many of the damn things Heath might've made, but then the man took a breath.

Just a regular human monster then.

"Because of that speech you just gave," Opal said.

"Does it seem like, if I gave that speech, that I'd be in here with you?"

The vehicle rumbled to life, its jets kicking it forward. Davin swayed with the acceleration, his stomach wondering what the hell was going on. Windows: turned out they were nice.

"Doesn't," Opal replied, "but it sure looked like you up there."

"Heath's been making lifelike copies. Not just killers, but replacements."

Opal sighed. "Of course he has."

"You don't sound surprised?" Davin waited till Opal glanced at him, and he flicked his eyes towards the guard. "Predicted this one?"

"I just assume my life is always going to get worse."

"That's a given, Opal." Davin leaned back, brought up his cuffs and coughed into a closed fist. Tapped his heel against the floor. "When have our lives done anything else?"

Opal resumed glaring, this time at the ceiling. Davin felt the guard's eyes on him. The captain coughed again, not bothering to bring his hands up this time.

"Have any water?" Davin asked the guard, who shook his head. "Silent type, eh? Don't blame you."

Rolling along on jets, the speeder tilted as it finally went around a curve. Davin went for another cough, leaning left with the turn. He curled over, turning his back to the guard. Coughed again.

"Turn around!" The guard snapped.

Davin didn't bother. Coughed. Ignored his throat telling him all this faking was going to have consequences later.

"You can't get the man some water?" Opal asked, putting just the right amount of exhausted indignation into the words.

Davin coughed again.

"Here," the guard said, marching forward a step, uncoupling his own water bottle and twisting off the lid.

Davin, cupped hands near his mouth, looked back at the guard, the solid face staring back at him. The black water bottle held forward like a grim peace offering.

"Thanks," Davin said, reaching for it.

Opal rose, wrapped her cuffs around the guard's neck in a single fluid move. She fell back between the benches, letting gravity whip the guard backward to the ground. Davin, grabbing the water bottle, stood and snapped a kick, knocking the little remote that'd activate the stun cuffs away from the guard's frantic hands. The tiny rectangle bounced off beneath the benches, so the guard went for his pistol instead. Pulled it from its holster, shot, a hair too slow to catch Davin's backwards dive.

The laser burned into the rusted interior, sparking up some smoke and splashing in a tiny ray of natural light.

Davin told himself the guard got a good look at the sun before Opal's chain-linked choke took him out.

"Remote's somewhere by you," Davin said, disarming the limp guard. "Kicked it."

Opal squeezed out from the guard. "Figures." She turned over, started the search. "Good play. Been a while since we used that one."

"Been a while since you and I were in cuffs."

Davin slotted the pistol away in a pocket, picked up the rifle. Standard issue, no advanced safety measures. Some of the things tied themselves to ID badges, to passcodes, but Eden wanted volume, and that meant cutting costs.

"Found it," Opal said, emerging from beneath the right side bench. Two quick presses and their stun cuffs popped off to the floor. "Where do you think they're taking us?"

"Nowhere we wanna go," Davin replied.

An improvised plan formed quick while they stripped the

guard of useful gear. No grenades, but a second pistol and a utility knife. Davin and Opal didn't have their wristlets—stolen by Eden—so the guard's emergency radio delivered some options.

"Ready?" Davin asked, the two standing near the hatch.

A red lock said it wouldn't open while the speeder was in flight, but the red lock itself was none too sturdy.

"I've been in these cuffs all night," Opal replied. "Let's get the hell out of here, please."

She stayed back while Davin unloaded several lasers into the lock, melting the thing off and springing open the hatch. Outside, a highway zipped by. Not exactly a prime evacuation option.

"Guess we do it the hard way," Davin replied.

This time they stood by the open hatch together, each holding onto the doorway with an open hand. Davin aimed straight ahead, held down the trigger and sent bolt after bolt flying towards what should've been the speeder's cockpit.

The shots burned clean through, right on to the outside. No pilot, hell, no cockpit in sight.

A drone hauler. Point A to Point B with nobody to bribe in between, no loyalties to question. Eden must've overridden its danger sensors too, because the craft kept on zooming. Its target loomed, too: Quito's big spaceport, rising up as the speeder neared a cresting hill.

"We never catch a break, do we?" Opal asked.

"Not one," Davin replied.

No sooner were the words out of Davin's mouth than the speeder slowed. Not a panicked breaking, but a gradual decrease until it moved along at a fast walker's pace. Davin and Opal glanced at each other and leapt.

The two caught the reason as they ran across the old concrete, stomping on weeds allowed to make headway in this era of floating cars: a traffic toll, charging anyone making entry to the spaceport's grounds and scanning them for dangerous weapons at the same time.

"Thank you, Quito!" Davin shouted as they ran.

"Shut up, you moron," Opal said. "We're not done yet."

"Celebrate the little things," Davin said as they hit the freeway's far side, then climbed over a pitted guard rail and dove into the grass.

"Once we have our people back," Opal replied, delivering Davin a no-joking glare, "and once those Eden bastards are dead, then I'll celebrate. You hear me?"

CHAPTER 9
SKYBOUND

Fulfilling Opal's oath wouldn't be easy from the grassy hillside, so the pair took up a stumbling wander through the brush, angling away from the spaceport till they hit a dirt path heading back towards Quito. A sunnier day than the last, the rays cut through the lighter alpine air and had Davin sweating. A headache murmured and his limbs dragged as sleep's lack crept on and adrenaline ebbed.

Vengeance, rescue. Davin repeated the two words to himself, trying to use them as leverage for a bit more stimulus, a bit more energy.

"You gonna keep muttering like that?" Opal said as they trekked along the dusty, tree-lined road.

"Was I talking aloud?"

"The whole way, captain."

"Might be my mind's finally going, Opal," Davin replied. "Just saw myself give a speech to the whole solar system while sitting cuffed to a cot. Thing like that'll mess with you."

Opal threw him an arch look. "If that's what's going to break you, Davin, after all the crap we've been through? C'mon."

"Get me some coffee and I'll be all right."

"Better be. We don't have time for a mental break right now."

Truth. Assuming Aya and Eden would stick to their words, the Nines, Alyssa, and her band were on their way to swift, silent trial and a toss out an airlock. They would be on their way to Eden's prison station already, could be dead by tomorrow.

That, at least, gave Davin some pep.

"At least we've done it before," Davin said. Quito's bustle played backdrop to the words, growing as they neared the city's outskirts. "Prison breaks are kind of our specialty."

"Might be worth wondering why that is."

"Thought we didn't have time for chitchat?" Davin flashed a smile, caught one from Opal in return. "Point is, we've got some tried-and-true methods."

Option one? Find a way into the prison, get to a control center and pop all the cells open. Hope the prisoners cared enough to fight for their lives, rescue the Nines in the resulting chaos.

"It's worked before," Opal said, "but I'm not betting on it here."

"Why?"

"You ever been in an Eden orbital prison?"

"Can't say I've had that honor." Davin tilted his head at Opal. "Have you?"

"Nope. Not planning on it either. But I've met rebels who took stints there," Opal said. "In fact, we had our own prison-busting missions drawn up, just never had enough people stuffed in them to make it worth it."

"So?"

"Right. These things, Davin. They're cylinders. Prisoners stuffed into cells around the outer edges. Every floor locked down at Eden's whim. They'll isolate anyone causing trouble and gun them down."

"Not helpful."

The dirt path found its way through some houses as they spoke, transitioning to paved suburbia. It was around noon, and people young and old bounced around the streets. Davin and Opal drew more than a few stares.

Hopefully nobody here cared to wonder why the face they might've seen this morning was going for a stroll.

Prison break option two: bust through the prison from the outside, blowing cells open, attaching an airlock, and sneaking out the good guys.

Opal had her head shaking before Davin was done talking.

"How're we going to get Mox and them suits? We'll just suck them into vacuum. Not something you want to see."

"Throwing cold water on everything?"

"My optimism's taken a hit lately," Opal said.

They veered towards a small shop, one selling a little bit of everything. Including, thankfully, coffee and sandwiches. A bathroom turned into a major plus, too, and the two reconvened on the curb to eat while bicycles and the occasional speeder zipped past.

Sitting there, hunched over in worn fatigues, a loose jacket over a tank top begging for a spin in the laundry, Opal didn't have an admiral's bearing. Her look across the street at nothing in particular didn't bring with it the murderous determination Davin normally expected. Opal's back also looked empty without her long gun strapped to it, a mainstay during her Nines time.

Pressed to pick an adjective, Davin would've called her haunted.

"Getting to you again?" Davin asked. A moment's glance around the area suggested the passers-by kept to their own business, probably wouldn't call Eden down on Davin's head. "Remember how we used to deal with that?"

"I'd go into the sims and blow up some bots," Opal said,

biting her cold bio-turkey sandwich one nibble at a time. "Or Merc would get me drunk as hell."

"Or?"

The faintest smile curled Opal's crumb-covered lips. "Or you'd pull me into the next job."

"Damn right. Nothing keeps you feeling sorry about the past like the future."

"Wasn't long ago I lost a war, Davin. Not a bar fight, but a war."

"You kept it from being a slaughter. Eden was going to win any straight-up battle, and you know it."

"That's not what I told the people fighting with me."

Davin sighed. "What were you supposed to say? Chin up, everyone, we're all going to die today?"

"Seems to work in the movies, doesn't it?"

Davin gave himself a thoughtful chew. Embraced the thick bread, the cheese. Real texture in his mouth. Sure, the day had been one big suck from the start, but he could hold onto this as a bright spot.

"Everyone knew it, Opal," Davin said. "We held on to Vi's gimmick, but everyone going out with you that day knew they probably wouldn't be coming home. They fought anyway, rather than roll over."

"Now Alyssa's thrown them away."

"Can't say her plan makes the most sense. She's done that before. With the androids. Remember?"

Opal finished her sandwich, popped open the canned cold brew and guzzled it before shaking her head.

"You saying we're not just planning a prison break, but a full on rescue of the whole organization?" Davin nodded, Opal laughed. "All that hero crap's going to your head."

"We saved everything once, we can do it again, and I've got an idea how."

Prison break idea number three: Take the inside track. Use the system against itself. New, space-age prisons had all the fancy tools, so they didn't need to feed and support so many guards. Get inside, subdue anyone who gets in the way, get back out.

"You and me versus the world?" Opal asked. "Feels like your equation's missing a few steps."

"Might be." Davin felt his eyes lighting up. Normally, he'd get that feeling after a whiskey, but now, whether it was the coffee or the turkey, invigorating inspiration struck. "But let me fill in those gaps for you. We're two of the baddest asses in the solar system, Opal. Time to remind Eden who they're messing with."

Talking through a prison break, a full-on revolution, took time. Getting around Quito, a sprawling city, also took time. The domed towns and space stations in the outer planets kept themselves compressed, made it easy to dash from one vendor to the next without scrambling through traffic-filled blocks in between. Not so in Quito.

Even without the traffic, finding what the two needed took longer than either expected. Eden hadn't let them take their luggage from Alyssa's building, and while they had the pilfered rifle and pistol from the Eden guard, that wasn't enough to break a prison.

Arms shops weren't exactly prevalent—they weren't prevalent most places outside the fringes—but a few questions and new, cheap wristlets turned up some options on the city's outskirts, ranges and power pack shops nestled into the overgrowth. There, Davin spent far too much cash arming up with what he could find, namely another rifle for Opal, a pistol for himself, and laser-sucking body armor for the two of them.

Not exactly military grade, but they shouldn't die with the first hit either.

An early dinner—rice, beans, lab-spun pork—and a rented speeder dropped the pair a half kilometer away from Eden's private docking bay at Quito's spaceport.

Dusk set in as the two ditched their slapdash ride off the roadside, sneaking again into the tall grass. Approaching from the back like this let them skip the spaceport's entry scanners, though Davin found the hike even harder with a full equipment load.

Earth and its gravity.

Ahead, Quito's spaceport sparkled with white lights. The occasional launch rumbled as one spacecraft or another shuddered off into the sky. Depending on the engine, the ships left black or blue trails, dissipating energy or smokey chemicals.

Nothing launched from Eden as they walked, both mostly sticking to silence. They'd spent the day together, dishing memories and ideas back and forth, and now they focused on the mission, the odds stacked against them.

Davin figured he'd bust out the jokes again once shots started coming their way.

Eden's docking bay didn't have the courtesy to sit undefended. A four meter-high fence wrapped the place, broken up by tall lights every few sections. The launchpad bled out from the bulky docking bay building, a gray concrete platform mostly unnecessary with today's tech. And yet, parked there, as if waiting for them, sat a small Eden shuttle.

"It's meant for us," Opal said when Davin mentioned their good luck. "It's still here because we were supposed to be on it this morning."

"Nice of them to wait."

"I'm sure that's what they're thinking." Opal flipped off her rifle's safety as they neared the fence. "I cover you?"

"Always a pleasure to have the sniper watching my back," Davin said. "Once the chaos gets going, make for the shuttle and get her warmed up."

"You know I'm not a pilot, right?"

"Just turn it on, I'll handle the rest."

Getting through the fence would've been tricky if they hadn't planned for it. Davin took the heavy clippers he'd been hauling over his back, hoping they'd be good enough to chomp through the chain links. The fence didn't have barbed wire at the top, didn't have warnings about electricity or other deadly defenses.

Luck of the location: Quito probably didn't have the commerce or Eden investment to warrant heavy protection.

"Here we go," Davin muttered. He rested the clippers against the first link, and snipped.

The link snapped, the metal breaking apart with a satisfying click. Davin glanced back at Opal, gave her a wink. Easy.

The hope held for precisely one more second, until the spotlights flipped red and a hard klaxon sounded its displeasure.

"Plan B!" Davin said, wielding the wire cutters like some sword. He jabbed them in at the links, snipping and snapping as fast as his hands would allow. "Almost through."

"I'm ready," Opal replied, set off a couple meters to his right. "Don't need to make the hole big for me."

"Not your size I'm worried about," Davin said, completing the circular cut.

He kicked into the cut piece, folding the loose section through. The hole wasn't exactly inviting—razor metal pieces glistened on every side—but a torn sleeve or a cut on the wrist wasn't worth worrying about.

Dropping the wire cutters, Davin climbed through his hole, getting the expected scrapes along his head, left leg, and an annoying snag on his right wrist that took an extra yank to get free.

"One coming," Opal said. "Taking aim."

A dark shape, followed by several more a couple meters behind, was cutting across the landing pad on a hard dash to the shuttle.

A reckless play, but Davin could guess why: prepped for launch, the shuttle's ramp lay down and open. Letting the enemy get inside would make everything suck loads, and probably get the pilot disciplined.

If Davin had his way, everything would still suck loads for Eden.

Opal's first shot flashed behind Davin as he started his own break for the shuttle. Rather than gunning for the lead form, Opal's laser hit a luggage cart near the following figures. The spindly, wheeled vehicle crackled with the hit, sparks flying.

"C'mon," Davin muttered, watching as he scrabbled from the grass beyond the fence onto concrete proper. "Be a hero."

Opal fired another, the red laser—low power—streaking to the right this time and beaming into a big Emergency water tank. The bulbous thing blew out steam, a whistling whine joining the alarms.

Eden's lead player kept on chugging, arms pumping towards the shuttle. The person's reinforcements weren't so strong-willed: Opal's shots had them backing off, diving for cover.

"So perfect," Davin said. "Now get yourself going."

"Already moving," Opal replied, her voice coming through their connected wristlets. "Don't blow my opening."

Davin, his rifle bouncing against his chest as he ran, drew his pistol and fired a couple shots at the coming Eden runner. Both went wide, both intentional misses close enough to disguise, or so Davin hoped anyway, the point.

He plugged a couple more bolts towards the water-spraying mess too, bursting more steam from the tank.

A little more chaos, a little more opportunity.

Perhaps a little too much chaos.

"He's fast," Davin huffed, picking up the pace as the Eden guy closed on the shuttle.

"Probably used to this gravity," Opal replied. "I'm through the fence. Lost a sleeve."

"You'll look cooler without it."

Davin put himself ten meters out, a straight sprint across clear grey. The Eden guy had half that. The shuttle's boarding ramp sat down and extended, friendly emerald lights running down its sides. Otherwise everything sat coated in dull red and blacks, as emergencies at night tended to be.

A bright blue laser lanced by Davin's nose, close enough for the captain to feel the heat. Too big for a pistol shot. Someone back there had a rifle, was fixing to use it.

"Opal?" Davin asked, making the mental decision to risk keeping on foot.

"Plucky bastard," Opal said, her red counters playing off the shuttle's front. "He's hiding again."

The same couldn't be said of Eden's leader. The pilot hit the ramp a couple seconds before Davin, feet pounding up. Davin had his pistol up, decided a roasted leg wouldn't hurt things too bad, and squeezed off a bolt. The shot missed under, vanishing through the slit between leg, ramp, and the shuttle's hull, continuing into Eden's night.

"Don't damage our ship," Opal snapped. "We won't get another."

"Thanks, mom," Davin replied, hitting the ramp and feeling its levers shift as the pilot told the shuttle to close.

Two long lunges had Davin inside the shuttle's small confines, not much larger than the busted prison van they'd stormed from this morning.

The pilot greeted Davin with a pistol. Davin caught the pilot's turn, her gun aiming where his head ought to be, and went to a crouch. Her shot blitzed over his shoulder, buried itself into an unlucky crash couch.

Davin countered, throwing his own pistol. The small gun twirled end-over-end to smack the pilot's face, prompting a curse and a stumble, and creating an opening.

A longer ship or zero gravity would've made Davin's bum rush a dicey tactic. The shuttle offered no cover inside, and if the pilot had more composure, more time, she could've torched Davin just about anywhere she wanted to. Instead, by the time she had her pistol pointed back the right direction, Davin had a hand on it, pushing the barrel down.

The pilot fired anyway, the orange shot flashing into the metal tiling at their feet.

"Stop it," Davin said, wrestling the pistol away, only for the pilot to ball up her freed fist and slug him in the stomach. "Ow, damn it."

He blocked her follow-up with his left hand, letting his right take the pistol and shove its hot barrel right up under the pilot's chin. She flinched away at the touch, but the shuttle's cockpit didn't leave her anywhere to run.

"Just hold still," Davin said, feeling his kidney throb. That'd been a good socking. "We're borrowing the shuttle, and you. After, we'll let you go. No harm."

"Screw you."

A fair response, all things considered. Nevertheless, Davin didn't have time to play insult tag.

"Your friends are going to be scorching us in a second," Davin said. "They start doing that, I'm going to shoot you and take my chances. You really want to die for Eden? 'Cause I guarantee they won't do crap for you."

The pilot didn't move a centimeter towards the captain's chairs, the flight sticks, the engine starters. Instead, she spat at Davin's feet.

When did people get so difficult?

"Davin!" Opal called, her voice climbing up the ramp into the shuttle. "It's past time to go! My power packs are almost empty!"

"Well?" Davin asked.

The pilot shook her head. "My family depends on this job, I'm not—"

Davin reached into his jacket with his left hand, brought out a small taser like the one the Eden guard had that morning. A little insurance.

Before the pilot could protest, Davin jabbed her with the stunner, let her sink to the ground. Davin, setting the pistol aside, stepped over the pilot and into the captain's chair.

Eden's launch console greeted him, its green logo playing around a white background. Small text across the bottom told Davin to scan his ID to get things going.

"Mind if I borrow this?" Davin asked the pilot, who twitched on the shuttle's floor.

He leaned to the side, grabbed the pilot's arm and its attached wristlet, tapped it against the shuttle's console, and the thing sprang to useful life, welcoming Zoelie to her shuttle.

"Opal, get on in here!" Davin called, slapping away at the sweet options now available.

The shuttle's engines spun up with a high-pitched, delightful whine. The interior lights popped on, and the ship's small but standard shields blossomed. Small arms fire peppered against the shuttle, the scrambling guards outside figuring out their buddy had lost. The rifles and pistols could hurt the ship, sure, but not with the energy-absorbing field in place.

Not unless Eden kept some real artillery at their small-time space ports.

"Please let that not be the case," Davin muttered.

He wrapped his hands around the shuttle's flight stick as Opal climbed. The boarding ramp clicked shut behind her, Davin's clue to rise.

"Guess who's flying again?" Davin asked as Opal poked her head up beside him. The obvious question on her face wasn't the one Davin had asked. "Zoelie didn't want the job, so I'm giving her time to think on it."

"I'll make her comfortable then."

Outside, the shuttle drew even with those red spotlights. The shields held steady, the ship pinging a mild note that told Davin it was taking pointless hits. Rudimentary radar showed nothing on an intercept course, though an incoming hail from Quito's flight control begged to be answered.

"What's going on over there?" said some poor soul when Davin acknowledged the call.

"Lots of confusion," Davin replied. "Don't worry about it."

"Don't worry about gunfire around my spaceport?"

"I'd call Eden and complain," Davin said. "I'm just following their orders."

While he spoke, Davin pulled up the planned flight plan, the route going right where he and Opal suspected: a particularly nasty orbital prison.

"I will," said flight control. "What's your name, so I know who to blame?"

"Heath Swane," Davin replied. "You tell'em Heath got bored and decided tonight was the night to ditch this town."

Figuring that just about concluded the conversation, Davin closed the transmission and glanced back at his crew. Opal made use of the shuttle's prison prep, taking stun cuffs from a locker near the hatch and rendering the pilot harmless. The taser's twitching effects seemed to be wearing off, going by the more intelligible curses, insults, and general vitriol spilling from the pilot's lips in both Common and, Davin guessed, Spanish.

"You okay back there?" Davin asked anyway.

"Fine," Opal answered. Zoelie responded too, calling Opal something particularly heinous. Opal laughed. "She's fun."

"Throws a good punch too."

If Davin's stomach still smarted, the shuttle showed no ill effects from Eden's desperate barrage. They'd pulled up beyond small arms fire by now, Quito vanishing beneath clouds as Earth's upper atmosphere turned into an ever-more cluttered starscape.

Would've been a time those dots were actual stars, too. Now Davin guessed almost all were satellites, space stations, or starships zipping around. The old stars would be back there, hiding.

"I'm sure Eden will get to you eventually," Davin muttered.

The shuttle handled its own piloting now, funneling along the pre-plotted course. All Davin had to do was sit back, watch, and try to convince their hostage to play along.

Eventually, the prison station would ask why the hell their shuttle was coming in so late, and unlike those little workers down at Quito's spaceport, the prison would have the weapons to turn the shuttle to ash.

At that point, the only thing that'd keep Davin and Opal alive sat behind him, and from the sounds of it, she still had some anger issues.

Time for the scoundrel to turn on the charm.

CHAPTER 10
BREAK IN

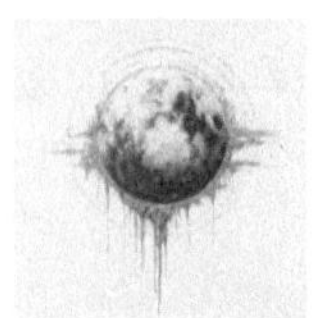

A pinch, a yelp, and an avalanche suffused with androids, plots, and dire straits left the poor Eden pilot with angry eyes and a twitchy right hand. Zoelie's fingers drummed on the seat's light cushion, one she pressed into good and hard as the shuttle climbed to catching orbit for Eden's personal prison.

Opal had traded spots with Davin, taking her lukewarm piloting abilities to the shuttle's front. Any minute now, the Eden prison would be asking a whole slew of pointed questions to which Opal had no good answers. She'd have to lie, evade, and spin, all things the sniper did as well as Davin sang pop songs at karaoke.

In other words, if Davin didn't get Zoelie and her passcodes, docking procedures, and general authority on his side, this was going to be a rough ride.

"You going to pay me?" Zoelie asked after mulling through all of Davin's nightmare scenarios.

"What now?"

Davin asked the question sitting to the pilot's right, across the narrow aisle splitting the shuttle. He'd debated whether to take the spot right next to the pilot, but that bubble-bursting proximity seemed a tad aggressive, so now he spun her way like an annoying passenger who just couldn't handle not talking to someone during the ride.

Zoelie's glare reinforced the impression.

"You're asking me to turn against Eden, who cuts my checks. Eden pays for my apartment, my dog, and my car, which has a crap rear axle waiting to snap," Zoelie said, her tone suggesting there were quite a few other demands on her bank account as well. "So if you're asking me to cut those ties, you'd better be willing to replace it with something."

"Guessing a clear conscience doesn't count for much?"

"Does it buy bananas?"

Davin winced, glanced towards the cockpit. The shuttle had cleared Earth's blue-white bar, the atmosphere's heat long replaced with cold space. Another couple minutes and one of those flickering dots in view would resolve itself into Davin's future home.

"Look," the Wild Nines captain said, dropping in a heavy sigh, "I didn't want to take the conversation this way, because you seem like a nice person—"

"I'm not. I do grunt flights for Eden. My life's a shell."

"My mistake." Davin nodded at nothing, nobody. "Does that mean threatening you won't get me anywhere?"

"Bingo, Bucko."

"Davin!" Opal called back. "They're hailing us. I can buy a minute claiming technical difficulties, but you'd better have something soon."

"Not me you have to convince," Davin muttered. The glowering pilot kept her arms folded, a tough crowd. "How about something else, then?"

"What?" Zoelie asked, not an ounce of trust in her voice.

"Adventure. Lasers. Action. A story to tell to that cutie at the bar you'd always want to talk to, but never felt you had something to say."

Zoelie blinked. A flush threatened to creep up, then

vanished into a scowl. Opal called Davin's name again, this time followed it with a curse.

"Well?" Davin asked. "Last chance to do something worth remembering."

The scowl settled, softened. Zoelie almost, almost smiled.

"You said you're the hero of Earth?"

"I did, and I guarantee you, this isn't going to be boring."

Despite Davin's words, Zoelie was about as boring as one could be as she batted codes and coordinates with Eden's prison station. The cylinder circling Earth dished out details, from flight speed demands to docking bay numbers, mixing them in with the expected questions about why she was arriving so late, who were her prisoners, and so on. Zoelie answered each question by casting blame where it belonged: on the universally mocked superiors. It'd been Eden brass who'd delayed her launch, it'd been an unexpected prisoner change-up that'd confused everything, and that also explained why the prison station had no names on its incoming manifest.

"Two saboteurs. Red Voice," Zoelie said, repeating what Davin told her when she'd muted the chat. "Ugly customers. I don't have any help here either, but they're cuffed and waiting."

The prison station took that as well as could be expected, protests and curses dying as inevitability took hold. Their docking bay changed to one for maximum security, and Eden's flight control said there'd be plenty of back-up.

Not exactly what Davin wanted. So he pitched a new story.

"Sorry, you'll want to change that plan," Zoelie said, playing along. "They're bio terrorists. They infected themselves with some nasty new virus. Get your vacuum suits on for these two, and I wouldn't risk more people than necessary."

More cursing followed. The docking bay changed a third

time, the new one requiring manual docking. Zoelie was asked if she could help escort the pair, which she agreed to, saying she'd already been exposed.

"And you're not dead?" came the question.

"Just lucky genetics, I guess."

The scintillating banter continued as the prison station rose out of the black, its silver and green shading doing little to make its vast rolling-pin shape appealing. View ports were few and far between, heavy plating covering the outside. Davin didn't have to guess why: Eden and Earth would plunk its worst prisoners up here, and none of them deserved a nice view.

Nor did they deserve a chance at rescue from some flunky with a ship and a death wish. The thick hull could take a crash landing and keep the bandits out, buying time for Earth's defense force to get their slow selves over with hot laser. So far as Davin knew, not a soul had escaped by means other than mortal or legal, and the Wild Nines had no hope of the latter.

Worse, hanging near the prison cylinder sat a battered frigate. Heath Swane's ship didn't coast alone: its bulk seemed to writhe as robotic repair ships scuttled about, replacing damaged plates and soldering new ones into place. This close to Earth, the work wouldn't take all that long, and then he could…

What, exactly? With his android doppelgängers running amok on Earth's surface, making a mockery of Alyssa's idiotic plan, Heath had no need to drift near a prison.

"Maybe he's that scared of us," Opal mused as the pilot turned the shuttle in for the last stretch before the docking. "Doesn't even trust an Eden prison to hold the Nines."

"The who?" asked Zoelie, whom they both ignored.

"I'm almost vain enough to believe you," Davin replied, "but I don't think Heath's that single-minded. Eden ought to be crowning him right now. He saved their asses, and might've resurrected the android program at the same time. He should be getting a hero's party."

"Guess you'll just have to ask him yourself."

"That'd mean talking to him. Figure if I see Heath, the first thing I'm doing is shooting a laser down his throat."

Opal frowned. "How d'you think that'd work, Davin? Shooting a laser down his throat? You have a pistol that tiny?"

"Shut it, Opal."

Even Zoelie, she of the perennial glower, chuckled.

Landing came and went with a smooth precision that clowned Davin and Phyla's continual jank with the *Jumper*. Not a reflection on Phyla's skill so much as how the dives they docked with ran their bays. Eden preferred strict standards, a haloed white square against black-painted metal giving the pilot a clear zone to park the shuttle. The rest of the bay, marked for sensitive prisoner drops, had biohazard signs blazing on the walls. Those swirling, interlocking diagrams mirrored onto the forest green uniforms of the Eden personnel greeting them, a foursome sealed head-to-toe in what could've been an ancient spacesuit.

Two carried stun batons in their thick gloves, one held a tablet tapping away, and the last moseyed their way around the shuttle as she set down, apparently curious whether there'd been any outboard stowaways.

"No way they can move well in those," Opal said as she and Davin took up positions on either side of the boarding door. "We each take a baton, and then the fun starts."

While Davin was a fan of Opal's apparent bloodthirst, he had some reservations about starting a brawl in a giant prison. Eden would have back-up, and they'd come running with lasers quick enough. Stunning these four wouldn't be …

"Wait," Davin said. "I have a better idea."

"I get nervous when you get ideas, Davin."

"It's not mine. Stole it from a movie."

Opal's sigh said all the wrong things, but by the time Davin finished the explanation, when Zoelie unlocked the door and lowered the ramp, the sniper had bought in.

Zoelie greeted the thumping pair climbing into the shuttle, the two galumphing guards with the stun batons. The pair looked past the pilot to Opal and Davin, both sitting in their seats with stun cuffs resting on their wrists. Glum expressions coupled with slouched shoulders and an affected sniffle or two completed the picture of prisoners looking forward to an eternity surrounded by space and steel.

Eden's guards told the pilot to scram. She'd have reports to file about everything while the shuttle recharged its batteries for the drop home, and Zoelie didn't protest, slipping past and down. Whether Davin's appeal and his promise of Alyssa's large bank account would work was immaterial now: he couldn't do a damn thing except hope the woman's conscience took his side.

At his side now but very much not on it was the Eden guard, looming over him with the stun baton crackling next to Davin's ear. The suit coated the guard's face in shaded plastic, a shield that made Davin's surprise surge—left hand gripping the baton's hilt while his right slugged the man's chin—easier.

The guard grunted, stumbled back across the narrow aisle towards Opal's seat. The sniper stood, threw her stun cuffs and the link between them over the guard's neck and pulled tight. The choking started as the guard's buddy, cursing, tried to raise the baton, only to hesitate. A tough problem: save your distressed friend, or deal with the enemy ripping the stun baton away from the same?

Davin helped the guard answer the question by taking that freed stun baton and jutting it, spear style, towards the person—the suits belied telling whether a man, woman, or android lurked beneath. The Eden guard jerked back, tripping over the thick boots, while their pal gurgled away next to Davin.

"Stop struggling and she won't kill you," Davin said, taking a light hop over the kicking boots.

Eden kept its prison spinning, generating enough gravity to keep bones and muscle from turning to mush, but a little twisting left a lot of lift for legs just off Earth. Davin's head brushed the shuttle's ceiling and he tucked his knees up into a tumble, leading with the baton in a display that might've fit in with a low budget circus.

His target had no idea what to do. With one hand steadying themselves after the unstable retreat, the other waved the baton at Davin's oncoming form. A simple thrust batted aside by Davin's two-handed grip, the swing turning Davin enough so his shoulder led the impact. The pair ground into the shuttle's aft, passing by the open boarding door.

Not quite the plan, that, and certainly not helped by the shouting beyond. Tablet tapper and their friend would be making all the wrong announcements.

Which meant Davin needed a new idea. The movie suggested a simple knock out and costume change would buy Davin and Opal a quick in, but without that...

The guard head-butted Davin, the hard plastic doing a number on the captain's right temple. Davin ignored the stars and jammed his stun baton's hilt into the guard's chest, before dropping off his right hand to grab for the guard's own wild weapon. The reach put Davin's back to the guard, had him sitting, as much as he could, in the guard's lap.

A ridiculous, terrible pose, but it kept the damn sparking end from numbing Davin's gut, so he held it. Dug elbows into the mushy suit, drawing grunts and groans every time, but small bruises wouldn't win this. And with fresh suited faces appearing on the boarding ramp, Davin couldn't afford to play the long game.

The shuttle lurched. Engines roared to emergency life, sending the shuttle on a sharp spin to the side. The tablet tapper and their comrade on the ramp flew off to rough landings, while Davin and his punching partner flew apart. Davin slammed into and rolled over the last row of seats, arresting himself with a delirious grip on an old cushion. Stun batons whacked around, their numbing ends turning off without pressure on the hilts.

During his rapid flight-and-flip, Davin had seen the cause for the shuttle's sudden snap: Opal, her guard dazed on the floor, had gone to the pilot's chair and used her utter lack of flying ability to send the ship into a frenzy.

"Davin!" Opal shouted. "Get your ass over here and fly this thing!"

Getting anywhere while on a tumbling shuttle, one spinning in place, was a challenge. Davin pulled himself into the aisle, watched as the choked out guard rumbled past, then lunged one row ahead at a time. Going for the biohazard docking bay had paid more dividends than expected, as its vacant space meant the shuttle could do the dumb maneuver without crushing itself.

At least for the moment.

"Set it down," Davin called back to the sniper, who was plopped between both piloting seats, gripping the console to keep herself steady. "We're not—"

"You're acting like I know how to do that," Opal snarled back. "I hit a couple buttons, Davin. I'm not a pilot."

She followed up the last by looking aside and vomiting some nutrient goop across the floor, a patch Davin dodged with another well-timed hop. This time he bounced off the ceiling and found rest in the pilot's chair, throwing Opal a sympathetic wince—his own guts were roiling too—and parsing what she'd done to the shuttle.

Slapping a few random buttons on a spaceship shouldn't throw it into a spinning panic, but Opal had managed to do the one thing that might: she'd restarted the maneuvering jets and slammed the steering all the way to starboard. Davin reversed it, and the shuttle sighed into a soft landing. The captain didn't wait for the ship to settle, and neither did Opal.

The sniper, wiping away the dribbling sick, lurched down the aisle towards the suited guards. Along the way, Opal scooped a stun baton off the floor, enabled its shocking stopping power, and jabbed it into the pair before they could do more than raise a helpless hand. Davin, following, grabbed the other weapon, and together the two stumbled down the ramp into the bay.

Tablet tapper and their pal lay crumpled along the side wall, flung at speeds high and hard into the metal. Neither one moved, and Davin didn't go looking closer. Whether they lived or died wasn't a question he needed or wanted to answer right then.

He'd prefer a low body count, but not at the cost of his own.

Zoelie waited by the bay's exit, mouth still agape at what she'd just seen. As Opal and Davin approached, Zoelie started to say that the pair were so screwed, only for Opal to jab her with the stun baton, dropping the pilot right there in the door.

"That was mean," Davin said.

"A kindness," Opal replied as they slipped beyond the door into the hallway beyond. "She'll have a ready excuse now, a victim of wanted prisoners. Eden won't fire her for that."

"Says you." But Davin could concede the point. Getting stun-stabbed by enemies was just another risk of Eden employment. "Now where?"

"Simple. Sanitation."

Opal's logic was hard to refute: neither she nor Davin looked like they belonged on the station. The place most likely to escape much inspection, most likely to be filled with bots instead of Eden personnel, would be the vast tanks changing prisoner's crap to consumables. Getting there from the decontamination bay could've been an impossible gauntlet. Instead, as Davin and Opal looked at the walls plastered with loud signs—all red, black, and official—the prison's dumping ground lay on their level, just to the right.

"Guess it makes sense to put all the infected crap near the incinerator," Davin muttered as he and Opal turned down the curling hallway.

Eden did its space prisons in much the same way as its ships: an attitude of slovenly sparseness. The walls and ceiling, aside from the official warnings, bore splotches and stains. Lines between plates spawned rusted tendrils here and there, while dust drifted from vents long left without a cleaning. At least soft air ran through, showing the prison hadn't neglected the absolute essentials.

"And they want this company to run the solar system? Really?" Opal said under her breath as they walked past dark rooms.

Vacant offices, supply closets, and unknown other hallways all sealed with blinking security scanners. That no alarm rang, no guards came pounding their way despite the shuttle mishap was both stunning and strange. Without much explanation, Davin wanted to chalk it up to Eden incompetence, but Heath Swane's proximity suggested something both dumber and more sinister.

"What, you think this is another ploy?" Opal asked as the hallway continued its wraparound. "Heath letting us stage a prison assault so his androids can wrap us up?"

"Seems as likely as anything else," Davin replied. "Eden's awful, but I can't imagine they're this lazy."

That question was again put to the test as they hit sanitation's entry, an inward double door again locked with a security panel. The prison didn't run on easily stolen ID cards, instead demanding both a fingerprint and voice identification to open up, a fact Davin discovered when he tapped the scanner and found little leeway.

"I could shock it," Opal said, flicking the baton on and off so little sparks shot into the air. "Maybe it'll short?"

"You're feeling violent today."

"Oh, I'm sorry Davin. Is this too much for you?"

"Just because Marc's not here doesn't mean you have to be mean."

Opal laughed, then reversed her grip and pounded on the double door with the stun baton's back half. The sound echoed.

Davin sniffed. "What're we going to say, that we're selling insurance?"

"If they're dumb enough to open this door, we're not going to say anything."

Also left unsaid was the plan if the door didn't open. Trekking back down the hall would, Davin had to imagine, run them into some sort of Eden resistance. Even if not, assuming every way off the level was locked meant Davin and Opal were stuck, and there were few hells more unappealing than a space prison corridor to be trapped in.

Davin was just about to voice that dire outcome when the door shuddered, slid apart.

"Well, well, well," said the man standing inside, one Davin did not, definitely did not, expect to see again. "Nice to see you after all this time."

The Wild Nines captain didn't say a word. He did cock his left fist, sans stun baton, and swing it.

Some people only deserved a punch to the face.

CHAPTER 11
OLD FACES, NEW IDEAS

Uros, the bearded, quiet rebel captain, had adopted a severe diet and a grungy, stained jumper. That beard, busy, red, and wild, seemed the only thing clinging to what the man had been, and Davin found his swing catching in its bristles, losing weight before connecting with Uros' chin. The man retreated a step, then burst out into a mad chuckle.

"After all this time, that's the punch you throw?" Uros declared as Davin eyed his right hand like he would a traitor.

Cold cocking had never been Davin's strong suit, but laughter? That was insulting. Now he'd have to go practice.

Opal's greeting measured better on human scales, the sniper reaching out and shaking Uros' hand before drawing the man into a friendly hug. After, Opal gave the captain a once-over before declaring the man looked terrible.

"The Eden lifestyle doesn't suit me," Uros replied, a rueful shrug following the words. "I gather it doesn't suit you either."

"Why would you say that?" Davin leaned around Uros, looked back into the dim-lit, rumbling nest behind the man. "We're adaptable."

"Because you're on the run." Uros's eyes twinkled as he spoke.

"That obvious?"

Opal snorted, then pushed past Uros. Davin followed, the door swishing shut. The space prison's sanitation works sprawled out, a multi-level morass of pipes, pools, and churning rotors ensuring every possible fluid, food, or chemical compound that could be re-used was cleansed and shoved back into the rotation.

The economics of life in space demanded no less.

Splatters and stains added color to standard-issue wall-hung notices and demands, all ignored by the listless prisoners working various areas, clearing too-thick sludge, trash, or their own demons from places they didn't belong. Uros didn't go much further than the few steps they'd already taken, surveying the place with them with his hairy jutted chin and an air of pride.

Not exactly the vibe Davin would've expected, given the nose-twisting smell and gut-rotting weight to the air, but everybody was made different.

Opal laid out the circumstances, the idea to break the Nines out and prove Heath Swane's gambit a lie. She didn't go into Alyssa's market-tanking master plan, an omission Davin didn't correct, because he thought the plan frankly insane. A consequence of too many hours left alone with her own thoughts.

Easier to just take a blow-torch to Eden's bits and wait for them to give up.

"Then let me ease your mind," Uros said as Opal wrapped up. "You won't need to break out your friends."

"Say again?" Davin asked.

"This is an Eden prison. Only a few guards. The ones you already hurt, I think, are about all on the station."

That sentence, after throwing Davin for a reality check, prompted more than one follow-up and a snappy answer from Uros. Those same outer space economics, coupled with Eden's desire to drop expenses by any means necessary, meant the prisoners were left to rule the roost. There were no escape pods, no shuttles to capture, no ways off the station, and if the prisoners didn't keep things in good working order, then they'd all die.

Which, so far as Uros could tell, would suit Eden just fine.

The token administrator and guard trio Eden kept stationed existed just to oversee supply shipments and dumping new arrivals into the central levels, where all the prisoners lived, fought, and accepted, sometimes with threats, their assigned duties.

"Who gives them their assignments?" Davin asked.

"It's a list, and people take the spots. You slack, you don't eat." Uros nodded as he spoke. "It works, mostly."

That a whole bunch of rebels, criminals, and random troublemakers would unite to keep a space prison in operation seemed far-fetched, but Uros made the compelling argument that staying alive, staying fed, and staying free from your own refuse tended to motivate people. Beyond that, Eden delivered cheap movies, books, and time-wasting tidbits to burn the days away.

"For some here, it's a better life than they had," Uros concluded, by which time Davin was rubbing his forehead and Opal leaned, eyes closed, against the nearby wall. "You might find it so."

"Yeah, but no," Davin muttered. "Not staying here. My ship's on the Moon, and there's people back by Saturn that're depending on us."

"Then you want to leave?"

"Uros, was it your capacity to see the obvious that brought you to the captain's chair?"

"That, and my good looks."

Davin blinked, took a deep breath which he immediately regretted, then coughed his way into another question.

"Any ideas for how we get out of this place?"

"Didn't you come here in a shuttle?"

Man, again with the obvious. Coupled with the man's revelations that Eden regarded its space prison as a money sink best ignored, Davin figured he might be overthinking things. Maybe, having made it here, they could waltz right in and take his crew out.

One step at a time, then.

Access about the station came courtesy of those keypads and daily code changes delivered to the prisoners who took every area's jobs. Decide on shoveling slop with Uros and you'd type in three-two-three-one and hold your nose when you arrived. Leaving was a simpler choice, one Uros explained by giving Davin and Opal directions to the space prisoner's central lift ring.

"Won't those guards get in our way?" Davin mused as Uros guided them back to the sanitation sector's exit, the man's shift far from over.

"They aren't paid enough. If they're moving, they will leave you alone."

The confidence in Uros's voice suggested more than one tussle that'd been left to lie. As Davin and Opal still had the stun batons, the captain didn't push the issue. Might be nice to lay out those Eden bums again if they wandered into range.

That their trek went without interruption vindicated Uros's judgment. Much as Davin hated giving the rebel captain credit, not a soul accosted Davin and Opal on their walk, and the central lift triangle did indeed come without security. A single button called the nearest lift, and when it arrived, the featureless cube split their options in two: on the left, a single button declaring the main floor. On the right, a keypad and a simple sign listing codes for the cell block levels and cafeteria.

"Enter the code, reach your destiny," Davin said,

wondering what'd happen if he started punching in random numbers.

"Keep those intrusive thoughts to yourself," Opal replied, slapping the single button and shifting her body to block Davin's reach.

"It's like you don't think I can control myself."

"Years of experience would prove me right."

Davin snorted. "You know, I could throw an insult or two your way, but I don't because I'm a nice guy."

"Is that so?"

Opal's smirk forced a reply with a sigh.

"Okay, it's because you could do terrible things to me with that baton."

"That's right."

The lift ended the awful conversation with a bold statement: the back wall opened onto what looked like sheer chaos. Eden's packed prison made dense use of its space, with the central ring giving a few stories to open air recreation before hitting a hard inner cylinder ceiling whereby food, entertainment, and other options waited via open lifts. The cell blocks sat atop the main yard, the central lifts and perimeter stairs the only ways up or down.

Prisoners demonstrated gravity's weak hold with wild romps, engaging in absurd basketball games, weightlifting, and other idle athletics that'd earned devotion in space's friendly physics atmosphere. Others lingered in dazed groups, tossing cards or gaping in simultaneous silent stares at nothing, the abyssal gaze that Davin had seen all too often among peers in Vagrant's Hollow as they contemplated a long, unchanging life.

Blending it all was a pulsating soundtrack, at the moment a thumping, ricocheting bass that made any spoken words unintelligible. The music echoed off metal walls, a mess of noise that nobody seemed to mind.

"Torture," Opal muttered as they stepped into the space. "That's what this is."

"Don't see anyone trying to get out."

"Give them a way, Davin, and I think we'll have a whole bunch of new friends."

The question, though, was where their old friends had gone? Mox should've stood out among this bunch easy enough, but the big man's exoskeleton failed to appear. Phyla and Merc didn't saunter up with sarcastic comments about Davin's late arrival, while Viola and Riley weren't lingering off to the side, confused and concerned by Eden's collected troublemakers. If the Nines were here, they'd been stashed elsewhere.

"Two options, then," Opal said as they continued to make their way into the mix, drawing no attention whatsoever. Davin told himself nobody would expect him here, so his celebrity wasn't recognized, yet it was a bit hard on his vanity that not a soul left so much as a lingering look on the captain. "We either scour all the cells searching for them, which I'm really not feeling, or we get a bit weird."

"Opal, you don't know how long I've been waiting for you to say that."

"What, weird?"

"Always so serious, it's time you went along with the Wild Nines peculiar brand."

"We have a brand?"

Davin waved the words away, asked Opal what she was thinking, and the sniper laid it out. They needed two things: to find their friends and convince Eden to land a ship here— or steal back the shuttle—for them to all ride out on. As for getting Eden to bite, Opal figured the easiest way was the hostage route.

"We go get those guys we tossed around, have them convince Eden to send in a rescue party, and let Mox take out his frustration," Opal said as she and Davin continued wandering around the great central grounds, earning casual looks here and there but nothing more personal. No Nines appeared either. "Then we coast back to the Moon, grab the *Jumper*, and disappear."

"Disappear? You want to give up?"

"I didn't, Alyssa did. Her crazy scheme to, what, get Eden's investors to force it to change course? Know what that sounds like to me? She's getting the yips. Going yellow. Losing her mojo."

Davin blinked. "I think I get it."

"Just like you did after Bosser went down. All those talk shows, all those thank-yous, and not once did you get anything for all of us."

The Nines captain squared off from Opal as they stood beneath the inner cylinder's flat bottom. The three lifts lazed up and down on thick beams, passengers as aimless as the ones waiting to board. A few nearby tables gave them company, most occupied by prisoners catching late night grub. Davin figured the hour might've been behind Opal's acerbic cut, but he wasn't going to let it lie.

She was giving him a test, seeing just how much fire Davin had.

If there'd been a slug of whiskey in his hand, the captain might've tossed some harder words, but as it was, after a long and not particularly great day, Davin gave Opal a squinted sigh.

"You think there was anything behind all that save some cash and a bunch of forms promising if I said the wrong word, I'd get thrown right into this damn prison?" Davin answered. "Eden needed its image buffed and I made a good show pony. I had no power, unless you wanted free drinks in the green room. I could've scored you those." Davin flipped on a grin. "Some were pretty good too, like this one with the pineapples in—"

"I swear, Davin," Opal started, but her argument petered

out into a shaking head. "It's late, I'm tired. Think we'll find our crew if we head up?"

"With our luck, I wouldn't bet on it."

Davin should've placed that bet, because the Nines were right where, if he'd have thought for a minute, his captain would've expected to find them: eating in the narrow cafeteria band, where nutrient goop dispensers offered endless, chalky options for the discerning convict. All five of the Nines, from Merc to Riley, sat clustered around a single table in the greasy circle.

As places went, the Eden space prison cafeteria continued the company's trend of sparing most expenses. The nutrient goop itself came from ten flavor tanks in the room's center, each stretching to the ceiling several meters above. Davin imagined vast pipes shuttled the awful stuff around at all hours. Nozzles at their end placed the goop into metal cups beneath handwritten labels describing the contents in colorful language both accurate and unutterable in polite society.

Not that this society was very polite, as the conversation drifting around, including the enthusiastic expletives shot from Merc's mouth as he saw Opal, put the prison cafeteria well into adults-only territory.

The Nines erupted from their chairs after Merc's outburst, drawing cursory attention from the other prisoners, who all returned to their late dinners upon determining the current chaos wasn't directed their way. Davin contributed, breaking into a short run to Phyla and wrapping her in a hug, one she returned with a tight enough grip to spark some worry.

"Did you actually miss me?" Davin said, pulling back.

"Always. When you're around, nobody bothers shooting at me."

"Because they're scared?"

"Because you're such an easy target."

Davin relaxed into a grin. "There we go, that's the Phyla I know."

Stories flew back and forth, adding color to the sudden abduction that'd occurred in Alyssa's Quito hideout a couple nights back. The various android clones had hit the Nines one by one, posing as their real-life pals until the proper chance came for a stun baton to the back. They'd been dumped on a shuttle and deposited up here without much word, without a single damn clue.

"But Alyssa's not here?" Davin asked.

"Haven't seen her at all," Merc replied, returning from the nozzles with some fresh, bluish nutrient goop. Opal started slurping hers, but Davin pushed his grumbling stomach away. Not quite desperate enough. "Not in the shuttle here, not before the attack on the surface either."

So she'd been arrested and shipped off somewhere else. A question Davin wasn't so sure he cared to answer.

"So here's the plan," the Nines captain said, drawing on the Voice of Authority every real captain had for times like these. "We're breaking out of here, getting our ship back, and . . . " Davin trailed off, running his eyes across the crew, seeing the thing every combat leader wants to find staring back at them.

Not loyalty, not happiness, but a burning desire for vengeance.

"We're taking out Heath Swane and his bots. Every last one."

Opal coughed. "And the rebels, Davin? Cass and the others?"

"Easy," Davin replied, leaning back in the stiff, plastic chair. "When we tear Heath Swane apart, we're gonna make sure everyone knows it was Eden's fault."

Confusion met his words and Davin let his grin grow wider. The suspense grew, and Davin figured he could let it simmer. Take a few bites of that nutrient goop.

It was, as Davin expected, terrible.

Phyla gave Davin the finger as she took her spot in the central level, the prisoners starting to fill it up after a long night in their hard-as-rocks bunks. Davin hadn't slept more than an hour, even counting a little bit of reunion fun with Phyla after his grand scheme won the Nines' approval. What, though, had sounded good overnight had a different feel in the morning, especially when it meant drawing everyone's attention to one particular bullet pilot.

You got this, Davin mouthed her way, his arms folded, hair wet after a fast shower with towels too thin to dry a desert.

The *Jumper*'s pilot didn't respond to that one except to raise her right arm, a metal nutrient goop cup in her hand. Phyla threw the container down, smacking it off the tabletop at her feet. The timing was precise, hitting in the slow transfer between bass-bumping songs—a musical assault that never stopped, no matter the hour, on this level—and getting a few looks.

Not many, because this was a prison and who gave a damn, but a few, and that'd be enough to get things spreading.

"Six hours," Phyla announced. "Six hours, and we're bringing this place down."

Davin repeated the time, calling out six hours and hearing it echoed across the level by Mox, Riley, and Merc. Opal and Viola would be saying the same in the cafeteria, crowded with prisoners resigned to another nutrient goop breakfast. They'd get stares, they might get questions, but neither mattered.

The time, the phrase, would be repeated, and it would make its way to the right ears.

Davin had sparked the fire. Time to fan the flames.

• • •

"Ready?" Davin said to Mox, meeting the man near the same lift he'd ridden in on with Opal.

They'd split for the rabble rousing portion, but the pair came back together for phase two. How many phases there'd wind up being, Davin wasn't sure. Best to keep plans flexible.

Mox, sporting the same loose, forest green prison jumpsuit available to anyone who'd ruined or worn out the clothes they'd had on arrival, grunted and slapped the call button on the lift's support beam. Davin's purpose in picking Mox for the role was already proving prescient: the big man's exoskeleton had a way of keeping people away, so nobody sought to join them on an elevator ride.

The metal man's hollow glare helped, no doubt.

Davin studied the lift's keypad, trying to find some intuition that might get them to Eden's administrative level. When blind luck failed—he tried the 1-2-3-4 classic to no avail—Davin tapped them back to sanitation's floor courtesy of Uros's insider knowledge. Mox settled against the lift's back, said not a word while the elevator descended, until the man squawked in surprise when his would-be rest retreated, becoming the door into the bland, branded corridor.

"You could have warned me," Mox grumbled as Davin marched on by.

"Gotta get my kicks somehow."

"I'll remember that next time you want my help."

"Betting you'll forget it quick enough." Davin spun while walking, threw Mox a cheeky wink, before sauntering back around. "It's part of my charm, Mox."

"Your charm's getting old, just like us."

"Young at heart, I say."

Mox's muttered expletive only made Davin's grin wider, though the shuttle's absence from the decontamination landing bay threatened to shrink it back. Phase two was a branching step, offering options depending on how Eden operated things, and if they'd left the shuttle here, then life would've been oh so much simpler.

Instead, Davin ticked the plan to the second line.

Eden's space prison, like just about any modern space station, had ways to get words just about anywhere you wanted them. The key, here, was getting the right person to listen. Outside the landing bay, a simple wall comm and keypad waited, installed so anyone in docking trouble could ask for help. The black screen offered no easy options, but Davin figured Eden wouldn't break emergency standards.

Four zeros on the lift's keypad might not get them anywhere. Four zeros on the comm did what Davin hoped: put them in touch with the bums running this place.

"Problem?" asked the same bored voice who'd been chatting with the pilot during their run-up. "And what are you doing down there? Residents aren't permitted in that corridor unless you're going to and from an assigned task."

"Residents?" Davin replied. "Is that really what you call us?"

"You live here. Therefore you're residents."

"Boy, Eden really has you roped, don't they?"

A sigh. "What do you want?"

"I arrived yesterday, in this bay right here. On a shuttle."

Davin leaned against the wall as he spoke, rolled his eyes at an arms-folded, similarly leaning Mox.

"The one that had the fight?"

"The very same."

"You're lucky we don't kill you for what you did."

"Well, here's the thing, I've come around," Davin said. "See, we took that pilot hostage. Made her land the shuttle or we'd throttle her into the next life. That, though, wasn't everything. We're space pirates, see, and we have that shuttle rigged to blow in about five and a half hours."

"What?"

"You heard me. Engine overload. Big boom. Nothing you can do about it, either, unless . . ."

Background noise came through the income, the fuzzy spray of voices away from the mic engaged in frantic back-and-forth.

"Telling you," Davin continued, "you won't find it. No matter how hard you look. We're pros. It's why Eden wanted us so bad." The conversation died on the other side, someone probably going to look at the utterly unaltered shuttle and find, indeed, no evidence of a trap. "Thing is, I've realized life's not bad in here. Free food, no debt collectors coming to skin me alive. Changed my mind."

Vacant hesitation on the other side. Mox rolled a finger, telling Davin he'd better spell the whole thing out rather than rely on Eden putting anything together. Probably the safer play.

"What I'm saying is, you bring that shuttle down here or tell me how to get up there, and I'll disable the whole thing. Your job's safe, nobody needs to know."

"I don't believe you," came the voice, but Davin could tell a dry throat when he heard one.

"Look me up. Davin Masters. Notorious criminal. A bounty the size of Jupiter on my head. You going to risk it all calling me a liar?"

"I, uh, give me a minute."

Davin glanced at Mox, tried to figure what gesture he ought to use to show his mocking confidence. He'd already winked earlier, and a finger snap didn't quite seem up to it. Nodding at nobody was always good, but when Mox reached out with a fist, the answer was easy enough.

A bump, a cough on the other line, and Davin Masters was in business.

CHAPTER 12
UNDER FIRE

Davin licked a finger, ran it through hair getting more and more wild. It'd been a long time since he'd sat beneath a barber's scissors, his look veering from swagger-filled captain into mangy renegade. Which, given where he was going, might serve him pretty darn well.

Eden had invited Davin into their home, and he was going alone, riding the lift solo into the sealed off level reserved for Eden's scant space prison staff. They weren't so moronic as to allow Davin to run up with Mox, a problem he'd have to solve while the Nines rallied the rest of the prison for a timed uprising in about . . .

Five hours.

In normal times, Davin might've used a wristlet, comm, or other device to set a timer. A not-so-modern convenience stripped away by the convict's spartan existence—what need did one have to track time in Eden's lifetime isolation? Nevertheless, monitors here and there did display clocks, probably to help keep prisoners on schedule. Davin had last looked at one on the central yard, dropping off Mox, before boarding a lift and entering the key code to send him flying upwards.

Hair as coiffed as a bit of spit and shine could make it, Davin leaned against the lift's back as it left the open area and disappeared into the station's sloppy white walls. The cafeteria and its nutrient goop zipped past, followed by ring after ring dedicated to the souls trapped here for, well, another few hours. A couple maintenance levels followed, given to all things power generation, oxygen scrubbing, and the other nuts and bolts Davin knew too well from the *Jumper*'s many quirks and quibbles.

If he had a comm—another reason to wish for one—Davin would be calling Phyla now for a last run-through, a wish for luck, and a sarcastic reply from the woman he loved telling Davin to pay attention, get it done, and don't be stupid.

That last an impossibility, just part of Davin's charm.

When the lift slowed, Davin folded his arms and put on a bemused grin. Sure, there was every chance Eden had cameras in the lift, were watching his every move, but bravado was always worth it. Especially when the doors before him opened to reveal a nervous quartet sans decontamination suits, with stun batons.

Davin had left his own stolen baton with the other Nines. Eden knew he had it, and no need to press their jumpy selves further.

"Howdy," Davin said, sliding up from the lean. "How're we doing?"

"Not great," said a craggy, bag-eyed man in the middle. The foursome all wore Eden's forest-green uniforms, though Davin noticed creases and stains aplenty. All four, too, seemed at the upper end of Eden's hiring spectrum, perhaps stashed here at their career's end. "I'm not keen on a bomb being on my station."

"Hopefully I can take care of that for you." Davin stuck his hand out, almost laughed when the bag-eyed man shook it. "Davin Masters, here to save the day."

"Tam Ways," the man said. "I run this station."

"And these?" Davin asked, running his eyes along the two other men and a bleary-eyed woman completing the Eden semi-circle around the lift's plain metal landing lobby.

"You don't need their names," Tam said, flicking his right hand to dismiss them. "We would prefer our staff stay anonymous. It prevents conflicts."

"Conflicts?"

"Some of our prisoners may have free friends. If they get out word, those associates may threaten our families."

"But not you?"

Tam stretched a craggy smile. "Not every name is real, Davin Masters, as I'm sure you've come to know during your auspicious existence."

"Ah, then you have heard of me."

Tam had, and explained that Davin's exploits had bandied around Eden's internal forums for years now. At first a hero and then a thorn, a rogue and a ruinous man who deserved nothing less than a laser to the eyes.

"To the eyes?" Davin quipped as they passed by personnel rooms not far off the prison cells in size and sparse amenities. "That's cruel."

"You've killed or hurt a lot of Eden, and therefore, a lot of our friends."

"Yeah, well, I'll claim self-defense."

Tam snorted. "Your type will always be violent, no matter the situation."

Thankfully, Davin didn't get the chance to ask what the hell Tam meant, as they'd reached the small docking bay reserved for private transports, small deliveries, and whatever Eden felt couldn't be trusted getting anywhere near the prisoners. There, much the same as it'd been the previous day, sat the shuttle.

One very much harmless.

Standing next to it, the glower having never left her face, was Zoelie. She'd received the same spruce up treatment

Davin endured, and seemed to be running on the same mix of adrenaline and caffeine that'd fueled the Nines for decades.

Sure, Zoelie didn't know the plan the Nines had concocted lower down, but the pilot had made the connection that proximity to Davin Masters meant 'the usual' was taking a long vacation.

"Hey there," Davin said as Tam hung back a step, whether because he thought a single stride might keep him alive if the shuttle went boom or because the man wanted to judge Zoelie's reaction. Either way, Zoelie grunted an acknowledgement and moved aside to give Davin a clear walk up the boarding ramp. "That's all I get after our conversation?"

"Conversation?" Zoelie's eyes flashed. "You took me hostage, almost killed me with my own ship when you pulled that maneuver in the docking bay. What do you expect? A smile and a hug?"

"Wouldn't hurt."

"It'd hurt me plenty. Get in there and fix my ship."

"You got it."

As Davin walked up the ramp, he noted two things: first, the docking bay was hard closed. Thick metal doors had slid across the opening into the black expanse of outer space, preventing an easy dash, doable if the bay had left itself spread with magnetic shields only. Second, Zoelie didn't follow Davin up.

Did Zoelie believe Davin had rigged the shuttle to blow somehow, or was she still choosing sides?

The answer to that troubling development didn't reveal itself as Davin walked into the shuttle's main hold, moving down the aisle and peeking out the windows to see the pilot have a brief, sharp word with Tam before leaving the docking bay behind. Tam pulled up a frown, folded his arms beneath his armpits in the classic pose of someone none too used to oddities.

At least it didn't seem like they were buddies.

Davin settled into the shuttle's pilot chair, the several screens powering up to show all kinds of fun details. First, Zoelie had charged up the shuttle's batteries to well beyond a usual flight's needs. Either Zoelie was planning on making a run to the Moon or she'd hedged her bets that what was coming might need some extra slack. Second, several plotted trajectories had been dropped into the autopilot, including one that had the shuttle floating out this bay and flying right back down to the decontamination level.

A perfect pickup that had Davin breathing his first relieved sigh in far too many minutes.

The Nines had persuaded Zoelie, and with her, the opportunity—

"How long is this going to take?" Tam shouted, the man preferring to yell up the ramp from his safe spot outside the ship.

"Just gotta make sure I get this right," Davin replied, dashing through a few pre-flight checks. "Wouldn't want to botch the job and set things off wrong, you know?"

"Please don't."

The shuttle passed its checks without issue. Ready to roll. Which meant, even though they were ahead of schedule, it was time to press go on this little enterprise.

Davin tapped the shuttle's comm to life, opened its link to the same flight control channel already set by Zoelie.

"Hey there, anyone listening?" Davin asked, conjuring up various lies, excuses, and sweet nothings he could use to get those doors open.

"I am," came Zoelie's voice, tight with something other than loathing this time. "The man who was here's taking a trip to the head, so make it fast."

"And here I was doubting you."

"I want that cash, Davin. If you don't get it to me by day's end, that shuttle's really going to blow up on you."

Oh, now that was an interesting twist. Could Zoelie have

rigged the shuttle to explode? Probably a bluff, but why call it if he didn't need to?

"You'll have it," Davin swore. "Mind opening these doors?"

"Tam's going to notice."

"If he didn't, I'd be worried."

Zoelie chuckled, gave Davin a five-second head start. One Davin used to withdraw the boarding ramp. Tam did, indeed, notice and started calling out this and that threat without moving or even drawing his stun baton.

"Where do you think you'll go?" Tam yelled as the ramp finished its withdrawal. "The doors are shut!"

"Thinking I'll try my chances. Better get running, Tam."

The Eden man cursed, seemed to decide Davin might be the kind of gonzo maniac to try ramming his way free of the station, and fled. Just in time for the bay doors to slide open. Davin goosed the shuttle's jets, found the calm thrum as the ship rose a few hairs above the floor. The flight stick didn't have the *Jumper*'s heft or bevy of accessories—and, could Davin believe it, he missed Fournine's lacerating commentary —but the Eden ship had top notch maintenance and turned like a charm when he nudged the stick to the left. A calm spin and soon Earth's great bulk sliced through half the black, the other a sparkling mess of other ships, stations, and . . .

Heath Swane's frigate. Still parked in close orbit to the space prison. Davin eyed the big ship, scarred from the *Jumper*'s surprise shuttle bomb way back out near Saturn. Enough firepower on there to blow the space prison to dust. That Heath would've done that already if he wanted to calmed some fears, but gave rise to others.

As Davin eased the shuttle from the docking bay and punched up the first plotted plan, towards the decontamination bay, the frigate seemed to wake. Turrets along the ship twisted, something Davin only knew because his shuttle lit up with warnings. Meanwhile, slits on the frigate turned yellow-white as docking bays opened, shuttles like Davin's own leaking free.

Having his gut turn to ice was never a fun experience, and this time was no different. The only way Davin knew to fight that feeling?

Take control.

As the frigate's turrets opened up, Davin punched the shuttle's throttle and prayed he'd live long enough to deliver the justice Heath so dearly deserved.

Dodging lasers in the prison shuttle felt too much like ducking blows after several Martian martinis: every move sluggish and apt to get Davin floored. Heath's frigate would have hard rounds, physical slugs that'd perforate the shuttle's slim energy shields like Davin's incisive repartee would penetrate dull dinner conversation, but the shuttle's damage reports were energy-only. Easy to explain: with the floating prison off to Davin's left, any wayward blast would smack the station. A laser would get sucked away by the station's own shields, but an explosive round might leave a mark.

Which gave Davin a chance.

"Tell me you're listening," Davin spat through the shuttle's comm system, opening the band wide. The pilot back up top would hear him, but she wasn't the important one. "I'm going to need a helping hand at the decontamination bay real quick, because this boat's not going to make it in good shape."

Any reply fuzzed out under the assault. The Nines captain winced as the viewport near his face flashed white and orange, the colors showcasing low-powered lasers meant to blow Davin's escape into a tumbling disaster rather than an outright annihilation. Or, again, sparing the prison collateral damage. Hits didn't shake the shuttle, didn't blow hull plates away. Instead, where Davin's jukes failed to evade the light speed zaps, the shuttle's wires melted. Circuits fried and metal boiled, creeping closer to a vacuum leak and Davin's swift death by asphyxiation.

A delightful end Davin had no plans to experience.

He pulled the shuttle hard to port, angling it into the Eden prison's smooth line. The shuttle didn't like that one bit, blaring fresh alarms about imminent collisions and the atomization that'd occur if Davin didn't adjust his trajectory.

"Whiner," Davin muttered to the ship. Fournine would've understood. "Shut up."

With the big station swallowing up the space to the shuttle's port side, the frigate's shots dwindled. Became more precise instead of a wild barrage. The old trick of ponying up to the larger craft still held true after all these years, targeting computers and ill-trained gunners had a hard time defining the small silhouette against the bigger station. At least, that's what Opal had said, what'd been a core part of rebel tactics in the last few run-and-gun years, and it seemed to hold true here.

Not that the shuttle was thrilled. Davin scanned the console, read enough integrity alarms—and smelled that classic, heart-stopping whiff of burning wiring—to guarantee this little box wasn't going through atmosphere again without major repairs.

Thankfully, it wouldn't have to.

Heath hadn't just launched lasers Davin's way: the frigate joined its guns with a shuttle wave. The svelte crafts, made for military work and thus packing more weapons, a shinier green frame than Davin's lumpy ship, raced in towards the prison. Some seemed to be angling towards Davin's own decontamination bay, while others raced for the prison's top bays. A full on assault, packing way more heat than Davin's little escapade demanded.

Whether that'd work out in the Nines' favor remained to be seen, and Davin didn't have much trust in his luck.

A few more lasers pounded into the shuttle as Davin scooted the craft into a hard turn into the decontamination bay. Davin pulled the ninety-degree shift with a hard push on the shuttle's starboard maneuvering jets, twisting the shuttle's nose into the opening while blowing its front jets to slow the ship down. Velocity in space was a tricky beast to calm, and the shuttle wasn't made for anything other than chill landings.

The viewport went from a split-screen between the station, black space, and Earth's blue haze to the red-washed decontamination bay, a swap that would've been fine if the slide hadn't continued to the bay's edge and the prison hull beyond.

Davin slapped the crash webbing across his chest, muttered a curse.

The shuttle ground into the bay's bottom lip. The viewport cracked and the ship wheeled as its remaining velocity made the collision a fulcrum. The shuttle's back end rose to span the bay entry's height, becoming the prison's newest vertical beam. Davin rocked from side to side as the shuttle ground into the prison's hull. Smoke, sparks, and more inane alarms told Davin the obvious: the man needed to leave, and fast.

Normally, evacuating anything in space required a suit for survival. The shuttle's shuddering halt seemed to give Davin the chance to climb back towards the shuttle's aft to find one, a trek he started by pulling off the crash webbing, putting a foot on the shuttle's console, and prepping to kick off, until he looked where he was going.

What'd been a few rows of sedate seats followed by a bathroom and small cargo slot had turned into a blazing disaster. Wiring dangled free from confines wrenched open by the impact. Bolts, rivets, cushions and shrapnel floated through the air in dizzying turns, some bits and pieces ablaze. Coupled with the blue-white sparks, smoke, and the techno-crunch of metal bending and breaking, the whole scene made a beautiful modern art canvas. It definitely told Davin any shot at getting back to a suit was impossible.

Spinning back around towards the console, Davin glared at the viewport's crack. The bay's floor lay beneath it, with the space station's outer hull and space itself still visible on the starboard side. Even if he punched through the thin splintering line, Davin would have to squeeze between the shuttle and the bay floor to get to safety, something he wasn't skinny enough to attempt. Any ejection from the shuttle's emergency options would be suicide here too, likely splattering Davin at high speeds into the docking bay.

"C'mon, give me something," Davin said, pressing his hands on the bulkheads around him and getting nowhere.

The shuttle was so shot up, but the only part keeping its integrity was the cockpit? Right here?

Davin cursed again, felt a pop in his left ear. A telltale sign the shuttle was losing pressure. Oxygen would vanish with it, dropping Davin into an unconsciousness he'd never come back from. Davin turned again to the cracked viewport. Not skinny enough, but maybe there'd be some miracle there.

Staying in the shuttle meant death, anyway.

One heel kick, then another, and the splintered line didn't spread. Glass meant to handle Earth's atmosphere could, apparently, absorb a Davin boot without much difficulty. The captain glanced around, his lungs starting to strain for every breath, and snagged a long metal chunk that'd once belonged to the shuttle's roof. The edges cut Davin's hands, adding bloody drops to the air, but Davin chalked the pain up as one more item in a long string of things he'd continue ignoring.

He swung the bar like a bat, slamming it into the viewport and, with the force, pushing himself back. Zero gravity was so cool in so many ways, and so bad in so many others. Still, Davin used the momentum, kicking off a passenger seat and flying forward, leading with the bar like an avenging angel.

That Davin and angels likely wouldn't get along didn't make much difference, that the momentum and metal shattered a hole in the viewport did.

If the shuttle had been floating free in vacuum, Davin would've felt his body temp drop. Would've found himself gasping for breath in the brief time before pressure took his insides and broke them free. Instead, he fell onto the station's floor, still trapped within the shuttle's crushed cockpit, but alive. The prison's docking bays, like most every station in civilized society, leveraged a magnetic, energy burning field to keep pressure, oxygen, and other essential bits and bobs where they belonged.

Another meter to Davin's right and he'd leave the field, drift into open space, and die fast.

Still, a look to his left, through the viewport's sparkling, sharp remnants, lay the shuttle's hull and crumpled supporting beams. A tangled mess of metal Davin couldn't hope to navigate. Couldn't squeeze through.

But he had to try, right?

"That you down there, Davin?" came the question, came the one voice Davin needed to hear right then, right there.

"Dammit, Mox. Get this shuttle off me."

Aided by his exoskeleton and gravity's flimsy grasp at the station's edge, Mox did, in fact, get the shuttle off of Davin. The extraction came with ripping metal, with Davin curling into a position not unlike the one he'd been borne in, and with flying sparks as the craft continued its collapse. The shuttle scraped on the docking bay's upper lip as it slid down into a shaky rest, a third of its battered bulk hanging beyond the magnetic shield into open space. Mox, breathing hard, stepped back from his feat and issued a single, sighing expletive.

"You think you've had it rough," Davin replied, crunching glass as he rose. "Try dodging lasers in that thing."

"I wouldn't put myself in that position."

"Yeah, yeah." Davin gave Mox a friendly smack on the shoulder. "Always surprised you're that strong."

"Batteries," Mox said. "Don't expect anything like that again for a while."

"Oh, don't worry. You can take it easy the rest of today."

Mox didn't chuckle, didn't give Davin a grin. A baleful stare, another curse, and the pair turned to the bay's exit. The crashed shuttle had an incidental benefit: with its damage to the decontamination bay, none of Swane's invasion forces would be able to slam in here, meaning Davin could set up a right and proper defense. Or, rather, join in the one Opal and Merc had already cobbled together.

Eden's prison wardens gave voice to the work before Davin saw it with his own eyes, their broadcasts warning everyone to return to their cells, calling for various groups to move away from other landing bays and lifts a clue that Davin's fellow criminals had bought into their chance at, if not freedom, then at least a satisfying fight. Davin's grin grew as he and Mox walked the corridors towards their level's main lift, the one that'd bring them back to the Nines, ready for a bold stand and, naturally, a rollicking getaway.

That grin, though, faded as fast as so many others in Davin's roughshod past when the captain tapped the lift's call button and received an angry beep in return.

"Locked lifts?" Mox asked. "Unfortunate."

"Guess we're taking the long way, then," Davin replied. "You have enough juice left?"

"For this."

Davin stepped aside and Mox delivered the goods, a one-two punch that dented and then broke through the lift's door into the long shaft. As with any good, up-to-snuff construction, gray rungs ran up the shaft's left side. Maintenance once again coming through to help the marauders. As Mox rubbed his hand, gloves scuffed from the impact, Davin offered to take the first step.

"You're the captain, captain," Mox said.

"So I am."

Davin heaved himself onto the first rung, glancing up to make sure no lift plummeted his way, and began the long climb. Hand, foot, one after another. Mox followed, and together they'd make the prison's yard soon enough. Perfect reinforcements to a fight that'd probably be well underway. Davin could dig that timing, could—

"The door's opening," Mox snarled, looking up past Davin to the level they were about to reach. The lift wasn't screaming down, but the doors were splitting anyway.

The reason why threw up a headache, had Davin wincing, because looking right back at him when those doors spread, wielding an almost-perfect replica of his shotgun, was his own damn self.

CHAPTER 13
KILLER COPIES

Okay, his own damn self if Davin had followed a rigid skin care routine instead of spending decades soaked in cosmic radiation amid outer space settlements, and embracing a hydration strategy primarily made up of booze in all its incarnations. Nevertheless, the android staring down at Davin was, it could be said, his spitting image.

Davin sure spat, anyway. A loud curse followed by the only thing he could do to avoid getting perforated by a bad-guy laser.

"Dive bomb!" Davin said as he kicked off the rung, plummeting down the shaft with Mox right behind.

A flash behind Davin's head proved his theory right: his robo clone wasn't here to play games. The laser wasn't followed by secondary shots, but instead the clank, clunk, and sinister slams as the androids opted for pursuit.

Davin would've hit the lift's bottom and pancaked himself save, again, his exoskeleton-equipped friend. Mox, who had many metal kilos on his captain, beat Davin down the shaft. He made a rapid grab and launch that cut Davin's descent and bounced him around the metal box. Mox landed hard, the exoskeleton creaking under an impact softened by low gravity. Davin followed, grabbing and kicking off rungs just enough to give Mox a catching chance.

Even so, wind blew from Davin's mouth as Mox's hands compressed his chest. Spots scattered and Davin's knee jerked, clocking Mox in the mouth.

"Dammit, Davin," Mox snarled, dumping the captain onto the shaft's floor.

For some reason, Davin had expected to return to the sanitation level, where they'd broken through the closed lift door. Instead, they'd fallen a fair bit further to the station's lowest point, where a thin exit smelled stale with disuse. That state ended quick, with Mox winding up his fist and smashing through with a single punch. The doorway flew off, scraping against nothing into an open space beyond.

Coughing, Davin grabbed Mox's leg and pulled himself up. "Sorry about that, buddy. Great save."

"Need to keep my human shield around."

"Say again?"

Mox flicked his eyes up, Davin followed and witnessed an android trio, led by the captain's own doppelgänger, jumping back and forth down the shaft. That they weren't firing indiscriminately said collateral damage was something best kept to a minimum, that they cared at all about such nonsense meant Heath, again, had other motives.

"This guy," Davin muttered, scrambling from the lift with Mox. "Why is it everyone we know's trying to play some complex game?"

"I'm not."

"Yeah, well, you're one of the good ones."

The pair straightened in the prison's basement, finding exactly what you'd expect to see in a little-used space: stacks of material, from stun cuffs to cots, replacement nutrient goop dispensers and oxygen filters. Row upon row spread before them, illuminated by soft white inset lights above. A small panel to the lift's left lit up as Davin took the first step inside, offering an at-a-touch catalog of useless crap.

"Want to bet there's only one exit?" Davin said, his voice coming back to normal as his lungs made a full recovery.

"No chance." Mox nodded ahead. "Two on three. Ready?"

"The Nines are always ready, Mox."

"I'm a Nine, Davin. I know that's not true."

The captain grinned, then broke ahead and right. Mox matched Davin for all of two strides before he bent, picked up the battered lift door. A squeeze narrowed the rectangle further. In a single motion, as Davin reached the first rack filled with replacement parts for Eden crap, Mox threw the door back to the lift's entry, just as Davin's clone landed in the space.

If Davin ever needed a picture of what he'd look like with a great metal spear jutting from his chest, Mox provided that visceral image. The android, complete with Davin's slight stubble, jerked and sparked around the thrown door's sharp edge. Melody's copy dangled for a moment, before Mecha-Davin smacked the bent door aside, raised the shotgun, and fired.

Mox, though, hadn't stayed around to offer himself as a target. Melody's green-glowing energy balls rocketed to strike random garbage deeper in the level. Davin felt loss's faint pang before twisting the sight into fresh possibility.

Mecha-Davin could die, and leave Davin a brand new Melody.

This new objective acquired, Davin snagged a long pipe off the rack and backed up against the level's curling wall. The space prison's long cylinder gave most of its edges a wrap-around flavor, and the bottom was no different. Davin crouched, watched the small hallway's entry into the large room. Mox had disappeared among the racks, plotting his own ambush.

If Davin could—

His clone wasn't the first one through. Instead, Opal's android clone marched in. The sniper's robo copy didn't carry her scoped killer, instead opting for bare hands. That those hands could pop Davin's head off his body like Davin might open a beer meant he ought to turn and hide.

Davin did the dumb thing instead, and swung.

Over his median length life, Davin had wielded a far-above-average number of weapons, but a meter long chunk of replacement pipe was new. The whistling sound as the tube swept through the air belied the hefty construction, some mix of plastic and plaster, smacking into the android's shoulder. Mecha-Opal lurched, as if Davin had shoved her on the way to the bar, while the pipe bounced back. Davin's hands shook with the hit, a tremor the captain took in literal stride as he followed through with a second strike.

Biology had a rough go when pitted against an android's kinetic computing. Mecha-Opal might've been lax on swing one, but she pivoted faster than Davin's eye could register, catching the follow-up and wrenching the weapon free. She raised the pipe as Davin tried to reverse his momentum, as if he could outrun the retaliation.

"Don't kill," came Davin's own voice, calling the captain to glance left, where his clone continued picking bits of himself out of the wound from Mox's toss. Next to him stood another Mecha-Phyla, because killing one of these things didn't count. "I'm not reading any cameras down here. Incapacitate only."

Heath Swane. What a goober.

Rejiggering her orders gave Davin time to clear a couple strides from Mecha-Opal, enough to put the pipe shelves back in range. With a hard yank and a loud scrape, the captain brought a fresh length to bear.

"Ready for the dumbest sword fight in history?" Davin said as Mecha-Opal brought her pipe into a double grip.

She did not respond to the taunt, putting another black

mark alongside androids in Davin's book. At least Fournine and the earlier models would crack back. Heath and Ava's creations had all the personality of an asteroid.

They hit like one too.

Mecha-Opal came at Davin with a sweeping cross, driving the pipe through shelving and breaking it, scattering the contents in a wild shower. The captain tried to block, but the pipe was far from an ideal shield, so random objects across the metal and plastic spectrum crashed into Davin's side, followed by Mecha-Opal's own pipe.

Davin's coat and clothes, unchanged since Quito—and likely smelling as such—soaked the hit, slowed from the plow through all the crap, with a bit more aplomb than Davin expected. No ribs broke, no blood poured free, but the captain still found himself mashed into the next row, half-buried under more pipes, screw boxes, and tools.

"Anytime, Mox," Davin snarled to nobody, planting his hand on the debris-strewn ground and earning scratches for his effort. Still, he stood, shrugging off the crud, and gave Mecha-Opal a sloppy grin. "Almost had me there."

Mecha-Opal answered with another swing, fast and aimed right for Davin's gut. Davin did what no android would expect, though, and closed, sidestepping the android's swing and putting his own pipe into Mecha-Opal's left side. The simple jumpsuit the androids all wore, dull in Eden's forest green, shredded with the strike, but the reinforced fake skin beneath had the pipe giving up. The tube cracked, Mecha-Opal didn't flinch. Instead, she dropped her whiffed swing and threw her left arm off the double-grip into a hard backhand.

As cheeks went, Davin always considered his quite the specimen. Sharp and tight.

No longer.

The blow cracked something in Davin's jaw and sent him flying across the level's central aisle to smack into yet more shelving. Junk cascaded around in a metal rain that would've looked right at home in some insipid comedy skit, save for the blood pooling in Davin's mouth, the spots dancing in his eyes.

Really, Davin needed to find poorer enemies.

"Bring him," came the order from Davin's android.

Mecha-Opal kicked debris aside as she walked up to Davin, the Nines captain unable to summon up a wisecrack as she reached for his hair. That dragging Davin would loose the fragile locks from his scalp was a point he started to bring up, iron-tinged wet words and all, until a hammer spun end over end to smack Mecha-Opal's too-perfect head.

Sure, if Davin had thrown the thing as hard as he could, the hammer might've left a dent. When Mox did the same, hitting fastball pitcher speeds, the same hammer detonated. Mecha-Opal's mechanical head blew apart in a fantastic sparking rain. Her body shook, froze.

"You alive, Davin?" Mox called from deeper in the level, following the strike-from-shadows strategy.

"Oh yeah," Davin said, standing, then giving Mecha-Opal a hard shove. The machine, bereft of its sensory inputs, toppled over with a satisfying clunk. "Couldn't have done that a bit sooner?"

Mox didn't reply, not giving up his position. A smart play, and not one Davin was going to make. Not when there was a guarantee to abuse.

Davin walked into the central aisle, swept his tongue around his chin to catch some leaking crimson, and waved at the android pair. Both had weapons raised, apparently running an algorithm to decide when deadly opposition over-ruled Heath's passion for publicity.

"Going to make it easier on you," Davin said, continuing to approach the androids, hands free. "Don't shoot, and I'll let you take me. You get to bag the captain, and my friend stays alive down here."

Davin's own android narrowed its fake eyes in far-too-realistic fashion, then nodded. "Your deal is acceptable. Approach without any false moves and we'll agree."

"Good bot."

Davin could imagine Mox's confusion, but the big man would understand soon enough. They'd surprised one android, but these two had lasers and might decide to just melt Davin and his friend. No sneaky hammer throws would work against that offense. Better to change the game.

Mecha-Davin took the lead, ignoring his spotty insides to grip Davin and swing the captain past him towards the lift shaft. Where Davin and Mox had plummeted and punched to get down, the android had an easier way to get up. Mecha-Phyla played rear guard with her laser raised, keeping Mox hidden back in the gloom. When the lift arrived, Davin walked right into the doorless box, followed by his own copy.

Phyla's android didn't follow.

"Hey," Davin said as his android punched in a code on the keypad. "We had a deal."

"I lied." Mecha-Davin raised his voice. "Kill the man. He isn't valuable enough to risk."

Before Davin could throw out a curse, the lift shot up and away, leaving Mox alone with mechanized death.

The slump against the side wall came as the rush receded. The lift continued its cruise upward, evident more from gravity's shifting tug than any change in the decor. Davin wallowed in his aching jaw—broken? Just marred? Who could say?—amid attempts to engage his android cousin in conversation.

Mecha-Davin didn't respond. He stood near enough to Davin for a quick reach and ravage if the Nines captain attempted anything funny, but otherwise adopted a monk's serenity as Davin peppered the bot with insults, invective, and interrogatory questions. When Davin accepted that he'd get nothing from the android, he closed his eyes and reran the plan.

Still viable, even with the unexpected bumps.

Heath Swane, though, remained an unknown. His frigate and these androids were more than just chance, and seemed to have a bigger objective than just tearing the Nines limb from limb. Lights and cameras being necessary pointed to an intended audience, but for what?

Another attempt to resurrect his pet murder projects as a viable product?

Davin found no clear answer by the time the lift stopped, back at Eden's administrative circle at the station's opposite end. When the door slid open, Tam stood right there, red faced and steaming. After sputtering in momentary confusion, Tam correctly identified the real Davin as the one without metal scarring and sparking wires in his chest, redirecting his ire only for Mecha-Davin to push the man aside.

"Follow me," Mecha-Davin announced to his biological counterpart as Tam bounced off the curling lobby wall.

"He's been in a bad mood," Davin said to Tam as the man coughed, caught his breath.

"Androids," Tam growled, falling into step with Davin. "What'd you do to get androids on my station?"

"Ask Heath Swane?"

"Who the hell's that?"

Davin chuckled, his jaw telling him that wasn't the best idea. "Betting you'll find out soon enough. Sorry about your shuttle, by the way. You'll find what's left in the decontamination bay."

Tam relayed he knew damn well what happened to his shuttle, stated the traitorous Zoelie was locked away in the visitor's cell. "If you don't want me to shoot her this minute, you'll tell me what else you've got going on."

"Figure you'd have noticed already?"

Mecha-Davin was taking them along a familiar route, past the barracks, including the pilot's timeout box. The docking bay would be coming up any minute, and with it, Davin had to guess, a swift ride to Heath Swane's favorite execution spot.

"They're riled up," Tam answered, a mix of gruff and befuddlement blending in a delightful way. "What we can't figure out is why. But I suppose it doesn't matter if there's more of these things on board."

"How many, you think?"

"Androids? Four shuttles docked. Including the one on this level." Tam's eyes unfocused as the man did some random math. "A couple dozen?"

Davin winced. Mox one-on-one with an android was bad enough, but twenty or thirty of the things could turn this whole prison into a mausoleum without much effort. At least, not without a particular trick or two.

He could really use a comm right now.

Mecha-Davin's reason for bringing Davin all the way up here instead of the mid-level docking bay they'd come in on became obvious when Davin saw the shuttle. Unlike the bare-bones military transports Davin was used to, had ridden here, this one belonged to the brass. Eden's decals were all over the green ship, but its boxy form shone with more care and better quality than its fellows. If the ship flew into a fight, Davin wouldn't be surprised if the bumps abounding the boxy shape would pop open to show turret teeth.

As Mecha-Davin walked into the bay—that the android hadn't bothered turning around once showed the machine's invincible confidence, a vain assumption Davin left alone—the shuttle opened up, its boarding ramp descended, and no soul appeared to greet them. Instead, Mecha-Davin turned around, faced Davin, and its head twitched.

"You okay there, buddy?" Davin asked as Tam scowled.

Mecha-Davin's difficulties snapped to an end with a straight-line stare back at the Nines captain. "Sorry about that," Mecha-Davin said, though the android's voice wasn't its own. Instead, the rasped, haughty tones belonged to a particularly punchable fellow. "It seems this android's been damaged. Something to add to your tab, Davin Masters?"

"Heath, the only thing I owe you is a sock to the jaw."

"By that bruise on your face, it looks like you've already had that yourself." Mecha-Davin laughed, an awful, tinny sound. "How do you like this new feature?" Mecha-Davin waved the laser rifle in its hands, swooping it through a few combat poses. "Remote control. Something the original models never had."

"Because they were designed to be neutral arbiters," Tam grumbled. "Not weapons."

"Oh please, Tam. Neutrality's dead. Eden has to show Earth it deserves support, and the best way to do so is staring you in the face right now." Mecha-Davin leveled the rifle at Davin. "A politician, a criminal, a rebel . . . We make our own version and out it goes. Free to change the narrative to whatever we want. Brilliant, right?"

Tam kept up his admirable, old-man scowl while Davin rolled his eyes.

"Heath, what's with you and justifying yourself to people you're planning to kill?" Davin said. "I don't care what you're planning to do, because you'll be dead long before you can pull it off."

Mecha-Davin's smile vanished. Puzzlement didn't replace it—now there was a feature Heath ought to work on—but the flat line and stiff body said enough.

"Dead? Davin. You're the one who's about to be dead. Along with your crew, and every rioter on this prison. Cleared out without the loss of a single innocent life." Mecha-

Davin stepped aside, gestured towards the shuttle with the rifle. "Now, if you would please get on board."

"So you can, what, eject me into space?"

"Something like that. If you would."

"Gee, you ask so nicely, how can I refuse?"

Mecha-Davin followed Davin up the boarding ramp, a journey Tam wasn't allowed to undertake. Despite grumbling, he didn't dare push the android, and the man disappeared back to his bureaucracy without raising a ruckus. Too bad, but not essential.

As Davin sat in the shuttle's back, Mecha-Davin forcing the issue with that rifle, the shuttle's ramp closed. The doors sealed and the jets spooled up. For the second time in little more than an hour, Davin was taking off into space.

For now, the plan held, but the seams were showing. Davin leaned his head on the hull plating behind him as the docking bay spun around, stars showing out the cockpit. And, drifting into view on the far side, the Moon's great gray expanse.

As good a sign as any.

"Heath, you listening?" Davin asked his android clone. Mecha-Davin glanced back and told Davin the Eden commander wasn't available, that it wasn't necessary at this point. "Oh really?"

The android didn't answer, returning to the pilot console. Setting some trajectory, and Davin could guess as to where.

A captain had to be ready to zig when zags weren't allowed, had to duck when he couldn't jump. Had to fight when he couldn't flee.

Davin rose. Took several floating steps up the aisle towards the android. Mecha-Davin turned, pointing towards the shuttle's aft. A command Davin ignored.

"You made a mistake," Davin said, nodding past the android towards the console. "Just there."

The android didn't flinch, didn't buy the bluff. Straight on.

Mecha-Davin had seen better days. Mox's door-busting blast had rent a big hole in the android's midsection, right where a human's lower lungs might've been. Dangling wires and scaffolding glimmered in the shuttle's placid icy light. With both hands empty, arms loose at his sides, Mecha-Davin seemed unaffected by the damage, but Davin knew better.

Or rather, hoped.

The laser rifle sat in the co-pilot's chair. Davin made a sudden dart that way, using his left foot to kick off the last passenger seat in the aisle. The android read the move with its impossible reaction time, snatching out and snaring Davin's left shoulder with its own right hand, a curious frown alighting on the robot's face. Standard self defense accounted for the obvious: grabbing weapons, punching the face, but Heath suffered from his own pride.

So when the android halted Davin's forward momentum, put the pilot to the brakes right in close, Davin jammed his hand in the android's open gut and pulled. Metal shards scratched—more stinging additions to a constant litany—but Davin found those wires, the tubes carrying lubricating oils for the bones and plaskin, and yanked.

Mecha-Davin saw the reach, struck Davin's chest with its free left hand. Davin let the hit come, focused on his grip as the android gave Davin more force than the man could ever manage alone. Davin's fingers burned, but an android's insides weren't meant to be gutted, weren't meant to withstand a good tug. The wires popped their holes, the tubes split, and as Davin flew back over the chairs, his hands held a fistful of robo-guts.

Coughing—this time, Davin might've earned a cracked rib —the Nines captain came to a rest back at the shuttle's aft. He let the wires drop, saw the grab's effects in the android's stock-still form. Unintelligible gibberish came from Mecha-

Davin's mouth, nonsense that found its form as Davin closed in carefully. The android was spooling off a damage report. Part numbers, percentage impacts, and all sorts of glorious minutiae Davin didn't care one bit about save for their effect: a dead bot.

"You pack a mean hook," Davin muttered, pushing the android over. Mecha-Davin's head thunked against the shuttle's port bulkhead, putting the android in a defunct lean. "Now, let's see what our friend had planned, shall we?"

The shuttle didn't bother hiding its secrets. The trajectory put Davin's course into an abandoned spot between Earth and the Moon, well away from ship traffic but within easy view of radar or curious onlookers. As to what they'd see, well, the shuttle didn't hide that either.

Heath, through the android, had set the shuttle's batteries to overload. A good old-fashioned self-destruct, meant to blow a ship away before it crashed into something important. In just a few minutes, Davin's beautiful bits would light up the starry sky.

CHAPTER 14
INFILTRATION

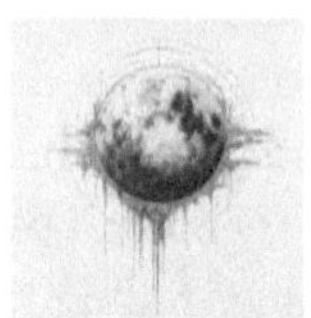

Davin had a whole crew, but not a one could help him now. If Trina or Viola had been on the shuttle, maybe they could've come up with a way to reverse the damage to the shuttle's battery chemistry, already too far along to get reverted with a button press. If the shuttle had a lifeboat, Mox might've dragged Davin to the rescue. As it was, Davin had dying thrusters and fewer seconds than one of Heath Swane's monologues to get himself somewhere safe.

Amid those limited options, only one made sense, and Davin swerved the shuttle hard port. The Moon and stars around it slashed from view, replaced with an ugly lump Davin had been aboard once before, wanted never to set foot on again.

"But fate makes morons of us all," Davin muttered to himself, pushing the shuttle into a straight-on shot at Heath's frigate.

The shuttle's console beeped, a separate tone from the pleasant bopping announcing Davin's imminent demise. Someone on Heath's ship must've picked up the changed direction, must be wondering just what Davin planned.

Joke's on them. At this point, Davin wasn't planning anything. All instinct, all hope.

He set the course, the shuttle indicating less than a minute till Davin made it. Either that, or he'd go boom and this would all end anyway. Davin turned, grabbed the leaning android, and kicked towards the shuttle's aft. The robot would've been too heavy in any normal situation, but here in the magical land of zero-G, the lifeless metal was merely awkward. Its head bounced across chair tops as Davin bounced aft.

"Sorry about that," Davin said to the bot as he bounced past the final row, swerving as his internal clock hit zero.

The turn revealed a terrifying glassy sight, lightning flashes zipping all around the shuttle as Heath's frigate tried to defend itself. Too little offense coming far too late. Davin scrunched himself up, slung across the crash belt, hugged the android close, and prayed to any listening god to make it through the other side.

Crash a spaceship into another one and you invited a cavalcade of calamities. Leaked atmosphere, fires, broken hulls and lost lives. When the shuttle struck the frigate's uppermost bridge, the private space where far too recently Davin had been tossed around by Mecha-Phyla, the Nines captain hoped it'd be as deserted as it had been then.

Not that Davin could tell, because he wasn't looking. He heard the shuttle's cockpit smash through the thick glass shield, heard the shuttle's own viewport shatter. The craft's metal frame dug into the dual-level space, crunching into Heath's domineering upper console, the thing's sheer size stopping the shuttle's grinding entrance. The crash belt held for a moment before snapping, and Davin shot forward in what would've been a soul-splattering experience save for one thing: the android.

Dragged back on its side, Mecha-Davin continued its cross-wise existence as Davin's battering ram. The Nines captain pulled up his knees, rode the bot's back as it ran first into the shuttle's seats, one line after another. Every break slowed Davin's momentum even as it jolted his teeth, even as his ears popped with the pressure changes. Chairs flew, sparks showered, gas and shrapnel filled the air.

Davin didn't let go, and Heath's androids proved their sturdy construction. After mashing through the last row, Davin and the remnants of his robo-clone crashed out into the upper bridge, tumbling through a fiery wall to bounce off the floor and roll to a bone-crunching stop. With the android turned mostly to mush, Davin let the machine go and lay on the metal floor, feeling the aches abound and cackling anyway. Behind him, the shuttle's aft jammed in the reinforced glass, leaving room for leaks but saving an all-out rapid decompression.

Burning blooms expanded before his eyes as the shuttle continued its collapse, those batteries completing their meltdown in lurid pink, blue, and white bursts. They were beautiful, but they'd also be the last things Davin ever saw if he stayed on that bridge one more second, so the captain lurched towards the exit.

Any smart ship in a vacuum emergency would slam shut doors to keep any leaks from spreading. Davin figured Heath's frigate would do much the same, and sure enough, the big double-doors had closed. A blinking red light above their middle suggested they'd stay that way.

Adrenaline, fear, trauma had a way of dooming or defining a person, and if Davin hadn't ever been in a situation like this before, with the very air alternately igniting or disappearing around him, the Nines captain might've given up right then. Instead, in a bleary glance at his ruined robot clone, he found inspiration.

He slapped the keypad at the door's side, the same panels along all the damn things that let you lock and let you talk.

"Target eliminated per orders," Davin spoke into the

microphone, as low and robotic a growl as his pressure-scarred lungs could manage. "Open the door."

A bet placed, a bet made that the smoke, sparks, and chaos would convince some Eden toady that the Davin making the call had insides full of circuits, not blood.

A bet made because Davin had no other.

Trace a common thread through Davin's life and you'd find steady beats where the captain had rolled dice and come up a winner or a dire loser. There'd been the gambit bringing the Nines out to Europa and Eden Prime for a steady job, a win until he'd decided to risk the crew by helping some soon-to-be dead inspectors on the down low. Then Davin had thrown everything in with Bosser to keep the Nines alive, a losing play corrected by betting Trina and Viola could twist an android's insides . . .

The list would go on and on, and Davin figured the ups would become downs often enough, but when the doors slid open, letting him lurch from the collapsing bay, Davin thanked whatever gods had given him the lucky day. He'd even earned an escape without a waiting, armed escort. Heath's frigate followed protocols well enough to toss anyone lacking a wrench and a death wish well away from the impact site, leaving Davin in a familiar circular anteroom with a hallway and a couple lifts staring back at him.

Death's retreat to the background gave a million minor problems their chance to shine, and Davin stumbled to his right as the doors closed behind him. He felt for and found enough grace to keep upright on the smooth, grungy—Heath's lack of sanitary discipline continued—metal tiles. He reached for his blurring eyes with a hand before remembering his fingers might be coated in who the hell knew what awful substances.

Space travel, space craft, were made possible by so many

nasty chemical constructs, Davin figured he'd probably go blind rubbing some sanity back into himself. So he squeezed his eyes shut instead, leveled out his breathing, took stock of the pangs and spikes, the bruises and twinges. Nothing came back screaming broken bones or bearing the dead heat hallmark of internal bleeding.

Davin could keep on walking, living, and trying to figure out a way back. Because a side trip to Heath's happy land wasn't part of the plan, and now the clock was ticking past the mark Davin needed to hit. Getting off this boat was step one, but before Davin could do that, he'd need to find a shuttle.

The lifts wouldn't help him, as they were in use, and anyone coming this way wouldn't be a friend. The hallway offered his only chance, and Davin skedaddled in a shambling dash. Any idiot scanning the cams would see Davin looking very un-android-like in his rough breathing, his shuffling steps, the curses muttered out alongside both. That the frigate's alarms and their minders were otherwise occupied with the crash gave Davin a break, one he couldn't find a damn way to use.

Doors and other halls presented themselves, each and every one a dead end, barred with a badge scanner. Davin tried, once, pressing his thumb to one, wondering if Heath had gone so far as to replicate Davin's fingerprint on the android, but the wild shot came back a bleeping negative.

Either Davin would get caught, or he'd run all the way to the frigate's far end and . . . get caught.

His lonesome spiral wasn't helped by people beginning to emerge. The damage control crews must've contained the crash, because alarms quieted and doors began to shunt open. Eden drones resuming their awful lives working for the worst bum Davin had known—quite an achievement, to top that list. At first, Davin ducked away here and there to dodge glances, a technique that worked for precisely two people before bumping him into a third.

She was backing out of a slim doorway, one marked for laundry services, and had Eden's strict, no frills forest green uniform on. A basic cap marked the woman, who Davin snap-guessed as somewhere around his age, as a functionary, one of those invisible cogs keeping the Eden machine rolling. She stopped, mumbled an apology, before looking at Davin with wrinkles creasing into confused worry.

"It's worse than you think," Davin offered as an opener.

Misdirection beat flat-out lying, and the bait worked, the woman turning away from the cart she'd been pulling and its heaps of clothing bins.

"What's worse?" she asked, her clipped accent putting her as an asteroid cast-off. "Because if you're telling me there's another batch to run today, I'm quitting right this minute."

Davin winced. "Sorry, it's why I'm wearing this. Accident down by the bays, whole lot of us covered in coolant."

The woman cursed while Davin nodded in sympathy. She shoved the cart back into the laundry room and pushed by Davin, heading, presumably, towards the bays. The laundry room door might've shut right behind her if a certain Nines captain hadn't stuck his arm in the way, followed it with his body, and soon found himself amid a churning clean machine phalanx.

Was it the clean laundry, the sterile room with its shelves stocked with cleaning supplies amid a sallow white light glow, or Davin's collected maladies, so recently discarded on the Moon only to be earned again, that slapped his focus into a new direction?

Davin couldn't answer, but the plan, concocted in nutrient goop's tasteless embrace, was beyond him now. Phyla, Opal, and the others would see as best they could that the prison faltered, that they could get the word out on a wide band that

Eden's androids were replacing bodies rather than burying them.

That was a larger mission, a broader objective. Complete the task Cassidy had set for them, that Alyssa had abandoned. A job that didn't pay damn near enough.

And if you couldn't get the cash you wanted, Davin figured you had to make up the satisfaction somewhere.

Taking Heath apart, and tossing this frigate on history's scrap heap, would go a long way towards balancing the accounts.

"Never liked you," Davin said, fishing a hand into the nearest basket, loaded with forest green uniforms. "But what's a guy going to do?"

The laundry room didn't need a keycard to leave, a break kind enough to give the newly dressed, still battered Davin a second wind. The frigate's soundscape had achieved a similar makeover, the calamity from Davin's crash apparently not rising to abandon-ship levels. Instead, calm voices popped over ship wide broadcasts directing this and that group, this and that squad, and some poor sap named Reff to and fro. Reff seemed incapable of finding the right way, as Davin measured the time it took to get to the next lift by steady cadence calling Reff from hither to yon and back again.

The cold halls, dotted with the same notices, groan-worthy slogans, and haphazard posters hung with Heath's standard lack of care for Eden regulations, treated Davin differently now. The cuts and sore muscles had fresh, clear purpose. He wasn't a victim, but an unknown assassin with a juicy target.

"Hey," Davin said to the first set he came across, a three-team combo hustling along in hunchback maintenance mode, their bodies covered in tool belts and hands pushing a decked cart laden with sealants. "Be careful."

The trio stopped, stared.

"You get a new update?" asked the first, a sweaty man who reeked of cleaning solution.

"Did I what?"

The three glanced at each other. Gave Davin, almost as one, a squint.

"Not once have any of you bots said a nice word to us," said the leader again. "I've been on this ship for years, and Captain Swane's androids are either giving orders or ignoring us. So what's changed?"

"Heath's found a heart," Davin said, then waved off the group, turning and quick-stepping down the hallway.

The goal had been to score a keycard, claim he'd forgotten his own or some other pathetic excuse. The turnabout had Davin questioning that plan at all: would the androids even need keycards, or could they just swish their palms over the readers? Maybe scan their crazy robot eyes?

Wait.

Davin stopped, almost tapped his chin until he realized the hallway had begun to fill. More people shuffling here and there, from more maintenance crews to staff returning to their regularly scheduled drudgery. No android would do something so pointless as tapping their own chin, so Davin kept his hands at his sides, resumed walking until he found the next lift.

The keypad mocked him, so Davin tapped the small red button in the panel's corner. Reserved for emergencies and idiots, and Davin figured he probably qualified as both by this point.

On the other end, a bored voice confirmed Davin's location and that he wanted a lift. When the voice, more robotic and lifeless than any android Davin had heard, demanded identification, Davin again suppressed the usual grand sigh he'd give, and barreled right into an explanation.

"Damaged in the crash. Can't access data. Need repair,"

Davin said, doing his level best to match the communicator's apathy.

Either he'd done a good enough impression, or the shift slave on the other end figured they needed an easy win, because the lift's keypad flashed green and gave Davin an entry. The lift's metal box, beyond the usual occupancy limit stickers, sported a single flyer promoting a weekly karaoke night in the frigate's mess. No other soul entered, and the lift set its target without Davin pressing a button.

"Now that's what you call service," the captain muttered, before recalling his own deception and setting his arms straight, his eyes ahead, and throwing a random twitch into his lips.

The frigate's maintenance floor wasn't just for androids, but everything on the ship that needed any assembly or repairs, including humans. Signs greeted Davin's exit, pointing him to the med bay, engineering, or the ghastly doom of the salvage department. Without knowing if his distant pal was keeping tabs, Davin headed towards engineering.

If one had a plan to escape a ship, the usual method was to find an evac pod and jettison yourself into fate's hands. Hijacking a shuttle or some other craft might be viable, but the amount of bribery, luck, and sheer computing chicanery required to do that was well beyond Davin's range. With bad odds in every direction why not try something different?

Rather than the isolated hallways on the upper levels, the maintenance floor operated in broad spaces. A central line with the lift stations on fore and aft bisected the frigate, and here, that meant splitting the level into uneven thirds. The med bay sat near the fore, just above the frigate's primary docking bays and below its bridge. It stretched back until it ran into engineering, whose vast swath occupied the level's entire rear half, using the central hall to divide itself into dueling sections.

One, meant to keep the frigate running, would've been Davin's primary interest save for the nattering man who described all this to Davin, who caught Davin as he left the lift. Covered in a thick coat meant to shield him from sparks, radiation, and who knew what else, the squat dude pitched himself as Davin's savior, ready to repair those broken circuits and get the would-be android back to slaughtering Heath's targets.

"Your name?" Davin asked, his second question after getting the level's layout. They were walking along the central hallway, a slow endeavor as people and carts covered in obliterated scrap zoomed everywhere. Relics of Davin's own crash, or so he supposed. "Mine is Davin."

"Davin mark three, to be exact," the engineer chirped back, then clucked his own tongue. "Oh, my name? Lamon." He crinkled a sweaty brow. "Asking me my name. Must be a new software update."

"Yes."

"Strange. You'd think I would have noticed, but then again, Heath's had us pulling doubles all month, ever since we tried to capture your, well, inspiration out by Saturn." Lamon shook his head, but kept up the smile. "Not that I mind. Not that any of us do. You don't choose Heath Swane's ship if you're not expecting a little crazy."

Davin said nothing. How would an android respond to that?

The non-answer worked well enough, as Lamon kept right on blabbing. This and that about future androids, about Eden's coming acceptance that the robots would once again return to their proper, exalted place, which Heath would be happy to deliver.

When, at long last, they reached Lamon's target door and

the man tapped his keycard against the lock, Davin managed not to sigh in deep, profound thanks.

Engineering, or at least the android portion of it, bore no resemblance to the setup Davin had last encountered on the frigate. No beds with bright lights, no helmets meant to scan your brain so some robot could mimic it. No, this looked and smelled like Vagrant's Hollow: a constant ozone reek, clanking noises as metal made contact with itself, and a steady stream of curses behind it all.

Workbenches longer than Davin was tall interspersed between racks filled with wires, plaskin tanks, and techno bits and bobs. Trina, the *Jumper*'s old mechanic, might've fallen in love at the sight, just like Lamon apparently had. Every wall sported hooks bearing tools, and directional lights followed spoken commands to focus on this, highlight that. Small floating bots that looked an awful lot like Puk drifted about, fetching tools and handling precision work the human engineers didn't care to attempt.

Viola had championed Eden's engineering for a few years, maybe she'd proliferated her own ideas across the fleet.

That little amusement aside, Lamon directed Davin through the buzzing maze to what Davin assumed was the man's own workbench. That assumption came with queasy support, given what lay across it.

Mecha-Phyla had been Davin's nemesis back on Ganymede and, too recently, in the prison, and now another copy lay here again, though this version wasn't going to jump off the bench and throttle him. For one, her chest and stomach were opened up like a box, sides flopping up and over, to reveal a nest of wires beneath.

"Third edition," Lamon said, every word laced with pride. "We've made so many upgrades from the first model. Your sequel's going to get them too. First and foremost," Lamon tapped on Mecha-Phyla's forehead, "this is all empty space. Turns out, everyone goes for the head first, so we're moving the processor down here, where it'll be wrapped in enough titanium to stay safe."

Lamon hesitated, his eyes flicking to Davin in search of a compliment. Whether an android would provide one seemed questionable, so Davin held his tongue. Lamon deflated, said they ought to have made the androids nicer, before touching a switch on the workbench's side. With a whir and a whine, the bench elevated itself, lifting Mecha-Phyla several meters up on extending poles at the bench's four corners.

Beneath, sliding out to cover the fresh opening, was another flat metal slat.

"Lets us handle interruptions without putting all the fun away," Lamon explained, waving at Davin to lay down.

Activity limited Davin's options. A sudden strike might knock Lamon out, but all those drifting Puks would see Davin zapped before he went more than a couple strides. At the same time, letting Lamon slice him up would be, well, a non-starter. Davin kept puzzling through his surroundings, discarding and pulling up new ideas as he stretched his legs out on the table, as Lamon leaned over and took a sniff.

The man frowned. Sniffed again.

Those eyes narrowed, the bright curiosity curdling to nervous suspicion.

"If there's one thing no update ever delivered," Lamon said, taking a step back from the workbench. "It's body odor."

CHAPTER 15
HIJACKED

I f lying atop a workbench had any benefits, they rested in the prodigious tools within Davin's reach. As Lamon declared his olfactory revelation, Davin found a wrench with his right hand and whipped the thing at the unfortunate scientist. The shiny, strong object found its mark square on Lamon's forehead, dropping the man with a silent thud to the ground. The wrench, bouncing off Lamon, wasn't so quiet as it clattered to the floor next to its victim.

By then, Davin had already rolled off the workbench to Lamon's side, leaning over the man and fishing inside his pockets for anything useful. His right hand snaked up to Lamon's neck, tugged off the lanyard waiting there. The first called question came, someone noticing Lamon's form and wondering how he'd wound up that way.

Davin, slipping the lanyard into his Eden uniform pocket, glanced up with too much hope. The questioning engineer stood to Davin's left, deeper into the level, but on his right, blocking the exit back to the frigate's central hallway. The bots, too, were getting reinforcements. The Puk clones, four of them, had corralled several engineers, and while Davin couldn't imagine the brightest torque-tuners in the galaxy would work for Eden, these dunces were smart enough to puzzle out a problem.

One Davin could solve with the same old playbook.

"I seem to have malfunctioned," Davin said, standing. "He activated my self-defense protocol."

Whether or not the androids had such a thing was immaterial. The words bought Davin hesitation, a chance to establish a route, shade instinct with an idea.

"He'll need medical attention," Davin continued as the cautious engineers and their bot escort approached. "I can take him."

"You'll take nobody," said the same engineer who'd asked the first question, a blasted woman who looked like she preferred to test her designs with live fire every step of the way. "If you're malfunctioning, we can't have you running around the ship."

Hmm. Davin might've been able to trick one engineer, but the whole crew, plus the bots looking at Davin now suggested a swift end if he decided on a rerun. Those looks, though, gave Davin a new opening: nerves around the eyes, tight grips on tools, and a reluctance to close even one more step reminded Davin of just what he was pretending to be.

Androids had always been killing machines, first and foremost. To all these goobers, if not the floating bots, Davin was a fast-moving fiend who could tear each of them limb from limb with or without a wrench.

Might be time to lean into it.

"I do not think you understand," Davin said, keeping his voice flat, even. "My protocols dictate wounded Eden personnel must be taken to medical. Any interference will not be accepted."

Oh yeah. The way the engineers twitched back had Davin fighting hard to keep a grin off his face. Phyla would be so impressed. Merc even more so. This was the acting Davin had spent a lifetime learning to pull off, and he added to it now by bending, putting his hands beneath the downed engineer, and realizing there was no damn way his middle-aged self could lift Lamon.

Instead, Davin straightened, turned back to his nervous crowd.

"I'm picking up a lack of trust," Davin said. "As such, I'm inclined to keep my hands free. You two, carry your colleague. I will escort you."

He pointed to the hardiest pair, ones holding diamond saws, and again suppressed the urge to chuckle when the duo dropped their weapons. Davin stepped aside as they lifted their colleague—Lamon's welt had grown into an ugly splotch, but Davin's sympathy was tempered by Lamon's choice of employer: anybody working for Heath Swane deserved what came their way.

With the engineers lifting Lamon, Davin followed the pair from the part stacks and workbenches back into the central hallway. The drifting bots and their fellow humans decided not to press any attack, the former because the latter suffered from that all important malady: cowardice.

Davin did his best to keep a stiff gait and a straight face as they reached the med bay. When one of the engineers beeped open the door, Davin announced his imminent return to the engineering floor for those promised repairs, and Lamon's carriers departed into the swirling medical chaos. A quick glimpse inside showed plenty of wounded receiving care, a mystery resolved by Davin's crash, or perhaps the invasion of Eden's prison hadn't been as robotic as anticipated.

More importantly, wounded meant someone had returned to Heath's frigate. A shuttle or two might be available, and Davin had a keycard that could get him to the bays.

This time, the lift took his tap without issue, and Davin rocketed upwards to a the level just beneath the one he'd rammed into. The keycard and Lamon's access offered escape . . . eventually.

The Nines captain had business first.

Heath Swane's frigate kept Eden's standard layout, though the top level with its android experimentation and second, now smashed, bridge was a tad unusual. As Davin stepped into the back-and-forth crowd, rumbling through afternoon tasks with the frenzy brought by combat action, he reacquainted himself with the ship's insides. Courtesy of the level maps plastered on the walls near the lift, Davin tracked a line to the bridge and headed that way.

He didn't have a gun, didn't have a weapon at all besides his fists, but Davin figured he'd come up with something by the time he found the Eden captain. The walk, falling in line with soldiers, technicians, and random Eden support personnel let those morbid plans flourish, blossom into a hideous multitude only to collapse back into a question as Davin arrived at the bridge proper, those big doors held open by constant traffic.

Killing Heath hadn't been part of the Nines' initial plan on the space prison, and, standing here, Davin found himself revisiting the idea. Murder wasn't a card Davin liked to play in the best of times, seeing as it usually led to bounties, pursuit, and the injuries he preferred avoiding. With Bosser, way back when, death had come via Viola's laser in a desperate moment. Marl had cast herself off the terramorpher.

Sure, Davin had a few ghosts haunting his steps, but if he walked onto that platform and took Heath out, what would that get?

A recording, certainly, of the Nines captain killing a man. Reputation ruined, legitimate bounties placed, and a forever stain on Davin's somewhat dubious legacy.

Taking Heath as a hostage seemed similarly impossible. What would Davin do? Grip the man by the ear and bellow at the whole bridge crew to abandon ship? Someone would take a shot at Davin before long, and he'd roast beneath the—

"You're looking good," said a familiar, awful voice right as a hand landed on Davin's shoulder. Heath Swane, separating from a pack exiting a nearby lift, grinned in Davin's face. "Not like we discussed, of course, you crashing into our ship, but I suppose Davin was never going to go quietly."

The hand on Davin's shoulder pressed, pushing the Nines captain towards the bridge.

"I improvised," Davin replied, the calm quandaries of a moment ago dissipating into frenzied confusion. "He was crafty."

"Oh, I know. It's why you're here. Too many people on Earth and around the colonies seem to like him. They won't buy his disappearance, unless you confirm it."

"As ordered."

"Indeed. Now, the prison is resisting more than expected. Your victim's colleagues are making it difficult, and I cannot have you announce our victory until it's complete."

"Announce our victory?"

The frigate's main bridge, like most Eden ships, splayed into a semicircle, with a raised platform in the center from which the commander could lord over the underlings manning terminals, comms, and cleaning the floors below. Soft blue and white lights bordered the room, bright enough to let footfalls find their path while giving shadows, and eyes dealing with dark screens, comfort. Heath made right for the central platform, pushing Davin along, and at his arrival, some Eden lackey found herself dismissed.

"Did Aya not send the package along?" Heath frowned, made as if to tap a standing comm before stopping. "No, that's not important yet. If casualties are high, we'll have to change the wording anyway." Heath nodded at nothing, turned back to the terminals. "Stay here. The moment I receive word the prison is in our hands, we'll broadcast. We won't give another voice a chance."

"High casualties?" Davin asked.

"On our side," Heath answered without turning around. "All the prisoners, and your famous Nines, are done. Tickets punched. They have to be, as an example. Everyone has to understand our androids are ruthless and efficient. Eden must have absolute authority, and I must be the one to give it to them. That's the only way we can ensure our research, our program, continues."

Davin froze for a cold second as Heath pronounced the necessary deaths of his friends, his family. The Eden captain's cold calculations were, as ever, worthy of a punch to the face, but the very line Davin had drawn a few minutes earlier broke. Death, murder, wasn't something Davin wanted.

But if you threatened the Nines, Davin would see you done in.

A more rational mind might've played out the scenario further, analyzed what might be accomplished in blending Heath's nose, blunt-style, with the rest of his face. Davin could've had a mind like that, but a long day's wrangling with death, destruction, and robot copies of himself had pushed the Nines captain into the comforting confines of his lizard brain.

So Davin swung the punch, and Heath, that damned monster, caught it. A reaction time too fast, too precise for the trim Eden captain. No way had this dude, this scurrilous android designer, found time to train in the martial arts. Davin's astonishment parleyed its way into widening eyes, but Heath only smiled, holding Davin's swinging hand in an iron grip.

Davin went with the left next, and again Heath countered, sealing both of Davin's hands in locking grips. The Eden captain maintained his chilling smile, as if this was some simple game and not an attempted elimination.

No cries for help, no mocking derision. Heath seemed stunned by the situation, the two of them in the bridge's center, surrounded by terminals and oblivious crew members.

When Heath's eyes twitched, the smile faded to a straight line, Davin cursed.

"Astounding," Heath said in response. "But you've once again proved my confidence is my undoing. No matter how many times I try to kill you, Davin, you somehow come through."

"Where are you?" Davin growled, jerking his hands with zero effectiveness. "What vent did you crawl into, Heath?"

"Oh, just my quarters, Davin." Heath's android copy spoke without moving, without relaxing its grip. "As you're no doubt seeing, I've become convinced of yet another android utility. Why put myself in harm's way, when one of these can take my place?" The android raised its arms, dragging Davin's captive hands along with them. "A lesson you should have learned, Davin. A whole crew ready to step into the fire for you, and here you are, leading the way?"

"Wanted to punch you myself."

"And you did! Admittedly, not to any real effect, but you crashed a shuttle into my poor frigate. A good ending, one to burnish your legend. A fantastic way to die."

Around the bridge, heads were turning, words murmured above the clicks, rings, and soft-toned beeps inherent to any ship's command center. Those heads saw Davin lifted off his feet, his mouth stretched in a bare-teethed snarl as his knuckles and fingers ached with the android's grip.

"Aya is quite the writer, do you know?" Heath continued, falling into his awful monologuing habit. "She's scripting a new release right now. It'll play with the video of your desperate crash, a dive to keep a shuttle filled with awful criminals from escaping. You'll remain the hero, Davin. So be thankful."

Davin told Heath just how thankful he was, and earned a

couple gasps from the collective audience. Not that a soul moved to help him, to dissuade Heath from what might've been a very public execution. Might've, if Davin didn't have one last gambit up his very stretched sleeves.

With a clenching of abs strengthened by their brief trip to Earth's surface, Davin kicked up his legs and pressed them against the android's chest. At the same time, Davin straightened out his hands, leaving the fists behind in a simultaneous slip that had the android's powerful, precarious hold sliding off Davin's skin. The Nines captain hit the platform on his back and kicked again, sliding himself across the floor and off, falling on a cluttered desk. A terminal bent under Davin's weight, twisting his fall to the side and dropping him further onto some poor flack's chair. Arm rests gave Davin a moment's pause before he rolled off those too, hitting the floor on his stomach, sheltered by the desk on his right and fleeing officers on his left.

"Arrest him," Heath, via his android, demanded, and while the words didn't stop the officer flight, it did signal their replacement by hardier forces.

That Heath himself didn't chase Davin with his android double suggested something else: the man remained a coward, even with his copycats.

Davin rose, hit his head on the desk, and cursed. The first Eden guard bore down on him, stun baton raised like some glorious justice about to be meted. Davin shoved the wheeled chair into the man's approach, taking the bastard right where no male ought to be struck. The baton faltered and Davin followed, lurching with the chair and using its arm rests— useful things, those—to hoist himself up. As the first guard stumbled back, looking rather green, a second took his place. The woman pushed aside Davin's chair thrust, meeting the opening with her stun baton.

The Nines captain retreated, putting his back to the desk as the baton swished through space. His hands found things to grab, and Davin threw them at his attacker. A flimsy notepad fluttered to the right, but the pen flew true, smacking the Eden guard in the face and drawing a yelp. Davin curled to his right, the baton smashing blind against the desk and splitting it down the middle. The bent terminal sparked as the stun baton unleashed its current, white flares and smoke hissing from chips fried beyond any use.

As he wrapped around the desk, Davin confronted the harsh realities of Heath's bridge. The circular end and Davin's place within it meant the Nines captain had nowhere to go. Before him the wrap-around continued, with Earth cutting a beautiful slice against the dark beyond. More desks and terminals filled the space, their occupants gone in the chattering, not-quite panicked flight. A sprint around the bridge would only bring Davin face-to-face with—

Heath's android landed with a hard thunk before Davin, a wild grin on the robot's face. The machine had no weapon, but those fists balled up into what'd likely be a devastating one-two combo. Especially with stun batons coming in at Davin's back. A pincer, and with it, Davin's likely demise.

If Davin played by the rules, anyway.

He rushed the android, bellowing out a wordless roar that felt damn good, considering. Davin raised his right fist and Heath's android sought to meet it the same way it'd dealt with Davin's earlier punch: grab, control, taunt. Good. The Nines captain slowed the approach, let his left stride drag on the metal floor. Behind him, the Eden guard came with her stun baton, the steps clear, hard, and victorious.

Davin planted his left foot, dropped his planned punch, and pivoted hard to his left, swinging his body around as the android, seeking to close an unexpected gap, reached for the arm it so wanted to grab. At the same time, the hard-charging Eden guard jabbed with the baton. Davin's twist cleared the way for the two would-be friends to meet in the middle, and, wouldn't you know it, sparks flew.

The stun baton treated the android just as it would any other victim, delivering a nerve-numbing surge right to the android's grasping arm. Hissing, fizzing, and spitting noises rose from Heath's expensive machine. The arm dropped and the android followed, though Davin didn't think for a minute the whole machine would be busted for long—even early androids had been hardened against attacks like this. The Eden guard, though, stared at what she'd done like she'd murdered a child, a dropped jaw and limp form giving Davin ample time to dash past her.

And into the chair-checked man, recovered from his brush with cosmic pain. The man lifted his own stun baton, though the sudden turn had scrambled his reaction time. Nobody expected a victim to dodge an android, and that hesitation let Davin sneak in an elbow to the guard's gut, throwing off the swing and, again, sending the man to the floor, groans going loud.

Which left Davin with a clear path to the bridge's exit. Except, of course, for the half-dozen more soldiers rushing in. They weren't armed with batons either, but rifles. Real weapons, and Davin had to figure they wouldn't be friendly. Yet, Davin had grown up in Vagrant's Hollow, and when security came calling into that busy mire, the oppressed had one advantage:

Confusion.

Davin ran at the soldiers, yelling that they'd knocked the guy down back there. The soldiers, probably responding to Heath's alarm, to the rushed exit from the bridge, wouldn't have received a briefing. More than that, Heath's best force would've taken major hits on Ganymede in the assault on Viola's home. These scrubs lacked the training, the will, and the knowledge to know how to handle Davin's wild panic, his waving arms, and his green Eden uniform.

At least, all that came through in vague hope as Davin ran towards the bridge exit. The soldiers slowed, glanced at one another in that classic hope that someone else might take the reins. One of the Eden guards behind Davin demanded the soldiers to shoot Davin, but the order, what it meant, and just who Davin was took too long to process. With a shove and a stumble, Davin ran through the bridge exit and into the crowd outside.

What'd started as an attempt to turn Heath Swane into sludge had turned into the more rational alternative: amid curious looks, shouts, and general chaos, Davin escaped. He jammed into a crowded lift, slapped the docking bay level button, and heaved a heavy sigh as four other Eden staffers stared at him.

"Long day," Davin offered to their looks, and if any recognized the man who'd just escaped an android, guards, and soldiers, they kept that knowledge to themselves.

Smart cookies, the bunch.

Ditching the lift put Davin in a familiar place: a central corridor with big bays opening along either side. Frigates weren't huge, but they could stock a fair shuttle complement, and, as Davin had heard, some were already coming back from Heath's subjugation mission to the prison. Medical staff ran Eden soldiers on carts towards the lifts, sparing little more than glances at Davin as he slipped past them. The first bays on the left and right were empty, but the third held what Davin was looking for: a landing shuttle, engines still warm. The pilot was standing by those nacelles, inspecting something, and Davin took advantage, broke into a straight dash towards the boarding ramp.

One boot hit the metal before the pilot noticed, yelling at Davin to stop.

As if.

The shuttle didn't have the prison's passenger seating, instead leaving a cleared center for equipment and two long benches along the sides for armed and armored soldiers to suffer during what would be, hopefully, short rides to their objective. That space gave Davin a clean run to the shuttle's console, a path Davin didn't take, instead side-stepping to the right once he'd topped the ramp.

The pilot pursued with panic's abandon, dashing up and in, only to hesitate when he didn't see Davin at the controls. After tangling with androids and charging stun batons, getting a clear shot at a confused target was a delight, and Davin roped the man into a hard headlock. A quick negotiation followed, with Davin spitting an offer for the pilot's life in exchange for departure codes and the man's swift exit. Eden's loyalty again proved loose as the pilot accepted the exchange with all-too-much enthusiasm, practically dancing down the ramp and off through the bay.

Davin had the shuttle's already warm engines spooled up, the maneuvering jets lifting his shuttle before the pilot disappeared from view. A slight rotation, a push forward, and his new ship graced the beautiful void. As he tossed the pilot's codes back to the frigate, the Nines captain opened the comm wide, trying to pick up anything, everything.

And hoping a certain voice would be on the other side, telling Davin how to save his crew.

CHAPTER 16
WHISKEY

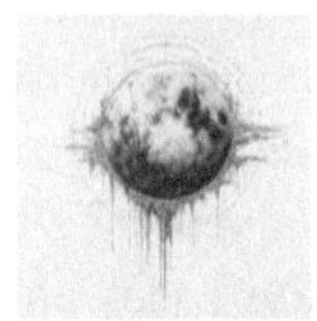

The lasers told Davin his codes were bad.

The frigate fired once Davin's shuttle cleared the bay's shield and put a few kilometers between itself and Heath's big boat. There'd been no warning, just a sudden spray that would've turned Davin to so much space dust if the shuttle hadn't been tasked for military duties, if its shields weren't already up from its retrieval runs to the space prison.

Energy crackled and the shuttle blinked alarms as Davin threw it into jagged evasion, kicking maneuvering jets on while throttling up the shuttle's engines. The combo let Davin shunt the smaller craft from side to side at erratic intervals, making it hard for the frigate's gunners to draw a bead. The bright rays continued, zipping past Davin to vanish against the Earth's bright halo to port, or off into the twinkling dark to starboard.

Missiles and hard slugs, the solid metal that'd pierce the shuttle's shields like Davin's jokes would a dead dinner party, didn't follow, suggesting Heath Swane hadn't picked up on this particular shuttle swiper. Those weapons were expensive, and where, after all, could Davin go?

The wide comm crackled with the wrong messages.

None emerged from the space prison, suggesting the bad guys still controlled the top command center. Instead, a request shot from the Eden frigate to Earth's perimeter defense force, alerting them to Davin's hijacking and requesting assistance.

When Earth's fighters replied to ask whether the shuttle needed capturing, Heath's lackeys demurred. Destroyed would be just fine.

That put half a dozen fighters on Davin's trail, even as he neared the frigate's maximum gunnery range. The space prison sat well behind Davin now, with the frigate placed between him and that hopeful return, making a run to Phyla and his friends worse than a suicide mission.

It'd be a stupid one.

Yet, flying straight on into Earth's teeth, a gauntlet that'd snap down on Davin if he tried a hard port dive to the big planet's surface, wouldn't play either. He had a narrow window to make a choice, and only one way offered itself as a chance.

"Mox, I wish you were here," Davin muttered, pushing the flight stick towards the big gray ball. Or rather, where the Moon would be in a few hours as its orbit brought the crater-blasted sphere into view. "But since you're not, I hope you won't mind me asking your friends for a favor."

Davin slid the shuttle to starboard and opened up the craft's comm, angling the communications towards the approaching Earth squadron. The lead pilot jumped on quick to Davin's greeting, demanding this, that, and other nonsense that Davin countered with a single word.

"Whistleblower," Davin said. "I'm running because I can't take what's going on with that ship, what they're doing. It's illegal, immoral, and terrible."

That Heath Swane's android program counted for at least one of those things only gave Davin's protest weight, enough to make Earth's pilot hesitate.

"You're claiming protection?" the pilot replied, after what Davin assumed was a quick look-up of the relevant laws.

Davin only had a fuzzy memory of the things himself, but you'd catch occasional news blurbs about disgruntled workers making crash dives off corporate vessels, seeking to divulge secrets for safety. Usually, that safety came from skin-flint working conditions, like spacewalks in suits prone to leaks or weeks on some asteroid with dwindling nutrient goop reserves.

Whether those poor souls who attempted the negotiations actually wound up with anything, Davin couldn't say. He didn't have time to follow-up, so he banked this particular request on hope.

"I'm claiming that frigate behind me is going to cause the solar system far more trouble than I will," Davin said. "Their captain's a right nut, and he's busy massacring everyone on the prison right now."

Another several second pause before the Earth captain clicked a reply, "The prison?"

Davin had to clarify while the Earth fighters continued to stream closer. The gaps in the Earth pilot's conversation suggested the man had two channels open, was getting persuaded by the powers that be on whether Davin's whistle ought to be left unheard.

Silence seemed to be the answer.

The Moon hovered in the distance, always both closer and farther than you'd expect. A few hours flight at top speed would get Davin in hailing range, a chance to schedule a landing, but his odds of lasting that long with these fighters coming in hot were somewhere between zero and, well, zero.

What other bluffs could Davin throw?

While chronicling a story about the assault on the prison, Davin cast his eyes about the shuttle. Packed for an offensive strike, the craft had deadly implements aplenty. Rifles, grenades, and armor packed the racks, gaps showing where

Heath's androids and their human counterparts had armed themselves, but more than enough for a one-man stand.

If the fighters decided to line themselves up and dock with Davin one by one, he might have a chance.

"I'm going to give you a choice," the fighter pilot said at long last. "Power down your engines and we'll let you wait until Eden comes and picks you up. In the meantime, I'll take your report and file it for someone to look into."

"Or you blow me to bits?"

"Glad we understand each other."

"Don't believe me, eh?"

"One man's word against another. I'm not big on killing based on hearsay, but I can't let you run away in a stolen shuttle either."

"Well, you could."

"I won't."

Davin drummed his fingers on the shuttle's dash, dancing near the thing's console. Phyla might dare herself to take on the fighters, thinking she could dance her way to the Moon. Davin didn't have the skills or the death wish for that. Nor did he have the time to wait for Heath to send a few androids along for a fatal pick-up.

His focus returned to the sprawling glassy shield between himself and the stars. The Moon grew in that picture, but what drew Davin's attention was a blur towards the bottom, a reflection cast by the shuttle's blue-white lights. A rugged, tired face that belonged to one of the most famous bastards in the solar system.

"Hey," Davin said to the flight leader, back through the comm. "You know who you're talking to?"

"No?"

"Davin Masters. Hero of Earth. A guy who already took down one bad dude and is trying to do it again."

Musing on the other side. The kilometers between Davin and the Moon continued to drop. The chaos, the fighting, the carnage back on the prison fell farther and farther away. Whether the Nines were still alive on that disaster of a station . . .

"Eden's frigate says you're lying. I'm inclined to believe them."

"You willing to bank your life on it?" Davin asked. "Any lasers come my way, I'll broadcast a video distress call to every craft within range. They'll know exactly who tried to shoot me down."

Davin could feel the captain's indecision through the call. Like playing cards or negotiating a better contract. Once he had the opponent off balance, it was time to offer an easy out.

"I'm heading to the Moon. I'll land there. You can radio ahead, tell'em everything, and if I'm the bad guy Eden says I am, then the Centurions will arrest me. Nobody needs to risk a thing."

Open a door, and, if you're lucky, they'll walk right through it.

Luna gave Davin a glitzy landing vector, swinging in low around the arcing glass buildings made viable through loose lunar gravity. Giant domes caught sunlight, their bends shimmering in rainbow lines as Davin flew the shuttle—or, rather, the shuttle's flight computer steered—into an isolated docking bay away from commercial traffic.

Earth's defenders had made clear Davin's ride was stolen, that the man was dangerous, that Eden wanted him dead.

Thankfully, most on the Moon treated Eden the way Davin did nutrient goop: a fact of life, but not one to love. That reality played out when Davin stepped down the shuttle's boarding ramp toward a slim greeting party, headlined by a particular Centurion all done up in her red-caped best.

"Commander Latrice," Davin said, splashing on his hangdog grin, trying to fight off the headache, the muscle pains of too many hours on active duty. "Not exactly how—"

"Shut up," Latrice declared, her sharp face and equally razor eyes adding to the hands-on-rifles stance she and her pals had going on. "I let you land on this Moon once as a wanted man and you threatened me. Now you're landing here a second time, and as far as I can tell, there's no backing up whatever nonsense you're about to spew. You belong in a cell or dead, Davin Masters."

Yet she didn't move to take him into stun cuffs, didn't shoot him on sight.

"But you have questions," Davin said, folding his arms. "Might be I've got answers."

"I don't have questions. Luna does. Earth does too, and I've been told in the last hour that I need to wring some answers out of you."

"And I'd be damn happy to give you some, but see, time's not a thing I've got. My friends are probably fighting for their lives right this minute, so—"

"You want help? You'll talk. You want your friends to live? You'll talk fast."

Latrice's suggestion aside, the docking bay wasn't the place for an interrogation. When Davin acquiesced, the Centurions marched him to a featureless box of a room just off the bay, a spot designed for hard questions and easy kills out of sight, should the party prove problematic. Davin sat in a cold chair, warmed by coffee and, yes, some infernal nutrient goop. When the Nines captain made a pleading ask for something, anything else, Latrice noted Davin's friends might be dying that very moment.

A hard negotiator, this Centurion.

Latrice, though, didn't have dumb questions, and they came from people with real power. Earth and Luna both had noticed Alyssa's supposed arrest, the odd statements made by Davin and other rebel leaders seemingly all on Earth's surface, in Quito, declaring the movement a folly. What served to fool the compliant masses smelled wrong to politicians, intelligence services, and Eden's various rivals, all of whom were happy to see the fringe fighters keep up their resistance.

"So answer," Latrice said. "Why did you say all those things? Is the war actually over?"

"Lemme tell you a secret," Davin said in between deep whiffs of the coffee. Sure, it was cheap, machine-brewed stuff, but a smell other than sweat, burning wires, and fear was to be treasured. "None of those people you saw were us. Or human."

Latrice didn't flinch, though one eye widened a hair. "Androids?"

"Sharp one, aren't you?"

That eye narrowed damn fast. "Explain."

"It's a power play, Latrice. Eden's not a monolith. You've got groups all pushing for their pet projects, and one of 'em's led by this joker Heath Swane. He's the puppy Bosser Oates left behind, and now Heath's trying to make his big dog move. Thinks he can swing things back in the robot's favor by making mock-ups of you, me, and everyone Eden needs to fall in line. Only thing left is to make the real versions disappear."

"Yet, you're still here."

"Hey, I never said Heath was competent. His androids aren't perfect out of the box, as I understand, so Heath wanted to stuff us in Eden's orbital prison until he confirmed the copies were good to go. At least, that's what I'm thinking."

Latrice tilted her head. "So Alyssa is there?"

"Not sure. Didn't see her." Davin swirled the coffee. "Put a gun to my head, I'd say she's the reason Eden's giving Heath the resources for all this. They're letting him play his games with us, but Alyssa went to more important people."

"Like Eden's leadership?"

"Look, Heath's little escapade isn't free. Someone up the chain's responsible."

"And who do you think that might be?"

Davin grinned, finished his coffee. "Only one way to know for sure."

Not for the first time, Davin found his assertions questioned by people who, for some reason, didn't trust a mercenary for hire, known gambler, and one-time murder suspect. Those questions didn't come to Davin's face, but were delivered by Latrice on the way to the *Jumper*'s distant bay, where she'd rested well away from the public eye since the Nines first dropped her days—and seemingly years, going by how Davin felt—ago. Pieces shuffled on a board beyond Davin's view, moves resulting in his being returned to his old ship under a heavy Centurion guard.

The *Jumper* had been restocked and restored while the Nines jaunted Earth-ward, part of a favor negotiated by Mox with his Centurion colleagues that now paid off as Davin slid into his co-pilot's chair. Latrice took Phyla's seat, though the Luna soldier admitted she had no talent for steering spacecraft.

"Davin doesn't have much either," Fournine, the *Jumper*'s once-android AI and a wise-cracking ass, announced. "But fear not, I'll keep the ship out of his hands."

Latrice frowned at the console before her, as if that would impinge the AI's spirits. When Fournine continued with a cheery systems check, Latrice returned to laying out the terms. The androids were enough of a public crisis that all parties, Earth, Luna, and Eden, had an interest in keeping them contained. Davin, given his cache, would have a chance to prove his assertions and, if true, would help deliver Heath and his collaborators to justice under Earth's interstellar law.

Proving those assertions would come about with a few friends, like Earth's defense force, Eden support craft, and those Centurions now clustering around the *Jumper*. Heath's frigate had already been ordered to cease operations and wait for further instruction while various curious vessels made their way into position. Davin pushed for a return to the Eden prison first, a chance to showcase the damages the androids were capable of, and a chance to rescue his team. Latrice, playing the intermediary, relayed that ask and the subsequent approval, paving the way for a surreal return to the prison on the *Jumper*.

Ordinarily, Davin would've spent those hours in nervous wonder, playing out scenarios while the distance to damages fell to zero. This time, he slipped back to the captain's cabin he shared with Phyla and dipped into a sedative, knocking himself out into a dreamless instant that had him groggy when Fournine's incessant alerts shattered the sleep.

While the *Jumper*'s pillows had the rumpled, weather-beaten quality earned by too many used years, Davin didn't have a cramped neck, didn't feel anything other than a hollow guilt when his eyes struggled open.

Lying in bed while the Nines fought for their lives, if they still had them, in Eden's prison?

Not exactly captain material.

"Neither is missing the action," Fournine said.

"What?"

"You mutter in your sleep. Every time, without fail, when you take the sedative."

Davin sat up, ran his arm across his eyes. "And you listen?"

"Oh, I record. Phyla and I listen to them later and laugh."

With the nagging image of his wife and ship's computer chuckling to Davin's unconscious mutterings, the Nines captain returned to the *Jumper*'s cockpit to find Commander Latrice right where he'd left her, albeit with coffee. Latrice sipped on the straw, lid, and cup combo required to make zero-G drinking possible, not otherwise acknowledging Davin's return.

Rather rich, considering his ship crawled with the red-cloaked Luna soldiers, all bumbling through the few curling corridors, packing the central area with their gear, and occupying the lavatories.

"You take a shower, or is that a post-mission thing?" Davin asked by way of greeting, sliding into the pilot's chair —usually Phyla's, but it seemed wrong to cede the space to anyone non-Nines.

Latrice didn't respond, her mouth occupied with caffeination duties. Instead, she nodded at the console screen before her. The rectangle had a single scrolling image, a circle and a dotted line, counting down the distance to Eden's prison.

Davin might have time to finish his own coffee, and then they'd be docking.

Fournine had clarified the developments while Davin developed his clarity in his cabin, explaining that Heath had declared the prison to be in active rebellion, that his soldiers were putting down the troublemakers, and any investigation needed to wait until things were safe. While nobody seemed thrilled with that idea, Heath had sent along broadcast clips taken from the prison's too many security cameras showing carnage, firefights, and bodies aplenty. The evidence persuaded Earth and Eden's other players—the corporation seemed inclined to push back on the accusations—to wait until peace was restored to make a push.

Luna, led by Latrice, disagreed. As she said, one of their own, Mox, was on that prison and she meant to see him off alive. A bold thrust, and Heath gave in, accepted the proposal. Latrice and her Centurions could land, find Mox, and get him off alive.

"Though he made clear the prison is not controlled," Latrice said as the *Jumper* angled towards a familiar docking bay, the smaller one on the prisoner's administrative level. "We'll be heading into active conflict."

That was evident enough in the activity rumbling throughout the *Jumper.* The fifteen Centurions Latrice had co-opted for the operation busied themselves attaching sidearms, rifles, stun batons, and protective gear all along their bodies. Crimson capes, so flashy on Luna and worn as much to identify the Centurions as for any real measure, would be left behind.

They weren't, as Latrice said, trying to impress anyone here. Rescue Mox, get out, that was it.

"Sure," Davin said, throwing Latrice a wink as he settled the *Jumper* onto the bay's floor. "That's it."

"It will be if you make our arrangement any more obvious."

"Davin's never been known for his subtlety," Fournine said via the console speakers. "In fact, in a statistical analysis, his actions and mannerisms most resemble a degenerate drunkard who—"

"Fournine, if you don't shut it, I'll wipe you."

Latrice chuckled. A strange sight on such a serious face.

Five Centurions stayed behind on the *Jumper* to ensure it remained where Davin had put her down. That made a full twelve-person squad with Davin and Latrice at its head walking down the boarding ramp and right up to a particular Eden officer. The woman bore a patchy resemblance to who she'd once been, a limp and a shaved, capped head hinting at further injuries beneath. Aya kept those cool eyes, though, and they glittered with scintillated rage as she locked on Davin. Two Eden soldiers flanked her, their fingers awful close to the triggers. The Centurions followed, fanning out in the small bay to form a semicircle behind their commander, a pure show of power that Aya seemed not to notice.

Any pity Davin might've felt for Aya's damaged form never found a hold, seeing as Aya had tricked Phyla into her near-death flight. The woman was Heath's right hand, dedicated to developing those androids at just about any cost. Davin and the Nines had left her burned and broken back on Ganymede, a move made in the aftermath of enough carnage to keep another shot to the head from seeming reasonable.

Seeing her now, Davin found himself regretting the mercy.

"You should be dead," Aya said flatly, ignoring Latrice and talking right to Davin. They stood a meter apart, well within range for a throat-crunching swing. "A thousand times over, you should be dead."

"I'm only alive because you suck at killing me."

Latrice flashed a look between them. "You two know each other?"

"Latrice, meet Aya. One of Eden's more evil monsters."

Aya swiveled, stuck out a hand. "As Davin said, I'm Aya, the ranking Eden officer on this prison, and I regret that we're not meeting under better circumstances."

"Because if you were, she'd try to make an android out of you," Davin added.

"Excuse me?" Latrice asked. "What?"

"If you haven't learned to disregard everything Davin Masters says, you will soon," Aya stated. "My superiors said you were here to retrieve a Centurion?" At Latrice's nod, Aya frowned. "Unfortunately, we haven't run across Mox. As you'll see, the prison is very much in a chaotic state. We are attempting to restore order, but the prisoners here seem to think they have a chance at escape. When a sliver of freedom appears to those who have none, they will fight hard for it."

"Well, obviously," Davin said.

Latrice held up a finger towards his face, as if that'd get Davin to quiet down. He did keep his tongue in check while Aya ran through the station's status, delivering a level-by-level breakdown that amounted to closing jaws snapping down on the revolting prisoners. Eden's forces had landed on the prison's top and bottom and were working their way towards the middle, where the main prison yard remained in the enemy's hands.

"Enemies," Davin snarled. "That's rich."

"Rebels? Prisoners? Idiots?" Aya replied. "I'm open to another term. I imagine you would know which fits best."

Latrice steered the conversation back to the point, stating that Mox would most likely be at the prison's core. The Centurions had no quarrel with the other prisoners, nor with restoring the station back to Eden's control. A simple extract, to which Aya waved her on by with a warning: the lifts were out. Any descent to the station's center would require using the emergency shafts. Latrice confronted that daunting prospect with an order to move, and her Centurions obeyed.

Davin didn't linger, though he did flip Aya a particular finger on his way out.

"Be careful, Davin Masters," the Eden officer called to his retreating form. "Everyone's luck runs out sometime."

CHAPTER 17
BAD ODDS

Up and down took on different definitions in space. Counting the levels tended to serve Davin well enough, with Eden's administrative hive near the station's top and, thus, their objective downward. The space prison's stairs didn't wind back and forth, instead adopting a tight spiral not conducive to an armored squad's descent.

"That's the point," Latrice replied when Davin pointed this out, the pair leading the ten Centurions down the wrapping, no-frills gray metal. "This is a prison, not a luxury cruiser. You make stairs like these for maintenance personnel, who won't be traveling in large numbers."

The converse was obvious enough: a single sturdy body or blockade could clog the stairwell against a rushing horde with relative ease. A simple way to keep a prison break from spreading, which might explain why these stairs were empty. At least, empty of bodies.

"Now that's ominous," Davin said, cutting off fear's twisting spike at the sight of bloody spatters several levels down. The spray seemed wild, vicious even. Not the sort caused by a laser's precise damage, but a more savage blow. "Where's the owner?"

Latrice didn't have an answer to the mystery, but she did raise her left hand in a fist. Behind, Davin heard rifles lifted and readied. A soft whine added to the space station's constant background churn. The music of interstellar warfare.

Davin's goal rested at level zero, the prison's main floor. Everything beneath that level earned a negative prefix, marking the station's center and giving travelers some idea of where they were. The station's top sat at level fifteen, and the blood spatters began at twelve and continued thereafter.

A little comfort came in ashen splotches, blackened plaskin bits and burned wires where a prisoner must've nailed an Eden bot. Like the bodies, though, any bulkier evidence had disappeared.

Latrice kept Davin's focus with silence, a stern and steady progress down the steps without the slightest concession to Davin's random banter. After she ignored his initial prompts, asides, and vague assertions that his friends could handle any attack, Davin dipped into the same ready resilience as the Centurions. His nerves might be calmed with a few choice words, but now was a time for action.

Or so Davin told himself.

The eighth level, right amid the prisoner bunks, stopped the march with a bad end. The blockade had arrived, courtesy of melted steps, bent rails, and what looked like a torqued prison cot shoved amid the curl. Not an impossible barrier, but given the mess sat right near the eighth level's open door, Latrice opted not to waste time shoving the debris out of the way.

As she took the first steps through the door, Davin poked at the barricade, looked at the arrangement. The cot's crunched form suggested it'd been punched up into place, and blast scarring on the walls above the melted steps said the defense had come from below. The Nines and the prisoners holding to the plan, then. Making any Eden assault a little harder to perpetrate.

That the androids hadn't tried to smash through suggested worse things: little fear they could subdue the rebelling prisoners by marching the long way.

Every one of the prison's bunk levels rolled out the same style, with prisoners slotted into single and double rooms along the outer expanse. Like a classic wheel, the circling corridor had spokes leading into the center every so often, where Eden's captives could find lifts, lavatories, a few token refreshment areas, and little else. The emergency stairs opened right into the lobby level, a would-be bland, silver expanse decorated with warning signs about proper conduct, punishments, and Eden's all-powerful might. That these signs had been defaced with enough suave to make Davin grin suggested Eden didn't care much about maintaining the look and feel.

As Tam had said, the prisoners here controlled their own lives.

Latrice signified the less fun elements in the landing with a short breath, snapping her rifle up to her shoulders, finger on the trigger. Davin, without his shotgun Melody—whose glorious bits had likely vanished in Earth's atmosphere—lumbered up the same with a Luna rifle on loan. The stocky thing, meant to match the Moon's lighter gravity, swung too fast in the prison's grippier environs, causing Davin to whack himself on the cheek and stumble. Latrice bumped him back upright with her shoulder, letting Davin take in the gory sight.

The stairs had been kept clear until the barricade, and now the Luna squad took in just where those casualties had gone. Several bodies lay about the landing, pressed into corners with bone-crunching efficiency, as if the blood and bone sacks were little more than tissue paper. Davin didn't recognize any —no Nines among the four corpses here, all in Eden-green prison uniforms—but he'd bet their family and friends wouldn't recognize them either. The androids that'd dragged these bodies here hadn't cared to keep them whole. Faces were based in, limbs bent in all the wrong ways, and the uniforms bore terrible splotches where stuff designed to stay inside had burst out.

The worst of it all was the smell. Burned hair, moldering skin, and bowels emptied in the wrong ways all swirled together in a space station that didn't make ventilation a priority.

"Keep moving," Latrice said, picking a direction from the hallway spokes on offer. "Stay tight. Don't shoot first."

A bold order, and one Davin damn sure wouldn't obey if he caught an android trying to off Phyla. He didn't speak up that treasonous intent, instead following Latrice's measured steps from the landing without a look back. The other Centurions mumbled to themselves, and one asked Latrice if it wouldn't be better to split up, to which Latrice shot back a straight explanation:

"Davin says Mox will be on the main level. Our job is not to secure the station, but our Centurion. We stay together, we try not to present a threat, and none of us dies."

Was it noble to walk into a war zone with no intent to stop the fighting?

Davin couldn't answer that question, but he couldn't argue with Latrice's words. He'd always strived to get the Nines in and out of bad spots all together, and she was doing the same.

Shame he'd have to screw up her plan.

"Not just Mox," Davin said, waiting with the bait until right that moment.

Latrice halted, the Centurions clustering behind her and Davin. "Say again?"

The malevolence in those two words almost had Davin retreating. Almost.

"We're getting the Nines out of here. All of them," Davin

said, taking care to let his fingers fall away from the rifle's trigger. "No arguments."

Davin had seen icy masks aplenty, but Latrice's face went downright frigid, with not a twitch, not a blink breaking her glare.

"These are my Centurions, Davin Masters. They go where I ask them to. Ask. Not order, but ask." Latrice flicked her eyes to the ten soldiers behind her. "We're a civilian detail. Trained, loyal, and deadly when we need to be, but we are not drafted. We have families and friends, lives beyond this station and your stupid plans. We're here to rescue Mox because we know he would do the same for us. The rest of your crew is your problem."

"The rest of my crew has no business being here. Eden took us by force."

"Then it seems like your problem is with Eden."

"Oh, it definitely is. But so is yours." Davin turned back towards the lobby, nodded past the Centurions, who matched his look back towards the battered bodies. "Those androids aren't going to stop here. Eden's going to pop them out like nutrient goop soon. Not just to bend bodies like pretzels, but to take the places of everyone who works against them. You're not just saving the Nines, Latrice. We're breaking Eden's hold, this time for good."

"Your plan." Latrice narrowed her eyes. "I assumed all of that was blather meant to get us to come along, but you're really carrying it through?"

"We get my crew back, this all ends. Today."

Latrice held her silence for another slow breath before raising her rifle, its barrel in Davin's face. "A vote. Centurions, this man is asking you to risk your lives to save his crew. He believes this would hurt Eden. He believes this could allow Luna to escape Eden's influence. I doubt it, but I will let all of you decide."

If Davin had another speech ready to persuade the

doubtful Centurions, he didn't get a chance to give it. Latrice's rifle commanded silence from the Nines captain, and he stood there as Latrice's troops voiced, to a one, that they'd come on this mission to rescue Mox, and that hadn't changed. If Eden's nose got a little bloody in the process, so much the better.

"Move," Latrice said when the vote finished, the result clear. "Davin, you're in front. You want to bluff your way into being the hero, this is the price."

One, with eleven armed and ready Centurions at his back, that Davin would gladly pay.

Replacing wandering prisoners and bland lighting with laser scars and crimson spatters turned Eden's prison from a soulless trap into a terrifying one. Lights had been shot out, caught by stray blasts or done deliberately to confuse. Shadows and sparks mingled with distant cries, cracks, and foot-shivering tremors. Blood's sweet scent flooded everything.

With the stairway blocked and the lifts inactive, Davin and Latrice needed to find a different way down. Davin figured that way could be found by following the carnage, as Eden's forces would've discovered, or made, a path somewhere.

That hunch bore out as they left the spoke's hallway, another debris barricade pushing them left. They walked past room after room, cell after cell with beds, chairs, and other junk lobbed in front of the doors. Narrow gaps offered spots for someone to poke through with a rifle or a sidearm, as if the prisoners were well-armed.

Or wanted Eden to think they were.

"Delay, delay, delay," Davin said to Latrice and the Centurions as they walked along.

"Why? What hope could they have?" Latrice replied.

"Me, obviously."

She snorted. "That can't have been everything."

It was, but Davin only shrugged and kept on. The minutes were crawling, and he'd taken long enough already.

The path down came almost all the way around the level's ring, a popped hole in the floor of the last cell. A hard drop to the next level, work done with blunt haste. Davin stared at the ripped metal, the jagged edges almost a meter across in every direction. Eden's prison had made the cost-saving play to keep its structure light, betting on the fact that there was no way off to keep its prisoners in line.

Fast work with a utility cutter and you'd get this.

"How?" Latrice asked, joining Davin at the edge. "Was this already here?"

"No. They bought it with their lives."

The Centurions didn't shed any tears. Davin didn't either. Wouldn't unless one of the Nines turned up sloughed against the wall in one of these corridors. After seeing Opal's fleet decimated over Jupiter, a few more random bodies failed to nudge Davin off course.

So he took the first jump down into the seventh level, which looked much like its upper neighbor. Latrice and the Centurions followed, and they found a similar barricade in the hallway beyond. Another wraparound, another hole, more bodies and burnt metal bits here and there. The first noises beyond the station's grind echoed as Davin dropped to the sixth floor. Distant shouts, laser fire's simmering whine.

"They're not dead yet," Davin told Latrice, picking up his pace.

That the Centurions matched his effort was a good sign. What waste it'd be for Davin to go through all that and still wind up alone down here.

The next few floors played a strange game with the carnage, at first ratcheting it up to wincing amounts on the fifth level, where Davin kept his eyes front and center to avoid counting the prisoners who'd lost their lives in the makeshift rebellion. The fourth and third saw fewer horrors, evidence less of better fighting than casualty costs and rapid retreats.

A mordant breather on death's edge.

The second level caught them up to the fighting, the air at the cut hole hot and spicy. Davin checked his rifle before dropping, the landing setting him in a crouch. If the bodies on the other levels had been shunted aside, a clean-up taken to ease approaching reinforcements, then they'd caught up to that gruesome work.

Three Eden soldiers—human, going by their natural motions and constant coughs amid the gut-twisting . . . guts—lingered beyond the cell, peering along the rounded corridor towards the action. Davin took them in, the sweaty sheen, relaxed sidearms tucked into holsters, and casual stances belying an utter confidence. They'd been in the fight long enough to know they weren't needed to win it.

Time to change those odds.

"Hey there," Davin announced himself with his hangdog grin, the disarming move that'd served to buy him a line or two with everyone from Bosser to Alyssa. "We're your relief."

The trio turned, that promised relief already pushing nods and happy sighs in reply. One bent to pick up a pack bristling with rifle batteries, med kits, and plaskin applicators. The middle, an older gent who'd patched his age-pocked skin with slapdash, mismatched remedies, grunted at Davin's words.

"Bout time," the man said. "We've been down here way over shift. Stolen shuttle's gonna cost Eden a lot more in overtime."

The woman to his right chuckled, Davin added his own laugh, then stopped as their faces changed to frowns, glancing over his shoulders. Latrice and her Centurions walking into the corridor, turning any thoughts of backup to something a fair bit darker.

"The hell's this?" the man asked, one hand drifting towards his sidearm.

"Your relief," Davin repeated. "Luna's got an interest in what's going on here."

The man took in the words with the brain-fried suspicion so common among anyone burning hours in a combat zone, and when his hand came up away from the sidearm, Davin figured it had everything to do with how many rifles were pointed his way. The other two Eden grunts, looking to their leader, let the abject fear fall from their faces.

What getting your life back could do to someone.

"The front line's around the corner," the Eden man said. "We're keeping it slow and steady. Precise. They don't have many weapons, but there's some good shots on the other side and Heath doesn't want his bots hurt bad. Otherwise, keep yourselves back and let the androids lead. They're better at this than you are."

"Staying outta the firing line's a plan I can get behind," Davin said, throwing in a token nod to keep things friendly.

Latrice signaled her Centurions to step aside and the Eden trio walked through, into the cell, and took a boost to get on their way.

"Long way back," Davin said.

"If you don't think they'll take the lifts, then you haven't been paying attention," Latrice replied, nodding onward down the corridor. "This is Eden's prison. Don't forget that."

Forgetting such a thing became harder as their group walked the outer ring, drawing closer to familiar cries echoing pain, punishment, and more than a little hopeless bravado. Android-themed invective mingled with the screams, as if the prisoners were trying to bolster their own spirits by declaring the bots useless.

Based on what Davin saw, the burned and battered bodies littering the hallway, Heath's creations delivered on their promise.

They caught the androids outside the last, unblocked spoke hallway. The quartet, a mishmash of unfamiliar faces, had the intersection under control. Two stood at the hallway's corners, poking around in tandem to unleash lasers via heavy assault rifles that few humans could carry alone, much less swivel with, even in low gravity.

The great guns unleashed steady blue-white streams every time Davin saw them fire, and he didn't need to witness the devastation on the other end, what would be liquifying cover and bodies in equal measure. That the prisoners had held out this long against an arsenal like this was a testament to the android's caution.

The bots spoke to one another, calling out *clear* and *fire* in a careful cadence. The two androids without the big guns darted here and there across the intersection, their eyes flashing before snapping the precise coordinates of their targets—two meters high, a quarter meter right—after which their gun-toting pal would turn and unleash hell at the spot.

Hopefully the prisoners had learned to keep moving.

Latrice kept her Centurions back around the curve, walking forward with Davin, their rifles pointed low. She'd forced Davin to try negotiating first, on the idea that they could go beyond the android lines, find the Nines, and escape without too much death.

Heath's robots took her overture with the same mix of placid stare and aggression Davin was used to.

"Turn around and return to your ships," said the closest android, one of the spotters, a milquetoast man who'd taken a few scalding hits to his bot self, every blast patched over now with fresh plaskin. "This is a combat zone, and you're not authorized to be here."

"Actually, we are," Latrice said, adopting more of a bluff than Davin thought her capable of. "There're several high value VIPs among the prisoners that we need to evacuate. Eden has given us permission."

"No, they have not," the android replied. "Your arrival has been anticipated and communicated. Our orders are clear. You are to turn back, or your lives are forfeit."

Oh, Aya. Always trying to get Davin killed.

Latrice stood on Davin's right, her rifle at her waist. Trigger hand a slight move from firing. Davin's own was already right where it needed to be, his rifle angled at the android's knees. Not a kill shot, but a crippling one. Behind the android, its supporting trio busied itself with another scintillating round down the hallway. The laser light cast Davin's target in a silver silhouette.

How many seconds would it take the Centurions to get into play?

And did it even matter?

The androids were only a couple floors away from dropping into the main level, and there had to be other bots climbing up from below. Waiting wasn't an option anymore. Davin had come back to save his crew, and that's what he was gonna do.

The trigger pulled easy. The orange flash hit the mark, burrowing a burning hole into the android's left knee. A human would've crumpled, cursed some nonsense in pain. The android shifted its weight without a hitch, its unharmed left arm pulling the sidearm from its belt as Davin sent a second bolt screaming into the bot's waist. The sidearm leveled, and the android's chest vanished beneath a salvo from Davin's left.

This time the android fell twitching and smoking to the ground.

He would've thanked Latrice except the other three bots weren't granting that opportunity. While one continued its streaming assault down the hallway, the other two snapped in eerie unison towards Davin and Latrice.

"Run!" Latrice shouted, as if there were any time.

Instead, Davin dove into an open cell. The space where

he'd been vanished beneath techno-fire, hot enough to singe his pants and superheat the air. Frantic breaths burned Davin's lungs as he rolled away from the doorway, spinning on the metal floor to aim back at the entry.

Not that it mattered. He was cornered, and cornered meant dead.

Opposite the cell door sat a bland, burned wall. Davin couldn't see Latrice, couldn't tell if she remained among the living. Another salvo blazed past, this time not angling at Davin's cell but the hallway beyond. Scaring back the Centurions.

A tactic, and a dangerous one. The androids were trapped. Those heavy guns would chew through power fast, leaving them helpless and—

A shape appeared in Davin's cell door. The weaponless android, moving fast. Davin's trigger finger was a second too slow, and a second with androids meant death. His shot flew where the machine had been, flying through the door to add another black dot to the wall beyond. The android bounded to the right wall, kicked off it, and grabbed Davin's rifle, using it to push the Nines captain back against the cell's rear wall. The pressure twisted Davin's head, filling his last look with a sparkly clean toilet.

What a way to go.

Davin's face felt like it was about to explode, but he ran his left hand along the rifle, popped the battery pack, and made a play.

"Time to die," Davin said, his words tight and mushed.

His hand raised the pack and the android did what Heath's programming ordered. The bot threw Davin away, smashing him into the wall above the toilet and buying distance from Davin's would-be suicidal play.

Preserve the androids. A bad call, Heath.

Not that Davin, splayed across a toilet with a useless battery pack in his hands and at least one bruised rib, could do much about it. The android, across from Davin, snapped the rifle in two and tossed the chunks aside. Took in Davin's battery pack for what it was, and realized any threat was non-existent.

"A pointless bluff," the android said, taking a step towards the Nines captain.

"Never," Davin growled, sliding down the toilet until he sat next to it like he'd had far too many drinks.

With his left hand, he slipped the power pack's cover up, exposing the battery's coils. What you'd do if you needed to charge the thing quick.

Or do something real stupid.

The android lunged, grabbing for Davin's neck. The Nines captain dropped the battery pack in the toilet, pressed the flush. Water rushed over the battery pack, its coils hitting the metal toilet as the android put its right arm on the seat, its left reaching to crush Davin's small life.

The toilet sparked, the android spasmed, the grasping hand a sliver away from Davin. His vision blurring as that rib made its painful presence known, Davin pushed by the stunned machine into the cell. He scrambled, feet and hands on the floor, towards the door, lit by fresh lasers.

Orange ones. Going the right way.

Davin gripped the cell door frame—there were the little nodules for laser gates, but Eden never deployed the things—and started to lift himself up. Made it halfway before something strong grabbed his ankle, pulled him to the floor. A twist put Davin face-to-face with that same android, its placid, wrinkle-free face.

The hand reached for him, and this time, Davin didn't have a single damned trick left.

CHAPTER 18
PRISON MASSACRE

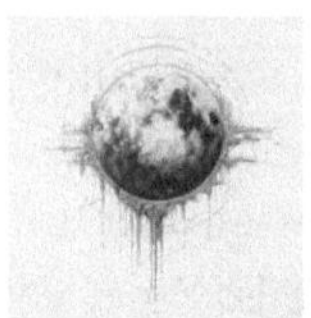

Life no longer bothered flashing before Davin's eyes. Maybe he'd seen his own replays enough times, but when the android's hand went for the throat crush, time didn't slow. Regrets didn't play out like a film on fast-forward. Instead, Davin started a strangled curse that evolved into a laugh when a hot orange laser burned the android away.

"Get up," Latrice said, continuing to pump energy into the machine.

The Centurion stood in the doorway, rifle up on her shoulder blasting away. As Davin sat up, he caught the android's smoldering body sparking apart, scattering molten bits about the cell. No white laser shadowed them from behind, an imminent demise put on hold as Davin rose, gave Latrice a knowing nod.

"Figured you'd rescue me," Davin said. "Knew it from the start."

"Did you?" Latrice spun back to the corridor, keeping the rifle raised. That told Davin the other androids were still around, though they'd apparently retreated towards the level's center. "Then you're worse than a moron. You cost me two Centurions."

Davin ran cold at the words, leaned out into the hallway and looked right. True to Latrice's words, a Centurion lay on the ground getting tended by another. Still, as Davin watched, the downed Centurion formed a thumbs-up with their hand. When no other body presented itself, Latrice's meaning became clear: one wounded, and one to tend them.

The other Centurions had already run past and taken up positions along the intersection. They spat sporadic fire down the corridor, the kind meant to keep enemies from slipping into the open.

"Not dead," Davin said, matching Latrice as she strode towards her wounded soldier.

Davin assumed she was going to offer encouraging words, but Latrice only bent down, took the wounded Centurion's rifle and tossed it to Davin.

"Since you lost yours," Latrice said. "They're going to follow, but there's no way she's making it back up through those holes. We'll need those lifts working."

The challenge in those words was clear enough: Davin had brought them down here, and Eden still controlled up there. He'd have to change that, or . . .

"You'd give me up? Me?" Davin asked as they returned to the Centurion lines.

"Came here for Mox. To save my Centurions, everyone else is expendable."

Latrice's tone, her refusal to meet Davin's doe-eyed, hangdog look left no room for negotiating on that score.

"Look," Davin said, peering down the spoke hallway and seeing a few burned prisoner bodies, smokey haze leftover from laser fire, and zero androids. "My crew's the best there is. We'll get your people out."

That assertion wouldn't be tested right away. First came a

slow advance down the spoke corridor, the Centurions clearing side rooms as they went. The action revealed the android's more gruesome habits: prisoners without mortal laser wounds had, to the man, their necks snapped. They'd been rush jobs, quick kicks from machines with too much strength and too little restraint.

"No mercy," Davin said as they neared the spoke's end, where the lifts and level's central lobby would be. He'd stopped looking at the bodies after the third, when the silence from all the others confirmed the pattern. "This is an extermination."

"Not a soul will care," Latrice said, returning with Davin to the head of the ten count force. "If this Heath Swane is trying to prove a point, the cost for this won't be high."

"Say that to their families."

"I won't, and neither will he. Or Eden."

Davin winced. "Always this cold, or just with me?"

"Focus, Davin."

Latrice and Davin leaned against the last bit of covering wall before the lift lobby. Centurions flanked their left side and their opposite. Latrice led the wheel, spinning around the corner and dropping into a crouch while Davin followed, his own rifle up and over Latrice's shoulder. If this level had been like the others, there'd be nothing in the lobby save an exit, another corridor, and another cell dropping down to the next level.

All Davin saw were barricades. Hasty ones built of chairs and cots. They'd been battered, shot through with no evidence of return fire—the prisoners wouldn't have much for lasers anyway. The shaky blockades were, however, intact.

As were the lifts.

"They ran," Latrice said as they took over the lobby, ignoring another four dead prisoners. A couple clutched broken chair legs, pathetic weapons in what'd turned to a desperate stand. "The lifts must be working."

"For them." Davin pressed the call button, received no

reply. "Betting that means they're chatting with Aya, letting her know we've picked a side."

"Expected."

That Latrice could continue her cold streak knowing the station's owners could regard her Centurions as hostile, that they'd be trapped here now unless Eden was driven away, chalked another point in her favor. She might have the personality of a wet rag, but Davin couldn't deny she stepped up.

Time for Davin to do the same.

The Centurions made for the barricades, beginning to tear them down, when Davin whistled their attention back.

"We're two floors up," Davin said. "I say we ditch the small drops and go big."

Now it was Latrice's turn to squint Davin's way, and his turn to grin.

The laser rifle beat out slug-throwers for more than one reason. A battery pack ran cheaper than solid bullets, sure, but the energy weapons were multi-purpose. Creativity found its cradle with these beam-blasting bad boys, and Davin took several spare packs from the Centurions to lay across a lift door. Mox's might could force things open, but without that exoskeleton, a solid blast would torch the flimsy barriers.

"You're insane," Latrice said.

"You're the one who didn't bring grenades." Davin judged his handiwork. Good enough to blow a hole. "That would've made all this easy."

"Explosives aren't a good idea in space. Or on Luna."

"We're in the center. No chance of a hull breach."

Whatever Davin's argument, Latrice backed her squad up all the way to the injured one and her caretaker, both advancing slow. Davin took responsibility for the blast and its trigger. Shuck the shielding, expose the battery to a low-grade laser, and the heat would set the little bricks to blow nicely.

At least, that's what Davin told himself as he took aim, fired from around the corner. The red laser, dialed down from combat-ready orange, hit the batteries and sparked up a merry flame. The glow turned blue and white as the battery packs succumbed, smoke and a few pops bouncing along, but when the flames died down, all Davin saw was a pile of melted batteries and a black sludgy spot on the lift door.

"Huh," Davin said, scratching at his chin. "Really thought that'd work."

"You watch too many movies," Latrice replied. "Now we try my idea."

The android's arm, separated from its body back in the cell, wedged between the lift's closing halves. Centurions combined their strength, gripping, pushing, and wriggling the arm until its hand-less stump burrowed into the door's seam. Once the wedge had its opening, Latrice had the Centurions wiggled the limb like it'd been electrocuted. Without preamble, the lift's doors shot open, revealing an empty shaft beyond.

"Standard safety protocols," Latrice said as she waved Davin ahead. "These lifts are made on Luna, and they'll always open if something's caught between the doors."

That Luna made the lifts wasn't surprising—most everything heavy was cheaper to manufacture on the Moon, asteroids, or Mars, where gravity didn't make shipping expensive —but Davin had to give Latrice credit.

"Don't," Latrice said as Davin loped over the lift's edge, starting down the rungs in every shaft. "It's a trick we use all the time at home."

"Then why did you let me try the battery packs?"

Latrice smirked, followed Davin. "You looked like a man who needed to be humbled."

The rungs, bare gray things bolted into the shaft on its

side, offered a narrow hand-over-hand option to descend one more level. Beneath his boots, Davin could see the point where the shaft gave way to the glass walls and open prison yard. Vague noises drifted up, the opening too narrow to reveal lasers, crushing bodies. The lift's box was visible enough, though: a dark square against the silver-white yard floor.

Getting so near the goal had Davin skipping rungs, releasing and grabbing a few further down. He held his breath as he dropped the last few into the glass shaft, where the rungs continued, albeit painted a soft white to blend in. Not that Davin noticed, because the view was enough.

The plan, hatched over nutrient goop that first night, called for a siege and an escape. Draw Eden personnel into the prison yard and overwhelm them, then take the shuttles and blast to freedom, all while exposing Eden's androids as fake copycats and killers. Whether or not that'd finally get Alyssa's investors to yank back Eden's murderous ambition was questionable, but it'd at least buy the Nines some cover to figure out what came next.

The siege played out beneath Davin's feet, with the yard's tables, chairs, and structures bent and broken into barricades surrounding the three lifts. Prisoners in Eden green uniforms mobbed the haphazard walls in a slow sponge towards the yard's right, starboard side, some holding stolen weapons while the rest played support. Their targets, Heath's androids and a few supporting Eden soldiers, hunkered down in the lifts themselves, turning out to spray fire before wheeling back under cover. Those reinforcements must've raced down activated lifts, or up from clearing out lower levels.

Both sides had losses, though the prisoners pulled theirs back to get what medical attention they could manage. Eden's, both machine and man, laid out on the battered white tile.

"Hours," Latrice said above Davin as they slowed their

descent, taking the battle in. "This isn't a few minutes of action. They've been at this most of the day."

"How do you know?"

"The routine. Your side has stations set up and used. They're passing out food and water, working in shifts. That doesn't happen in a short engagement." Latrice mused, humming to herself. "What I wonder is why Eden is bothering to let this continue. This is their station. They could drain the oxygen from this level."

A risk the Nines had talked about, that Opal had broached and Viola rebuffed. For the same reasons Alyssa wanted to twist opinions, Eden was in enough hot water as it was without massacring a space station's population through suffocation.

"It's different when they're out by Saturn, but most of these prisoners came from Earth," Davin said, resuming the climb down. "Eden needs to show they're not monsters, that they have a good excuse."

Davin scanned the yard, hunting for his crew, and spied Mox first. He'd made his way back up from the shuttle hijacking, seemed to be housing some nutrient goop near the yard's fringe. Phyla was next to him, her red hair flaring hope.

If she lived, then this whole exercise was worth it.

At the same moment, the shaft shook. Davin looked down, saw several bright blue-white laser streams emerge from all three lifts at the same time. Androids advanced, laying down burning lines that chewed through the barricades, burning prisoners behind them as tables and chairs proved woeful protection. The machines, two or three from every lift, advanced.

"Time's up," Latrice said. "Eden knows we're close, and they want this thing over."

"Then what are we waiting for?"

• • •

Davin fell five rungs before grabbing the next, keeping his style from busting his bones. Nevertheless, his point made, Davin continued skipping down the rungs while blue-white laser chewed through his allies and their makeshift defenses. The glass lift shaft gave the scrambling retreat a clear view, prisoners realizing their commitment to a sketchy cause didn't stretch to suicidal limits. Eden's androids—Davin counted eight, plus four more Eden soldiers offering support—advanced with the implacable doom afforded those who knew they'd won the battle.

Or, at least, believed they had.

The Nines had been playing the commander's role, giving orders from the back. Not the hero's stand, but one that'd let them leave alive, and a damn smart move. They joined in with the wild retreat, not bothering to rally a broken, overwhelmed, and ragged force. Mox himself scooped up Phyla and Merc, running with them towards the level's farthest band. All they'd find would be solid wall and a few more pieces of furniture. That, and seconds more time.

Opal, Viola, Puk, and Merc scattered after them, scrambling over blazing bodies and broken chairs. Davin wondered what they'd be barking to one another, what desperate ideas they'd be throwing around. Send Viola's bot on a bombing run? Have Mox try to punch a hole in the prison's hull to suck them all out into space, hopefully destroying the androids in a final flipped finger to Eden?

All unnecessary, if Davin did his job.

He hit the lift's metal roof as the androids reached the barricades. Letting their lasers die, the machines tore through the burning remnants, flinging the bits into the air like poor fireworks. Davin figured they had to have seen either him or the long line of Centurions descending the lift shafts, but none bothered turning back, spitting fire his way.

And the reason came clear as the lift juddered into an ascent, rocketing up several meters in as many seconds.

Davin wheeled, brought the rifle up to his shoulder, and fired at the cabling attached to the lift's center. Meant to hold weight, not resist an attack, the cabling frayed at the first and snapped at the second, just as Latrice hit the roof next to Davin. What'd been a rise became a fast fall. The lift didn't stay centered either, swinging to Davin's left and bashing against the glass wall.

Did Eden build their lift shafts for battle?

They did not.

Davin would've sighed at the predictable realization, but instead he jumped to his right, dropping the rifle and catching a grip on the lift's upper edge. His stomach swung as the roof went vertical, the side at his feet shattering the glass wall and driving the lift's cube through. Glass cascaded over him, but Davin was more concerned with the heavy weight on his ankles. Latrice had a good grip, one that didn't hold as the lift struck the yard's floor. The Centurion flew free as the lift threatened to roll on over, ready to squash Davin.

Until the lift stopped, victim to some cosmic force or . . .

Davin glanced down, saw Latrice on the ground, two androids next to her. One, the big laser cannon slung around her waist, had both hands up holding the lift. Good instincts, keeping them from getting squashed. The second android, spared lift duties, angled for a killing throat snap on Latrice. The Centurion threw up her arms in a cross block, a flimsy defense. The android pressed Latrice's arms against her chest with one hand, went for her throat with the other, ignoring the Centurion's kicks at the android's ankles.

So Davin dropped, landed with a face-full look at the gun-toting, lift-holding android, whose vague, gritty mug resembled some action movie actor Davin couldn't name. Cocky quotes offered themselves and Davin, at immense pain to himself, turned them all down to dive towards Latrice. The Centurion dodged one throat grab with a sudden twitch, buying Davin a second to reach Latrice's rifle, slide it with his hands, and pull the trigger.

Kicks might not earn an android reaction, but burning off an ankle sure did. The android's second throat strike swung wide left, scraping the floor as the machine tried to balance on one leg. Latrice rolled to her right, dragging the hand holding her arms with the motion, and the machine toppled to the ground.

Davin worked fast, flicking off the straps holding the rifle to Latrice. He snapped them free, brought the rifle up to angle on the one-legged android still making for Latrice's murder, only to hear bending metal overhead.

"Oh, c'mon," Davin muttered, swinging to see the second android tossing the entire lift his way. The metal block eclipsed the stale white lights, flecked Davin with falling screws, and gave the captain no chance.

The rifle's orange bolts, fired up at the lift with nothing more than impotent fury, scored a few dark marks as Davin's doom fell towards him. He kicked back as he fired, an effort to spare, perhaps, his head from getting mashed. The ceiling disappeared, then snapped back into view as Davin slid in reverse. Latrice yanked hard on the captain's shoulder, a heave clearing Davin from the falling lift with a centimeter or two to spare.

"And I always wanted to be taller," Davin said to himself, his toes touching the lift's battered roof.

"Get up," Latrice snapped, grabbing her rifle from Davin's hands. "No time for jokes."

"Wasn't joking."

Latrice swiveled, aimed, and blasted down the one-legged android, whose lurching disaster had been scrabbling towards the Centurion. Davin made it to his knees before the lift broke apart before him, the second android bashing through the thin shell. The machine wasn't single-minded in its charge, those plaskin hands earning nicks as they tore shrapnel to use as improvised knives. Faced with all that ugly, Davin backpedaled, keeping his feet as the android lunged.

Two stabs failed the fatal range test, drawing pinpricks on Davin's chest and adding ruin to the fresh jacket, shirt, and jeans the captain had worn off the *Jumper*. Rather than continuing the attack, the android flicked a piece left, the jagged edge slicing right into Latrice's rifle. The weapon spewed sparks and Latrice dropped it, cursing as she pulled a stun baton from her belt.

On his back heel, Davin felt a barricade's beginning. He reached back, yanked a busted chair leg free and considered his odds. The android must've been doing the same, as the bland man machine wheeled away from Davin and darted at Latrice. The Centurion tried a frantic cross-swing with the stun baton, a blow the android dodged with a duck too fast and flexible for a biological body. The arm holding its shrapnel dagger darted it in once, twice, a third time into Latrice's legs and stomach. The Centurion staggered back, fell, wet crimson spreading.

Davin's swing caught the android on its too-perfect skull, the chair leg's flimsy plastic shattering. The fake hair flattened, but Davin felt no skull give way, saw the android reverse its stab. The captain dove left, towards the ruined lift, and the android's swiveling strike slid overhead. A miss.

Considering his opponent, a damned achievement.

Rolling on glass and metal was the opposite of pleasant, but Davin kept his momentum, a move he'd had way too much practice with in his life. Rising, Davin felt the android's follow-up coming in hot and he broke into a stumbling flight, dashing with the lift on his left back towards the disaster that was the yard's center.

The other eight Centurions had descended the ruined shaft with rifles firing, laying into androids with less than total success. Davin couldn't see all that much with all the smoke from missed shots, but the continued blasts going in both directions suggested a fight well underway. The androids and their unnatural accuracy were making easy work of the Centurions too, forcing the Luna soldiers into desperate dives. Two bodies, rifles flying free, smacked the ground not far before Davin, their owners groaning, bleeding, and very much out of the fight.

Their weapons, those rifles, were not.

Davin had a step on the android, and that meter let him scoop up a fallen rifle, wheel around, and pull the trigger without aiming, with trust. Androids were the deadliest things in the solar system, but they had a single-minded ferocity that put this one right where it needed to be: a straight-on rush to Davin's heart. Davin's at-a-glance shot wasn't perfect, but the laser burned into the android's leading arm, set for a cross-cut with its glinting metal shrapnel. Like a muscle shocked, the android's arm lost power with the blast, the weapon falling from limp fingers to the ground.

Which did absolutely nothing to stop the android's bulk from bashing Davin and sending him flying.

The fleet, floating rush as Davin's limbs went akimbo ended fast as he whacked into an intact lift shaft and landed on his chest. The metal floor chilled Davin's cheek, and he held to one positive: this spot wasn't yet covered in slicing shards. Yet, his ribs hurt, his head fuzzed, and he knew, he knew, that android wasn't far behind.

Stand up.

Davin repeated the words to himself. Didn't speak'em, because that required breath he didn't have, but the captain repeated them again and again until he made it to his aching knees. Blood dripped in his mouth, a sweet taste from a cut lip. His tailbone protested, and those already-cracked ribs left no doubt Davin's remaining life, short as it might be, wouldn't be happy.

Except his ribs weren't counting on a face, on a hand to emerge from the smoke, nor the cries and the curses. Red hair tangled, blue eyes sharp, Phyla had a hand swinging beneath Davin's shoulder. Her legs added their strength to his, and they both straightened.

"Not the best rescue," Phyla said by way of hello, a slight grin flipping her lip. "But I'll give you points for style. Cracking a lift shaft?"

"Not my idea." Davin let Phyla drag him backward. "How're we holding?"

"Four androids left, by my count, though this smoke makes it hard to tell."

"And us?"

"Not enough, Davin. Not nearly enough."

CHAPTER 19
IMPROVISED ACTION

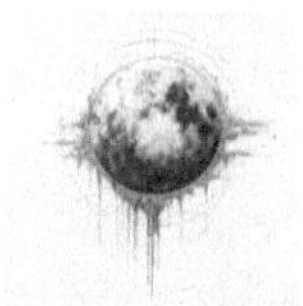

Davin hadn't ever played with Dominoes, but he understood the concept well enough: line the pieces up, hit'em, and if you'd done it right they'd all tip over in perfect order. As he and Phyla bought distance from the broken lifts, Davin was forced to concede these dominoes weren't falling as he'd hoped.

The Centurions were fighting a desperate skirmish, their numbers cut in half and drawing even with the remaining androids. Heath's machines had the Luna soldiers trapped on rungs in the lift shafts while they darted around behind cover, beneath smoke. The prisoner resistance, as Phyla informed him, had broken down amid the android fire, with the convicts flat out running as certain death lost favor to a bland existence onboard the station.

And the Nines had little left to change the equation. Mox, Merc, and the others were trying to find an angle, but taking on androids without weapons wasn't a good idea. An all-out rush to grab dropped rifles in the level's middle stood out as a tactic, though Davin had to figure they'd lose a couple in the attempt.

He couldn't order that. Not now.

Which left something different. A zig.

Davin's specialty.

"Puk!" Davin yelled, a shout that mingled with all the random awful noise around them, and one he repeated as Phyla, confused, stared at him. "Get your bot butt over here!"

He and Phyla were on the debris-strewn outskirts of the prisoner's barricades. Latrice, likely dead, lay lost in the middle's wreckage. Littered with busted furniture, some burning from laser blasts, Davin tottered this way and that as every step landed on some crap or another. Between shouts, Davin hacked as his lungs filled with smoke and torched scents of things sure to cause body-wracking cancers in the years to come. Phyla looked like a wraith, her hair and eyes standing out against a blasted prison jumpsuit coated in soot. Davin figured he wasn't much better.

"It figures you'd be alive," Puk said, Viola's floating pal zipping in over Davin's head. "Merc and I had a good bet going, one I just lost thanks to your uncommon resilience."

"We'll chat about your loyalties later," Davin snapped, nodding towards the center, the only firefight still going on. "Need you to run some interference."

"Interference?"

"Buzz the androids. Hit their communications with every code word in the Eden library."

Viola had spent years toiling in Eden's engineering sector, and Davin had to believe she'd continued to use Puk as her third hand. Heath's androids might be updated, but they'd still be running Eden software, maybe built on Bosser's old platform. Throwing a thousand darts at it, seeing if one might stick, was worth a shot.

"And if nothing works," Davin continued, "distract."

"Your trust in my intuition is heartwarming, Davin. Try not to get me killed for nothing."

Puk, the bot's little fans whirring, zipped towards the lifts on a mission that was probably suicide, yet infinitely necessary.

"Puk doesn't have a heart to warm," Phyla noted, frowning after the little bot.

"Neither do you," Davin said, flashing a scoundrel's grin as Phyla rolled her eyes. "C'mon, let's not blow the little orb's chance."

The goal, as Davin broke into a hard run towards the lifts, his battered body aching with every move—adrenaline remained the best, the favorite drug—was to get a rifle. Any rifle. Phyla matched Davin stride for stride, their steps moving from busted plastic to glass. Overhead, the Centurions retreated up the rungs, giving up firing lines to protect themselves. The androids noticed, their blue-white assault fire shifting back towards fleeing prisoners.

Not that their targets could run far. Fresh screams echoed, and Davin hoped none belonged to his crew.

Callous? Heartless? Evil, even?

Davin could live with any of those, so long as the Nines made it out of this.

Puk's interference broadcast went unheard by the humans on the level, but the evidence was clear: the android fire cut off, the whine's disappearance throwing Davin for a second before he remembered lasers weren't a constant part of life. The smoke died as they hit the shaft trio at the level's center, two lifts still in their slots. Three Centurion bodies lay around the gaping hole at the shaft they'd all used, small fires eating at their bodies.

But not their rifles. The stun batons. The former lay on the ground, and the latter hung loose from belts no longer tight to broken waists. Davin and Phyla didn't need to say anything, they just darted in for the dropped weapons.

A bolt, hot orange, flashed by Davin's head and he slipped, on instinct, into a slide. The Nines captain twisted as he went, scooping up his target rifle and aiming towards the attacker. Not an android, which explained why Davin wasn't dead, but an Eden soldier. His wide-eyed look, and sloppy hold on the rifle, said Eden's gunnery training hadn't prepped the man for combat.

Hadn't prepped the man to dodge, either. As the poor sop tried to re-orient, angle the rifle low, Davin squeezed off two shots, each plugging the soldier in the chest and dropping the soul.

Davin didn't waste time, rolling over and yanking a stun baton from the fallen Centurion at his back. He rose with the baton in one hand, the rifle in the other, the whole shabby, blasted picture feeling like home. A home he and Phyla had run away from for a while, but now they were back, and as Phyla took the Eden soldier's weapon for herself, a dozen fond memories flitted through.

"This again?" Phyla asked, looking at him.

"It's what we do."

Another blue-white cascade flashed through the smoke and Phyla grimaced.

"Then let's do it, before the Nines are back to just you and me."

The four androids grouped up beyond the barricades, heading in a straight line towards the level's outer perimeter and keeping firing lines towards the center. The Nines and prisoners had scattered, working their way like repelled magnets around the level to dodge fire and stay alive. Anyone who made a dash in towards the lifts found themselves blazed down. The Centurions, hung up in their lift ladders, weren't descending either, with Latrice not giving orders and death seeming inevitable if they dropped.

A rescue mission for one didn't seem worth losing more.

Puk filled Davin and Phyla in on all this, the bot returning unscathed and unsuccessful in his code barrage. Heath's androids had been upgraded, the trick rendered useless. They'd need the old-fashioned route to render these robots to ruin. And for that, Davin would need numbers. He'd need the Nines.

"We'll provide the cover," Davin said to Puk. "Tell them to break to the middle. There's weapons here. Then we overwhelm the androids together."

"Your confidence, as ever, defies logic."

"Just do it, Puk," Phyla added, the two of them crouching behind a blasted table.

The androids prowled beyond, moving in a clean-sweeping unit. Cut off from Eden resupply, the robots swapped salvos for precise shots, lining the air with an orange or blue blast for a second before falling dark again. After each attack, eerie silence resounded, the strikes so accurate the targets didn't have enough life left to scream. Drifting conversation died, as did the prisoner's numbers.

"It's a total execution," Phyla murmured. "This isn't about restoring order."

"It's a showcase," Davin replied. "Heath's made that clear. Ganymede didn't work out for him. This is try number two."

"A showcase for who?"

"You want my guess? It's Earth. Not Eden, but Earth that Heath's aiming this at. The planet wants order on command, Heath can deliver it."

Phyla digested the words while Davin peered back through dwindling smoke towards the level's center. The busted lift that'd nearly turned Davin into a pancake sat off to his left, and near it lay Latrice. Too far to tell if she still lived. He would've broken her way, but the androids had taken that route through the barricades and would have a clear firing line. Maybe, against faulty humans, Davin might've tried the sprint.

The androids wouldn't let him live through it.

"It's the same fear, isn't it?" Phyla said. "They don't trust us, because we live out here."

"Don't trust, but don't want to enforce. That's what

Heath's betting on. We sprawl out across the solar system and maybe beyond, Earth loses power with every kilometer. Androids get to be their strike force, their soldiers. Nobody has to leave Earth, and they still get control."

"But why does Earth care?"

"The real question, Phyla, is who on Earth cares. Answer that, and we know who Heath's dancing for. Then again, seems like we're jumping ahead here."

"Saying we should blow up some androids?"

Davin grinned at Phyla. "Read my mind."

Whether Puk had delivered the message or not, the androids had gone about a quarter of the level's distance in their perimeter sweep along its northern band, immolating prisoners along the way. They'd pass out of Davin's sight line soon enough, forcing Davin and Phyla into a dash across deadly space. Worse, if the robots kept moving, they'd get to the level's far side, where the rest of the prisoners, and the Nines, had clumped.

That just wouldn't do.

Davin wheeled, fired without aiming. Two shots, fast and likely misses. Davin didn't bother to watch, instead diving away to his right, across Phyla. Lasers replied, melting through the table and confirming Davin had attracted the wrong attention. He didn't rest, scrambling on past Phyla as she took her own potshots, then she joined him in a sprint along the inner barricade circle towards its southern end. The androids kept up their fire, the flashes blinking around Davin's eyes.

"Now!" Davin called, breaking right and through a blown part in the makeshift barrier.

Phyla escaped with him, branching to the circle's outside as lasers burned holes behind her feet. Smoke, surprise, had bought them a few misses, but the androids would be coming now.

"I'd say we got their attention," Phyla said, breathing hard.

"Mox and the others had better use it."

"We can't just sit here."

"They're computers, right?" Davin asked, both of them pressing backs against the overturned tables, chairs. Butts on the ground. Before Davin spread a bloody yard, full of bodies and smoking ruin. To his right and left, the barriers continued. "We want a chance, we have to be human."

"Ought to be easy for you."

Davin nodded. "We do what they won't expect. Attack."

Phyla cursed, but she readied her rifle anyway.

Easy to say, stupid to do. That's what ran through Davin's mind as he curled right, thick Centurion boots crunching over drying blood, burnt plastic, and, here and there, the soft white Eden tile. The fight continued like a long day, dwindling action that wouldn't quite stop as the carnage settled. The androids weren't executing anymore, they were hunting, and Davin hoped they'd follow the trail right back to the level's center. He kept himself low, Phyla following, with the rifle tucked up near his chest. If an android popped out ahead like some scary prank, Davin would blow it away.

If the machines attacked from anywhere else, Davin would be dead before he knew it.

Starting on the level's southwest side, Davin and Phyla circled northward, hugging the battered barricade. At the first android-blasted gap, Davin slowed, took a peek. The deadly foursome had made their way back inside the inner circle, backs to each other's backs, with implacable faces gazing out in all directions. Davin slipped back, gave Phyla a nod.

Time to see if they'd bought the Nines enough time.

She scooted in front of Davin, leveled into a crouch with her knees on the ground. Rifle ready. Davin brought his weapon up to his shoulders, took in a breath and held it. Felt Phyla's ready nudge from her foot against his ankle. She fell forward, twisting to angle the rifle right where the androids ought to be. Davin stepped to his left and ahead, turning with the move to get a perfect angle.

Apparently his sneaky peek had been spied, because both Nines found themselves facing four androids and their assorted weapons. Aimed, ready for fire, and Davin, even as he pulled the trigger, figured he'd at least go out blasting.

A silver orb flashed down as the first lasers flared. The androids aimed their shots at Davin, four sniped bolts going right for Davin's head. Puk caught them all, the burning lights blowing the poor bot from the sky in a superheated puff a few meters away from Davin's face. The Nines captain didn't dance back, didn't scream or fall away, didn't mourn a bot that Viola could, hopefully, rebuild.

Instead, like Phyla, he held the trigger. Orange bolts sprayed back at the androids, Davin pushing forward as he fired. Phyla let her rifle stream for a long couple seconds before curling back behind the barricade. Davin felt heat brush his back, his right leg, a fire so hot that he fell forward, pitched onto the tile. Agony skittered up and down his right side, a sensation he knew too damn well.

One he didn't have time for.

Using his elbows, Davin crawled ahead towards the next gap. He'd get there and—

"Behind!"

At Phyla's voice, Davin twisted—his vision blinked black as his wounded leg dragged on the ground—and brought up the rifle. An android appeared in the gap they'd just left, wielding a rifle in either hand. Each weapon pointed a different way, a feat of strength and targeting acumen that might've wiped them both out if Phyla wasn't a damn pro.

She shot the android as it landed, smoking the machine's side with a steady orange stream. The hot laser burrowed into the machine's side and through it, melting circuits, wires, and the metal holding it all together. The android's top half split from its legs, falling forward to sprawl amidst the other debris.

The bot still fired its rifles, a last command spewing orange across the ground. Flame trails lingered. Phyla put a final end to the android with several more shots, then frowned her smoke-smudged face Davin's way.

"You're hit."

"I'll live," Davin said. "Won't be running anywhere fast, though."

Phyla started his way then stopped herself, glaring towards the gap in the barricade splitting them as if it were personally responsible for this problem. Which, Davin supposed, it kind of was.

"Stay here," Davin said, putting one hand on a chair pile to steady himself. "I'll keep going around, you look for a shot. Three more."

Some earlier version of Phyla might've tried telling the wounded Davin to trade spots, to not do something so stupid, but the years they'd spent together coiled into the nod she gave him. The crinkling around her eyes saying *I love you* better than any words could've. They knew each other, in every way, and in that ruined prison Davin realized this was a life he very much did not want to lose.

Lurching along the barricade didn't feel heroic, nor did his hard-breathing crouch as Davin reached the next blown gap. Another peek confirmed the android trio had decided to set up shop around the lifts, each lugging one of those high-powered laser cannons. Abandoning the clean sweep for a strong position, but why?

Reinforcements?

With the remaining Centurions trapped up the battered shafts, the androids definitely could just wait for more Eden forces to show up. The Nines and what prisoners were left didn't have the arsenal to dislodge the three. A charge from all sides might earn some hits at massive cost to their lives, an idea Davin discarded even as it formed. He had no way to talk to anyone, to set up a signal, with Puk gone.

Stepping out for a shot didn't seem like a great option, either.

The burnt furniture held a better answer. Thin chairs and tables. Clumped enough to make targeting hard, but Davin didn't need to be perfect. Just good enough to draw some attention without killing himself. He shifted to his right, put the rifle up against the leaning table and its attendant clumped chairs.

"C'mon, it's not the worst idea you've ever had," Davin muttered.

The rifle spat orange into the table's plastic white, burning straight through and streaking towards the androids. Davin only saw a dot haloed in orange and black, one he filled with several more bolts until the barricade around him began bursting with blue-white fire.

Davin dropped, let his wounded leg lead him to the ground as the air overhead immolated. He clutched the rifle, listened to the whines around the level as Phyla and the others picked up his plan. As the heat above dissipated, Davin climbed to his feet, brought the rifle up to the barricade, and found two androids left. Both had their cannons roaring, scattering fire against incoming attacks around the level. Davin sighted the rifle on the rightward robot, took actual aim, and pressed the trigger.

The lasers burrowed into the machine, right around the robot's waist. One struck the big gun's battery pack, bursting it into pink-green fire. The android collapsed as its partner wheeled Davin's way, only to find itself dropped by an enterprising Centurion. The Luna soldier fell as she fired, spraying bolts in a wild descent arrested with a desperate grab of the rungs, her rifle left to dangle by its strap.

Davin knew that move: a suicidal play, meant to crash into the enemy even if it shot the Centurion first. Buy a second for the following soldiers. Instead, she'd finished the fight.

For the first few minutes, nothing changed. The level crackled with fires burning themselves out, the groans of the wounded not finished off by android fire, and the space station's churn. Davin ventured into the dissipating smoke, keeping the rifle up as he approached the androids and checked each one, dropping an extra shot into a couple whose eyes still twitched. His right leg burned, but apparent victory dulled the ache enough for him to limp around.

Latrice numbered among the living, pale and glassy. The four remaining Centurions circled up around her, first aid kits coming out to handle the stabs. Davin watched as Phyla found him, as the survivors began their cautious approach into the level's center. The two working lifts zipped up and away, a detail Davin registered and did nothing with.

If Eden decided to send another android swarm down in those boxes, the machines would be trapped, gunned down without mercy. He figured Eden would know, would—

"You lucky bastard," Merc announced, walking with Mox into the level's center. "How'd you make it through all this alive?"

"Cheating death, as per usual," Phyla answered for him.

What could've been a cheery reunion under better circumstances went sour as Merc detailed injuries. Riley, Viola, and Opal were all hurt, all laid up at the level's outskirts. Shrapnel, lasers, and, in Viola's case, a broken ankle earned from a bad drop on the levels above. The androids had come in precise and furious, slaughtering most of the prisoners and throwing their plans into chaos.

"The only thing that saved us," Merc continued, "was how cautious they were. Like Heath didn't want to lose his toys, so they gave us chances to run away and regroup."

Mox had counted ten androids in total, a smaller force

than Davin expected, until Phyla reminded him this was a prison. The people inside weren't supposed to have weapons, and they'd lost most of the two hundred or so prisoners as it was. What little remained of Davin's winning cheer withered when he counted fewer than twenty still standing. Heath had demanded a slaughter and received one.

The metal man himself ought to have numbered among the dead, being left in a one-on-one match-up against Opal's android copy. Mox ditched off the duel as a quick affair, brought to an end by the android's faulty logic.

"She thought I was a normal, weak man like you, Davin," Mox said, tilting his neck to either side as if to accentuate the black metal wrapping his shoulders. "She caught my first swing with her hand and the pipe wrench tore off her arm. The second caved in her head, blew her sensors. From there, it was ugly."

"Geez," Merc said. "Mox, why aren't you bashing them all in for us?"

"Because I got lucky, and Davin's failure set up my success."

"Okay," Davin said. "Enough about my failure. Congrats on being a badass, Mox. Don't stop now."

"New plan," Davin said as the group circled up, Latrice joining with a lean on a Centurion shoulder. "What we saw here could happen anywhere. This has to end today."

"We're ready," Mox answered the unasked question. "Tired. Real tired. But ready."

"Good, because we're going to keep moving."

The *we* in that announcement turned out to be Davin, Phyla, Mox and Merc. A devil's quartet if Davin had ever seen one. Latrice and the Centurions, despite fuming over a mission gone very sideways, agreed to help the remaining prisoners and Nines crew hold the level against fresh assaults.

How long they'd have to stand guard without more help would depend on, well, how far Davin's swagger and a hefty supply of pain-killing drugs, courtesy of those Centurion aid kits, could carry him.

Viola took the news of Puk's heroic sacrifice with a sigh. She'd rebuilt the bot a couple times already, and made a habit of syncing Puk's memory to several different back-up spots. Opal, with both arms burned by bad blasts, had drifted into unconsciousness. Merc's cocky guise slipped when he looked her way, but Viola promised she'd be well-taken care of. Riley, like Viola, had minor injuries, but Davin figured the guy would be about as useful in the coming mission as a drink of cold water.

As for the quartet, they stocked up on what they could. Some leftover nutrient goop shuttled down prior to the fighting, stolen rifles—Mox hefted one of the android heavy cannons for himself, and a couple of those Centurion aid kits. There was no fanfare when Davin, leg wrapped and creams applied, said it was time to go.

Eden hadn't sent the lifts down, wasn't responding to calls. Not a surprise. Aya might be watching their every move with popcorn in hand, debating with Heath about when they could declare victory. Davin hoped she choked on a kernel.

Anyway, that the lifts had gone up was a good thing, because the Nines were going down.

CHAPTER 20
SCARRED PLANS

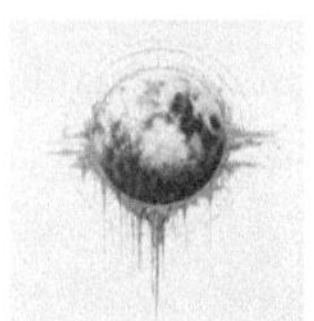

Before a mission, the Nines always assembled in the *Jumper*'s cargo hold. They'd check each other's setups, confirm battery packs were charged, accessories were clipped to belts, and repeat the plan to each other. A ritual at once necessary and bonding. Davin, Phyla, Merc and Mox did the same now, standing near the lifts while the remaining prisoners and Centurions shored up what defenses they could.

Mox held a heavy cannon, his exoskeleton more than able to heft the monstrous weapon. Cables ran from the long laser gun to a big battery pack strapped over Mox's shoulders. Almost like the big man's old mini-gun back on the *Jumper*, and plenty fearsome. Beneath the gear, Mox's shiny black exoskeleton pushed out the forest green Eden jumpsuit, bulky ridges spidering about his arms and legs all the way up to his neck. Like all of them, exhaustion played about Mox's features, wrinkles driven by age and exertion brought to the fore by sleep's unmet demands.

Phyla and Merc matched each other, their marred jumpsuits offering little space to attach anything useful. Even so, they both stuffed pockets with extra packs for their rifles.

Merc, the lean pilot, kept up the swagger as he scoped several rifles, landing on a fallen Centurion's weapon.

"Trust Luna more than Eden to keep their gear in good shape," Merc said when Davin eyed the choice.

"So long as you bring it back," Latrice, sitting on a chair and breathing slow, said. "That's not yours to keep."

"What's your damage policy? Cause where we're going, she's not likely to come out clean."

"Prison time. Breaking rocks."

Merc laughed. "Noted. I'll give her back in one piece."

Davin, thanks to his change in the *Jumper*, had a real setup, albeit one burned and battered by the fighting. Still, he had a belt with clips that he put to good use. A Centurion aid kit found its way onto his back, drugs from another already numbing his burned leg. The Nines captain wouldn't be winning any footraces, but he wasn't sitting this one out.

Not with vengeance on the menu.

Merc offered to lead, and Davin gave him the go-ahead. The pilot started off down the left lift shaft. The fragile courtesy doors had already been shattered by wayward blasts, letting easy, albeit crunchy, access to the rungs along the shaft's side. Mox took the last spot, slinging the big cannon over his shoulder. They descended fast, or at least as fast as Davin's wounded leg would let him. All the while, they rehashed the new plan, not all that different from the old.

The Nines had wanted to lure Heath into an all-out response, trap him on the prison and take him out. That Heath had sent Aya instead, along with a few androids, confirmed he was a damn coward. Confirmed the Nines would have to go to him.

"They can see everything we're doing," Davin said, just above Merc as they kept going down. "I don't understand why they're not responding."

"My guess?" Phyla said. "They're dealing with bigger problems."

"Bigger?"

"Earth, Luna, and all their eyes. Alyssa had one thing right: Eden's a company with investors, with people who don't want anymore disasters. Heath pushed for this, and now that it's gone sideways, they have to clean it up."

"By killing us all?" Mox rumbled. "They have Centurion blood on their hands now. Once Luna knows, Eden will lose access to the Moon."

Mox's words made Davin twitch. The proverbial chill followed. Once Luna knows. Heath wouldn't be dumb enough to let that happen, but just killing the Nines, the prisoners wouldn't safeguard that. The prison had cameras. Any disgruntled employee could pull the footage, send it . . .

"They're going to blow the station," Davin snarled. "That's how they hide everything. That's why they're not sending any more androids at us. It's an evacuation, a wipe."

"That's quite the play," Phyla said. "Does Heath have the stomach for it?"

"The man believes in androids. He's risking everything. The man won't care if a prison goes boom to keep that dream alive."

"Which means what, a timer's ticking somewhere?"

Merc snorted from below. "Any station in Earth's orbit has to have a self-destruct option. Has to be thorough, too, so big chunks don't land. They'll have the trigger up top."

Too far to climb on the lift ladders.

"Keep going," Davin said. "They'll need time to evacuate everyone."

"They've had time," Merc countered.

"Then climb faster."

Merc did, dropping rungs like Davin had done farther up. A tricky move Phyla managed. Davin tried, but his leg flared at the hard impact several rungs down, and his arms, already feeling like lead weights, burned. Mox didn't bother to catch himself, simply jumping into the shaft's middle and plummeting the last few levels to the station's bottom. He landed with a loud crunch, the exoskeleton catching the weight and converting the kinetic energy into the power all that metal needed to keep moving.

The lift doors down there were already gone, courtesy of Davin's earlier escape, and Mox ran through as the rest caught up with him. The corridors were quiet, the androids that'd struck down here apparently among the ones dead up above. Mox, of course, knew where to go: the docking bay.

The corridor's silence spread to Davin and the others. The white metal walls splattered with Eden posters offered no evidence of war, no stink of burned bodies or curling smoke. Groans, screams, and shouted orders swapped with a space station's gentle thrum. The trio walked quietly after Mox, giving room for the last few hours to fill the gaps.

The first body was a shock. Always. Davin had seen his first at a far too young age, bumbling around Vagrant's Hollow until a fight's noise drew him, Phyla, and Lina. A little too much anger, a knife's quick cut, and a person's life ebbing out onto the dusty street. He'd stared then, but learned soon to look away fast.

Less chance of nightmares that way.

Now, though, Davin was seeing carnage by the dozens. Europa, Ganymede, this damn space prison. How many ghosts would he collect before all this ended?

"Snack break?" Merc offered, nodding his head to a closed door on his left.

The sign outside suggested a break room, and, Mox opened it with a single smash. Inside the squat room were plain lockers, stuffed with nutrient goop and canned coffees, juices, and fizzy waters. A plain bump in an otherwise absurd day.

Not that the crew enjoyed it. A snatch and run affair that had Davin alternating plain black coffee with strawberry nutrient goop—tasted like old chalk, no matter the flavor.

They hit the decontamination docking bay several minutes later, nary an alarm or call from Eden to explain themselves, to cease, to offer terms of surrender.

Davin cursed and Phyla asked why.

"Because they really did leave," Davin said. "I keep hoping people aren't going to be so heartless, but here we are."

"They're willing to let us die for their jobs, their dreams," Phyla answered. "Screw'em."

The decontamination bay gave Davin exactly what he expected: a thick door and a warning that the atmosphere inside had been compromised. The wrecked shuttle waited, still jammed along the docking bay's length. As with any docking bay, a nearby room held spacesuits and emergency gear, stuff Mox pulled out and threw to Davin, Phyla, and Merc. His exoskeleton rendered Mox a hard partner in this bit, the Centurion putting on a helmet and its attendant oxygen mask. He'd keep his breath, but a trip beyond the station would freeze or scald the man.

But a space walk wasn't the idea.

Smashing into a damaged docking bay wasn't so easy. After a couple of hard, ineffective whacks with his fist, Mox backed away with a shaking head. He waved off the others, then leveled the high-powered laser cannon.

"Don't you dare miss," Merc said, taking cover behind Mox along with Davin and Phyla.

His voice puffed into their ears on the near-field comm relay connecting each of the suits.

"If I do, I'll make sure to hit you," Mox replied.

But the doors made easy targets, and the white-hot cannon melted through resistance meant to seal oxygen, not repel an energy assault. Hissing began and ears popped as Mox burned a line along one side, severing the sliding door's connection to the walls around it. This time, Mox's fist warped the door, bending it far enough with a second swing to let a careful walk through. Davin, witnessing the whack through a thick helmet, announced pole position. He bonked off the metal with that same helmet on the step-through, but avoided any ruinous tears from the torched, battered door.

There was debris everywhere, but otherwise the docking bay remained peaceful enough. The lights had died, replaced by headlamps on their helmets. Davin didn't stick around for a thorough inspection, instead loping along to the damaged shuttle. The craft had smashed so hard into the station, the front end looked like a snub nose. Davin angled towards the rear, where, outside of laser scoring, the vehicle was intact. Its boarding door hung open, the panel popped out by the crushed roof and on the ground.

"You really did a number on this one," Merc said. "Remind me never to let you fly again, Davin."

"Lotta enemy fire. Not my fault."

"I would've dodged it, right, Phyla?"

"We both would've, Merc. There's a reason Davin doesn't touch the stick unless it's an emergency."

Saving the insults for later revenge, Davin climbed into the ruined shuttle, picking his way along the seats until he came to the smashed pilot's terminal. Broken, unable to fly, but the shuttle hadn't exploded. Wires splayed everywhere, but Davin didn't spy severed lines. It'd been a crunching hit, but ships these days kept their comms well-secured.

Nobody wanted to be stranded without their mayday.

The screen had shattered. There'd be no fancy interface. But Davin felt beneath the terminal to the narrow analog layer meant for those times when everything had gone wrong. He found switches and flicked them, one by one. A nested port let loose a dangling plug when Davin pulled it open, and he yanked it free, then set it into the suit's comm relay up by Davin's neck. Without atmosphere, nothing Davin said sans suit would go anywhere. When he plugged in, though, Davin heard the euphoric crackle.

"We're up and running," he said, the words traveling both to his friends and out along the shuttle's open band.

Only, Davin didn't want to talk to the void. He had a specific target. Without a functioning console, he had to do things the old fashioned way, and get his target to come to him.

"This is a dead man," Davin began, "a ghost, and a reckoning." He slowed, threw Phyla a wink she probably couldn't see through their visors. "Heath Swane, if you're listening to this, tune to my frequency, and let's decide how your dream dies."

Davin rattled off a band at the end, twisting the analog dial beneath the crumpled terminal to the desired frequency. Now, to wait, all while the space prison's presumed destruction ticked closer.

"Think he'll answer?" Merc asked, hanging with Mox at the shuttle's back. "Very ominous though, Davin."

"That's the idea," Davin replied. "Heath's the kind of guy whose imagination will create a worse picture than anything I could say."

A man so warped by a singular obsession that any threat to it would drive him beyond rational response. And Davin did have a good threat: he could dance back to that open band and deliver what'd happened on the space station to everyone within hailing distance. Out beyond Mars, that might not amount to much.

Around Earth?

Davin would have an audience of billions, and most wouldn't take kindly to a story about androids massacring prisoners.

So when Heath's voice crackled over the comm, tired and angry, Davin couldn't help but grin.

As negotiating positions went, sitting aboard a busted shuttle that, itself, was crash-landed into a space station likely to self-destruct, offered little. Being an underdog put Davin right where he belonged, though.

"You'll tell Aya to stop the space station from blowing apart, and then you'll send us a proper pickup," Davin said, taking care to talk evenly, cocky, as if this was all expected.

"Because you'll reveal my little subterfuge, Davin? Is that your threat?"

"Glad we're on the same page."

Behind Davin, Merc, Phyla, and Mox waited. Their oxygen tanks, small and meant for quick in-and-out action, dipped lower. As low as the station's blow-up clock?

"I'm waiting," Davin spoke again, as Heath hadn't. "Agree to the terms, or I start talking?"

"And if I play it slow, Davin? If I keep you bantering long enough for the station to explode? Tell me why that won't work."

"Because I have insurance."

Heath laughed. "You have nothing. Only—"

Davin opened up the comm. Back to the wide band. "Hey there, this is a Centurion squad on Eden's prison. We're in need of rescue, and Eden's set the station to self-destruct. Please advise if you're able to assist."

A little nudge, and a spin back to Heath's frequency.

"How'd that play?" Davin asked the void, hoping Heath waited on the other end. "Now, you blow this up, people are going to ask questions. You want me to get them asking the right ones?"

"What happens, Davin? I send the shuttle, leave the station spinning, and then what? Where do you go?"

"You bring us to your frigate. We have a nice chat. Settle all this."

"A final meet? On my frigate? Davin, that's foolhardy. Even for you."

"My problem, Heath. Your solution."

Davin stared out the crunched cockpit. Shattered glass, bits of his own blood among the shards. His cool wavered. How close he and the Nines, how close Phyla had come to dying because of this man. He needed to take a shot, needed to—

"Davin," Heath said. "Do you know what I will do to you? You will land on our frigate, and we will capture you. I will make androids in your likeness, and they will crush your little friends. One after another, they will look at who shot them, choked them, broke them, and they will see you. I don't know your dreams, Davin, but I know your legacy, and I will ruin it."

"Good. Send us a lift up top, then we'll catch a ride your way. I'll be waiting, pal."

Davin closed the comm channel. Nodded back towards the docking bay.

"He's a monster, isn't he?" Merc cracked as they left the shuttle. "Almost makes me wish we had Bosser back."

"I don't," Phyla said. "Bosser was smart. Heath's a moron with Eden's cash in his pocket."

"And a whole bunch of androids."

"Fournine and ThreeTwelve were better. Not sure why, but these all seem off. Deadly, sure, but with the numbers we've been up against, we should've been immolated by now."

"Been thinking about that," Mox said as they made it through the ruined bay, back to the corridor. "Betting it's on purpose."

"Getting philosophical now, Mox?" Davin said.

"Practical. Androids used to just kill. Now, Heath has them doing more."

Lying, giving speeches, working in teams rather than as lone bounty hunters. Davin wasn't savvy enough with tech to know whether any of that might twist an android's combat effectiveness, but if Heath was screwing up his battle bots, all the better.

.   .   .

The foursome played pitch and catch on that idea while they walked to the lift. The box was already waiting for them, doors open, not a single dead body in sight.

What a treat.

One sarcastic remark from Merc comparing lifts to climbing the rungs and the quartet hit the station's top level. Any access locks had been removed, the keypad giving them a cheery green light. That freedom extended off the lift too, into the cramped warren usually dominated by Eden admins. Empty now, Davin and the others explored. Mox went towards the docking bay to wait for Heath's shuttle, while Davin, Phyla, and Merc broke towards the prison's control center. Thankfully, Eden's signage was up to the task, and a couple of short halls brought them to the prison's brain.

Not unlike a starship bridge, the circular room had terminals everywhere. Also like starship bridges, where so many spent so many hours, slices of life abounded. Family pictures flashed by on digital frames, plants and their attendant growth lights lingered in nooks, and a board assigning workday music choice responsibility, upcoming birthdays, and a word-guessing riddle in dry marker completed the picture.

"Never like seeing this," Merc said as Phyla went right to the central terminal and started tapping away.

"What, plants?" Davin asked.

"All of it. Reminds me that our enemies aren't just faceless losers that deserve a laser."

"Doesn't mean they didn't choose to get in our way."

Even as Davin said the words, Zoelie came to mind. She wasn't here anymore—they'd splashed by her assigned bunk and it'd been empty—and that didn't bode well for her. Heath and Aya didn't seem the type to forgive anyone who went against them.

And Davin hadn't even paid her yet.

"I get we're supposed to be heartless in all this," Merc said. "That's the soldier's job, right? Fight the war, win it for everyone else to benefit? But man, it'd be nice going up against pure evil sometime. Like in those movies, the bugs, aliens, whatever? Guilt-free, you know?"

"Like the androids?"

"Hell yes. Gimme more of those."

"You'll get your chance," Phyla said, glancing back from the terminal. "There's a shuttle coming into the bay now."

"The self-destruct?" Davin asked.

"Not seeing it. They've left these terminals unlocked too, so they want us to know. Heath's keeping his word."

"I'm sure he'll twist it."

"Then we'll twist it back after he's gone," Merc said, patting the rifle slung over his shoulder. "C'mon, let's go see our ride."

Davin asked for a minute and received it, taking Phyla's spot at the terminal and tapping around until he found the prison's broadcast system. Opening it wide, he sent out a message telling the Centurions, Latrice, the Nines, and whomever was left of the prisoners that the two working lifts were clear. They ought to take a ride up here, get some better medical help.

"And Viola, Opal," Davin said, "there's a ship waiting for you that I'm betting you'll be happy to see."

"The *Jumper*'s here and you're sending us in a shuttle?" Phyla snapped as the trio walked back towards the docking bay. "Why?"

"Because we jet out in the *Jumper*, Heath's going to blow my baby apart. We'd never get onto his frigate."

"Get a full crew on the *Jumper*, though, and we might give that frigate a beating," Merc mused. "This close to Earth, fry those engines and it's going to sink into atmosphere fast."

Davin squinted at the pilot. "Didn't you just get done

saying you didn't like killing people? Lotta paycheck pushers on that frigate, Merc. They deserve to die for Heath?"

Merc sighed. "This is too messy, Davin. I just want to get Opal outta here and lay low for a while. Have a stardust martini and watch Saturn's rings."

"Stardust martini? Too sweet." Phyla stuck out her tongue. "Give me something that burns and I'll join you."

The Great Drink Debate carved up the remaining minutes til they reunited with Mox and watched Eden's shuttle put the final touches on its soft landing. A small bay forced the shuttle to nestle in nice and close to the *Jumper*, the pilot performing the task with enough skill. The ramp went down and, with Davin in front, the Nines foursome went up.

When he saw who sat at the shuttle's controls, Davin couldn't help but chuckle. "We were just talking about you."

Zoelie glanced back with her perennial sour expression. "Great. Sit down."

"A question first, if you don't mind?"

"Why'd Heath put me here?"

"Always suspected you were smart," Davin said, coming up and sitting in the chair next to her. Phyla and Merc took the next closest spots, while Mox, too large to fit in the seats, hung at the rear where he could brace himself against the walls.

"It's a deal. I fly you back to the frigate, he doesn't ruin my life."

"Why you, though?" Davin pressed, a vague unease blooming as the pilot powered the shuttle up, dipped it out into space. "Heath could have an android do the job."

Zoelie nodded out into space, then tapped the center console, killing the comms. Davin noticed the slightest moisture around her right eye, a tear that didn't quite want to escape.

"Because, Davin, this shuttle's toast in three minutes."

CHAPTER 21
HUNTING

Davin didn't hesitate, neither did Phyla. From behind Zoelie, Phyla surged up and grappled the Eden flyer, putting the pilot in a hard headlock against her own seat's back. Davin leaned over the pilot's console, expecting to see a ridiculous countdown timer, a directed power surge to the engines, or a trajectory that'd send the shuttle diving into Earth's atmosphere at a vector best described as 'belly flop'.

"Spit it out, now," Phyla was saying as Davin scanned the console, found no immediate indicators. Merc let fly a few choice curses. The pilot coughed. "Talk. Or I snap your neck and we figure it out after."

"Harder than you think," Zoelie gasped. Davin gave the pilot his most disappointed look. "Breaking a neck isn't easy."

"We've done it," Davin said. "Plenty. Explain."

Phyla let her arm slip, though a single jerk would bring it back real quick.

"He's going to shoot. When we're clear of the prison," Zoelie said. "Heath knows there's no Centurions on here. At least not any he cares about."

"And you agreed to fly this suicide mission to save your

life?" Davin turned back around, found the flight stick and sent the shuttle starboard, across the prison and away from the frigate. "Doesn't make much sense to me."

"Because you're a renegade. A random. I have family. Friends. People Heath said he'd go after if I didn't."

"The man lies, Zoelie."

"The man has androids, Davin."

"If there's not a bomb on the shuttle," Merc ventured, "then we're good, captain."

Folding his arms, Davin centered himself against the console, put his back to the stars and stared at the crew he'd dragged with him on this little revenge mission.

"I'm saying, you got me and Phyla on here. Best pilots in the solar system, if I'm being fair," Merc said. "That frigate's going to be manned with auto guns or a few Eden burnouts that couldn't crack the front lines." Merc's grin grew as he talked. "Even if we're in a crap boat like this one, they won't touch us."

"We won't let them," Phyla affirmed. "Not after all this."

"I was going to suggest going back, getting in the *Jumper*," Davin said. "Can't imagine Heath's going to open up his docking bays for us."

"He won't have to," Mox said from the back. "You already gave us an opening. I'll make sure it's big enough."

Zoelie, Phyla ushering her out from her seat and into the shuttle's aisle, where Mox came up to guide her, with all the kind certainty that said a wrong move would be her last, shook her head and cursed again.

"Heath's going to—" Zoelie started, only for Davin, ceding his half to Merc, to put a heavy hand on her shoulder.

"Heath's not going to do a damn thing. He's going to watch this shuttle crash dive into his ship, panic, and forget you ever existed." Davin threw on his scoundrel charm. "And by the time he remembers, he'll be dead."

"Bingo," Merc added. "Now, if you'd all strap in, this is going to get a little crazy."

Davin found his spot in the first row, leaned forward with his elbows on his knees to watch his two favorite pilots put on a show. Merc took the primary controls, with Phyla volunteering to dance with the shuttle's shields and auxiliary systems. The Eden craft wasn't quite the crap box they'd flown up from Earth in, its role on Heath's frigate giving it stiffer shields, heavier plating, and a single light turret up on top.

Just enough firepower to clear riffraff from a hot landing zone.

Merc kept Davin's spur-of-the-moment starboard course, letting the shuttle wrap most of the way around the prison before pushing it into a steep dive. Earth's blue majesty conquered the dark, save for the prison's dagger edge off the starboard side. The shuttle hummed as Merc throttled up the engines near max.

"Going to smash us into Earth?" Zoelie asked. "Do Heath's job for him?"

"Dolphin kick," Merc replied, not looking back. Phyla whistled. "You ever fly a real ship, maybe you'll learn some real moves."

The namesake maneuver started as they hit the prison's bottom point, Merc pushing the engines past their safe point for a hot second. He pushed the flight stick forward, the shuttle shoving Earth out of view as the craft tumbled in a hundred-eighty-degree spin.

"Firing now," Phyla said, tapping on the console.

Flashes lit the shuttle's windshield as the craft completed its turn, now looking right back at the space prison's bulk. Fiery glows in reds, blues, and whites flared and dissipated, save for the shuttle's laser, which bounced into the space prison's shields. Those added to the crashing light as Merc kept the throttle up, the shuttle working to kill its velocity and head back up. The craft rattled, the outside continued to spark, and they drew real, real close to the space prison's bulk.

"Think we got their attention?" Merc asked.

"Think so," Phyla replied. "Now let's see what they do with it."

A splash, a reverse, and a sudden charge. The dolphin kick done right distracted the target, earned a response, and Heath's frigate didn't disappoint. The big ship had been hanging in orbit near the space prison, but now its engines added their glow to Earth's shiny glory. The frigate's nose began a slow rotation towards them, a move that'd bring the ship's hefty forward batteries to bear.

It also put a particular crash zone right in their sights.

"Here's where it gets fun," Merc said. "Ready, Phy?"

"Been too long since I hit someone in the mouth."

If Heath's pilots suspected the move, they sure did nothing to dodge it. Davin, downing another round of painkilling pills pilfered from the Centurion's aid kits, tried not to blink as the shuttle bore down on the frigate. Merc and Phyla bucked the small ship, chasing the frigate's shots so any corrections would send the fat lasers wide. A strategy that'd work until the frigate's gunners figured out the play.

Too bad they didn't have time.

"Mox, get up front," Phyla said, taking calling duties while Merc handled the juking. "We're going in backside first."

"Brutal," murmured the Eden pilot.

Davin agreed, and that sentiment bore out three minutes later. Mox stayed in the slim aisle splitting the seat rows, clutching the chair behind Davin's neck, and so they both had a great view as the frigate's busted bridge, still boasting the wrecked remnants of Davin's first stolen shuttle, filled the windshield. Makeshift sealant swamped the crash sight, goo-like substance filling all the gaps. Might not be a full seal, but close enough to keep a bad leak.

All that work, waiting to be ruined.

Heath's gunners had proved their ineptitude, failing to score any significant hits, which let Merc slide the engines and flip the shuttle. A nauseating turn followed by a crunching crash. Davin's head whipped forward, back, and his stomach threatened to toss those oh-so-necessary pills.

"Looks empty," Merc said, flipping off the shuttle's various doomsaying alarms. "Engines are damaged, but they'll still spew heat."

"Fire anyway," Phyla ordered. "We scorch the room."

"You're insane," Zoelie snapped. "You might blow us all apart!"

"Androids don't need air to breathe. Heath might've sent them in here. You'll do better if they're all melted first, believe me."

Davin nodded, felt the shuttle hum as Merc turned up the main engines while firing the maneuvering jets in reverse. The craft tried to shiver free, might've if Merc hadn't kept pushing it into the frigate's thicker hull. The scraping sounds tore at Davin's ears. Flames licked the forward windshield before dwindling oxygen stole them all away.

"Think that's all the burn we're going to get," Merc said, killing the thrust before the shuttle forced through a rough escape. "Not seeing anything out there, though."

"Then mask up," Davin said, "and let's get off this boat."

Mox led the way, kicking off the shuttle into zero gravity. Everyone else followed, including the Eden pilot, who wore the shuttle's only emergency evac suit. The bulky things made fighting hard, made a sudden, back-stabbing change of heart harder, so Davin pushed the donning and told her to go behind Mox, with Davin at her heels. Merc would bring up the rear, rifle ready.

The same thick doors Davin had conned his way through

last time stared at him again, the bridge around them now thoroughly destroyed. The combined wreckage of two shuttles and a few dozen terminals drifted around, illuminated by sputtering lights left by repair crews. If Davin had been worried about mashing some innocent engineers in the landing, he found no evidence there'd been anyone here. The only blood left in the place lay splattered on the right side, a remnant from Davin's own collision.

"Quiet," Mox said, bounding towards the door.

Gravity's absence came as a surprise: big ships like the frigate could rotate when they wanted to keep boots on the ground. Imperfect, but more practical than the other main solution scattered throughout space travel in magnetized clothes and shoes. The *Jumper* kept things floaty, so Davin and the Nines adapted well enough to the weightless drift, but Zoelie flopped around in her suit. Merc couldn't suppress a laugh.

"Focus," Phyla said, her voice coming through the comms into their ears. "Mox made a good point. No alarms. No crew, rescue or otherwise, coming through to shoot us."

"Means Heath is nice enough to let us leave vacuum," Davin replied. "Break us through, Mox."

"Working on it."

Phyla threw Davin a glance, which, even with the oxygen mask taming the worst of her suspicion, had an obvious tint. This ambush was already too easy. The frigate's gunners had failed to pierce a predictable strategy, and now, despite taking time to get out of the ruined shuttle, nobody bothered to blast the Nines in this coverless, floating bridge?

Davin could worry about a nefarious plan, but it was easier to assume Heath was an overconfident moron.

Mox skipped his fists this time, angling for a scrap metal piece, only for the thick doors to slide open. They stared at the lit landing beyond, empty and whistling as pressure popped.

"Don't think. Go," Merc said. "They close, we might die out here."

Merc had it right, and Davin followed Mox through the doors. Phyla and Merc jumped with the Eden pilot, the trio flying into Mox's waiting hands. The smooth floor didn't offer much traction in the zero-G confines, a factor Mox ought to have weighed in his choice: he joined the threesome and they continued in an odd ball until Mox collided with the far wall, back first. Behind Davin, the open bridge doors shut with a hard click, followed by pops as the frigate worked to replace lost air.

On a smaller ship, opening the doors like that might prompt such violent decompression as to tear the ship, and idiots like Davin caught in it, apart. The frigate's size left them all alive, though Davin figured any doubts as to Heath not having a plan were gone.

"This is his game now," Davin said as his friends righted themselves in the landing. "He'll tell us where to go next."

"And we'll listen?" Phyla asked. "Sounds like a bad plan, Davin."

The Nines captain gauged the landing. Two lifts, both shut with red keypads. The hallway running along the level's length was likewise sealed off by an emergency door. Another side room sat to Davin's left, the only opening. Inside, a quick peek revealed a lame break room and attendant lavatories.

"Welcome," Heath's voice came over the ship's broadcast as Davin shook his head at the Eden stock. All nutrient goop and cheap coffee. "Somehow, Davin, you and your crew remain a problem. You've thrown what should have been a simple plan awry, so I have nothing left. You get what you seem to want, me and the destruction of my androids. You shall not, however, hurt my crew any longer. They are leaving as we speak. As for you, come find me with the ghosts of your victims."

Davin nodded as he listened to Heath's little speech. The

man did like to hear himself talk. When it wrapped, the right lift swung open, its keypad green.

"He really cleared his ship for us?" Merc asked.

"Could've let me go with," Zoelie muttered.

"He will," Davin said. "Heath wants us. We go down the lift, you wait here, and I bet he'll give you the out."

"Think so?"

"Sure do," Davin said, then pointed a finger to the open lift. "Let's go, people. Heath wants to make this easy and I'm inclined to let him."

Concerns about traps, ambushes, and other crap weren't worth worrying over. The Nines were well beyond borrowed time by now. If something waited on the other side of the lift ride, they'd either smash it to pieces or die trying.

"You really think Heath will care about her?" Phyla asked after the lift doors closed, the small box shuttling downward.

"Nope," Davin said, "but I don't want to cover her. We take care of Heath, we can come back and get her later."

"That's mean, man," Merc said.

"I'm a practical guy, removing problems one at a time. Now, check your rifles, because the next one's almost here."

Ride a lift in Zero-G and you'd better be ready to flip to the ceiling. The Nines executed the roll in almost perfect synchrony, save Mox, who just stuck a hand over his head and let that ballast keep him level, if not comfortable. At least it was a short ride.

The lift opened onto a dark, quiet level. A bunk and block floor, meant for storage and sleep for unessential crew. Dim blue lights glowed here and there along the floor, emergency options in case power failed. Seeing as the lift worked just fine bringing them here, Davin doubted the frigate had suffered a local outage.

"Heath's got a dramatic flair," Phyla noted as they exited the lift, rifles up and at the ready.

The pilfered headlamps offered the Nines good views as

they advanced aft-ward, one floating kick at a time. Locked doors and halls offered targets, all of which Davin ignored, the fuzzy memories coming into focus.

"Do you remember, Davin, when you were first here?" Heath's voice crackled through again. "I see Phyla is with you. I offered you both peace then, a chance to end the war. A clean compromise. No more death. You rejected the offer. Instead, you injured innocents and fled to cause more carnage. You were a hero once, Davin. I was heartbroken to see you fall."

Merc stifled a laugh. "This guy's either drunk or on something I'd very much like to try."

"A game," Mox said, low and serious. "He is playing with us."

"But why?" Phyla asked.

The answer to her question would need to wait. They'd arrived at the right cargo hold, a fact made clear not through Davin's recollection but because it was the only door so far unlocked and evident. Davin stared at it. Fought off exhaustion, the ache in his leg, and tightened the grip on his rifle.

"If Heath has any androids left, they'll be in here," Davin said. "We go in, flare out. I'll advance head on."

"No, captain," Mox said. "You go right. I take the center."

Mox patted the hefty cannon and Davin couldn't deny the logic. He kicked off a step, let Mox get into position, then punched the big button on the keypad. The door whisked open, revealing more dark blue diodes, stacked crates, and a single form far back amid the stacks. Davin caught a glimpse as Mox's headlamp found the silhouette, the flash revealing an Eden uniform and nothing more. Too fast to catch anything else, but after the ship's eerie emptiness, it was nice to confirm they weren't alone.

Davin mimed zipped lips, flicked his left hand forward. Stale air and spaceship sounds filled in the senses. He slipped right, his knee continuing its dull protest. Crates, bins, and lockboxes stuffed metal shelves bolted to the floor and ceiling. Little lips kept the containers, each section labeled with a number and a name, in their spots. Shadows stayed steady around Davin's headlamp as he advanced, rifle raised. Phyla tailed him, while Merc held the exit, watching for any retreats or come-from-behind attacks.

Side-eye glances confirmed Heath's obsession with Bosser's first android attempt had been all-consuming. The boxes held parts, from extra limbs to early processors and plaskin molds. The names, Davin realized, weren't the owners, but the android models. TwoSix, OneThree, and so on, a mechanical life litany that offered up unsettling questions: were these boxes all that remained of the bots?

And wasn't that a good thing?

Even strides eventually brought Davin to the first turn, a hard corner. He steadied himself, waited for Phyla to tap his shoulder, and the pair did what they'd done so well. Davin swung out low, dipping with the rifle up while Phyla came after, aiming high. Headlamp beams illuminated a box-filled length all the way to the back wall's gray blot. Not a thing waiting for them.

Blue-white flashes lit leftward, rapid for two seconds before cutting out. Metal tore, a curse echoed, then a thump.

"Go back," Davin whispered. "I'll keep on."

"No damn way. We're together."

Phyla's tone brooked no argument, so Davin gave none, advancing as he rose back to standing. Two strides brought him to the next cross, an intersection he traversed with another low swing, though this time Phyla kept her aim down the long passage. Nobody in the cross, but Davin did spy something bulky on the ground, way back in the center. A moment's squinted inspection confirmed: Mox's laser cannon, ripped apart and tossed on the ground.

How had there not been more noise?

Either way, Davin hadn't come all this way to lose Mox.

Chasing an ambush was a sure way to get yourself killed, though, so he pulled away, motioned Phyla to keep going towards the back. His steps went faster now, every footfall padding out his sure reasoning on the split-up, the rationale that Mox could handle himself better than any of them. That Merc would see anyone coming and . . .

Do what, exactly?

Davin broke into a run, Phyla whispering his name, frustrated, but keeping up. As he passed the intersections, Davin wheeled with the rifle, keeping on the move. Nothing for the first three, and with one more until they hit the rear, Davin's light found a mark.

Heath Swane, standing over a senseless Mox. The metal man's huge frame lay facedown on the floor, headlamp blasting into the ground and haloing the pair in white. Heath turned, saw Davin's look, and as the Nines captain sighted the rifle, the man ran forward. Towards the exit, over Mox.

"Cut him off," Davin snapped, heading towards Mox.

Android heads, some with skin and some without, leered from their containers. Not a welcome addition to his nightmares. Davin crouched as he neared Mox, the headlamp showing emptiness all the way down the hall to the room's far side. He swerved as he reached the big man, sending light down the middle towards the exit.

An empty exit, no Merc in sight.

Keeping his left hand on the trigger, Davin felt for Mox's head, his breath. Hot, thin, alive. Whether Mox had been thumped hard on the head, drugged, or stunned, Davin couldn't tell. Any relief came and went, orange flashes to Davin's left suggesting Phyla had found someone to shoot.

"Hang tight," Davin whispered to Mox, starting off down the center passage.

A loud crash to Davin's left had him swiveling as he hit the next intersection. Launched in the loose gravity, Phyla flew hard and smacked the rear wall. He spun the opposite way.

The wrong body floated towards him, kicking off the shelves in near silence. Aya catapulted herself into a straight-line dive at Davin's midsection, a move that might've worked if Davin hadn't been playing the game for so long, hadn't learned to trust instinct. Instead, he had two long seconds to draw a bead, two long seconds to sight and pull the trigger.

Zero gravity could be fun, but if you bounced the wrong way, there wasn't a damn thing you could do to change your path, and Aya's path was dead in Davin's sights.

The first orange shot took her in the shoulder, the second in her chest, and the third made a ruin of her head. Davin dropped as her body floated on overhead, the lasers doing nothing to stop Aya's momentum. She ricocheted off the wall behind Davin, where Phyla had flown by just before, and clanged off.

Clanged.

Davin cursed again, spun back to Mox and bounced towards the metal man. He spun as he floated, aiming back along the central corridor. Charging up after him, kicking with all too much precision, was Heath Swane. Or rather, the man's android. Smarter than Aya's version, or perhaps just luckier, Heath's bot hadn't stranded itself into a straight line launch. As Davin turned, the android kicked the right side and zipped away off to that side. Davin let his back hit the rear wall, not far beyond Mox. He threw a look left, saw Phyla's crumpled form. Blood oozed from her, drifted into the air.

"She's alive," came Heath's voice, over the frigate's speakers. "I'm not brutal, like you are. This isn't a game, Davin. This is a reckoning. Your way against mine. The final act's arrived. Time to play your part."

CHAPTER 22
ZERO GRAVITY DASH

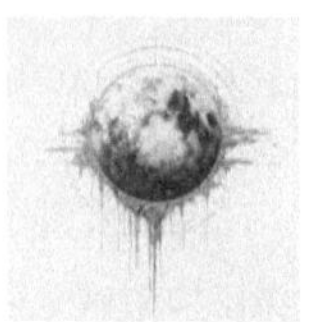

Davin didn't leave Vagrant's Hollow to solve mysteries. Running cargo, working security, or going up against maniacal goobers didn't require detective-style sleuthing, but he'd picked up a bit of insight over the years, and Heath's little end note, about Davin playing his part, tilted the scene.

He still stood near an unconscious Mox. To Davin's left, crumpled against a wall, lay Phyla. Merc . . . who knew where the fighter pilot had gone? Also, somewhere in this dark maze was an android. One that probably should have killed Davin by now.

The connections, the stress, the too-long swirl since the prison plan had kicked off crashed in among the curiosity. Davin put his back to the wall, kept the rifle ready, and tried not to drown.

"I'll make sure they live, Davin," Heath's voice came back up. "But you, you cannot. A forfeit, a price to pay for all the pain you've caused."

"What is it with you and your proclamations, Heath?" Davin grumbled, too low for anyone to hear.

"Walk out of here, Davin. Into the hallway. The lighting is better there."

Davin squinted at the doorway on the bay's other side. Took a breath, raised his voice. "What in the hell are you talking about, Heath?"

"I thought I had a dream. Humanity's perfect protector. No judgment, always ready, never making mistakes," Heath continued. Davin, perhaps in spite of himself, kicked off the wall, started the slow flight forward. "We found it's a lot harder to cover our problems. Androids aren't human, but then, they are in a way. Reflections of the people who built them. You proved we were far from that goal."

"Glad I could help."

Davin drifted over Mox, saw the big man still breathing. Yet, did Mox's hands move? A knee rise? If so, better not to stop, give anything away.

Heath's android didn't make an appearance, so Davin kicked forward again. The headlamp swiveled in the dark, catching bins full of body parts.

"Success in our worlds comes from adaptation, Davin. Change to suit the circumstance, and that's what I've done here. You've already seen the best way. Copies. Of you, me, and every person of any value. Eden will profit, yes, but more, the research will continue. I'll never have to stop again."

"Always about you, isn't it?"

"Of course it is. We're the star of our own lives, aren't we? You certainly enjoy the spotlight, Davin. I've decided I'd quite like my turn in it, albeit for a real accomplishment. Not accidental celebrity."

The exit door grew near. Heath's android hadn't show up yet. Neither had Merc. The dim blue diodes marking the transition seemed a poor gateway between worlds.

"But I understand you're not in the charity business. So I'm making a proposition. I'm done trying to kill you, trying to undermine your band. Whether you have some divine protection or too much skill, I can't seem to win this way. It's time to try something new."

Davin floated through the doorway, into the hall. To the left, the corridor continued in night-like gloom deep to the frigate's aft, where Heath's crew would be evacuating. To the right . . . Merc, hanging limp in the air. Adrift without gravity, eyes glassy. Breathing.

Behind the pilot stood Heath. Another android, or the real one?

"Heath?" Davin asked, raising the rifle.

"Shoot me, and your friends die," Heath replied, putting a hand on Merc's shoulder, pulling the drifting pilot down to cover his body. "We'll fire on the prison, obliterating it too."

"You'd start a war with—"

"I don't care, Davin. I don't care. I'll be dead if you do that anyway, and the people on my team believe in the same dream I do."

The hair on Davin's neck rose. Androids didn't have dreams. If Heath was out here, then his android definitely waited back in the cargo chamber. Angling to make a move.

"Then what's your play?"

"Shoot me," said Heath, only not the Heath by Merc, but the android. The one floating out next to Davin in the doorway. The robot had his hands raised. "Do that, and your friends get to live."

"Now," the real Heath said. "No more talking. Shoot, and your Nines survive."

"And me?"

"You'll be charged, convicted, and killed, Davin. But I think you knew that, coming out here. So go on. Press the trigger. Save your crew, like you've always done."

Easiest request ever. Davin pulled the rifle's trigger, lanced another brilliant orange bolt right into the android's chest. Right where Heath had moved the processors. The android didn't scream, moan, or twitch. Those connection severed in a millisecond, zero-G keeping the machine afloat as its joints went limp.

"And now," Heath said, "I have you. Murder, cold blood."

"That wasn't," Davin said, swiveling and putting the real Heath in his sights. "This might be."

Heath shoved Merc ahead, the unconscious pilot hitting Davin's weapon and knocking aside his aim. Davin elbowed Merc aside, pulled up the rifle. Heath, kicking, flew fast down the frigate's cargo corridor. The man banked right, rebounded off the wall to cut across into the lift, and Davin shot again.

Hit again.

Hard to tell how bad, whether Heath's insides were molten mush or if Davin had grazed the man, seeing as Heath's momentum kept him right on floating into the lifts. Sparing a pitying glance for Merc, Davin kicked after Heath, bounding along the hallway, angling left, and seeing one lift door close.

And another one open.

Eden soldiers. Armed, armored, and with weapons out. What might've been a tidy exit from the lift was complicated by gravity's absence, their kicks and pushes bunching them up. Davin, flying into the landing lobby, fired at random. The rifle spat, scoring hits on the ground, the lift doors, and the ceiling while Davin tried to right himself. He imagined it looked either ugly or hilarious, depending on the perspective, but for the Eden soldiers, it was a step too far: they backed into the lift, the soldiers in back grabbing the uniforms of their forward friends to stop momentum.

Davin hit the wall between both lifts feet first, bunched his legs and kicked back towards the corridor. He flipped again off the jump, spraying more shots at the lift and the six or so bodies crowded inside. If the first round went wide by chance, these went wide by choice.

Heath's crew had been undertrained, had been toyed

with, and were working the paycheck game. If they shot back at Davin, he'd do what he had to. Until then, like Zoelie, these morons deserved to go home to their families and find another job.

"I'm such a saint," Davin muttered, angling his hit on the corridor's wall to kick back down towards the cargo bay.

Greeting him, looking at the smoking corpse of Heath's android, was a bleary Mox. He had Phyla under one arm, Merc in the other. Tired eyes asked the right question.

"All a setup," Davin said. "We gotta go aft, to the other lifts."

"You didn't get him?"

"I had a shot, I took it. Probably ruined his day."

"Not his life?"

"A man can dream, Mox."

The exoskeleton gave Mox a hefty edge when it came to launching down a long hallway. Doorways gave kick-off points, Davin following the metal man's lead as they zipped along like a pair of discount superheroes towards the frigate's aft end. Every few breaths, Davin would squeeze a few bolts back down the corridor without bothering to look.

If he hit anyone without aiming, their luck was so bad they deserved it. Otherwise, the cautious batch would hopefully stay away.

That strategy didn't work for the frigate's aft lifts, whose own class of dubious recruits came drifting into the corridor ahead, just as confused as their counterparts. Mox, flying at them like a reckless meteor, drew panicked fire. Davin saw bolts bounce beneath, above, and around his friend, who took to pin-balling off both walls, the floor and ceiling, every bounce serving to pick up speed.

"You're gonna overshoot!" Davin yelled as they neared the lifts, the Eden soldiers dropping back into cover.

"Better than being shot," Mox roared in reply.

The frigate's absolute aft lay beyond those lifts, another

bulk room probably devoted to more cargo. Food, uniforms, the like. The engines and open space would be beyond those walls. At Mox's speed, he might just find out what would happen if he—

"Keep going," Davin yelled after his friend. "Don't stop!"

Davin didn't either, bounding with abandon. The Eden soldiers must've seen Mox go by, must've thought the danger was over, because their rifles nosed into the corridor. Tough to do a snap turn without gravity, tougher still with Davin triggering warning shots their way. Those tentative pokes dashed back, and Davin flipped them the finger as he sped past the lift landing.

Turning to use the exoskeleton like a carapace, Mox pulled Phyla and Merc in close as he hit the corridor's concluding door back first. The portal crumpled, blew off sparking hinges, the flashes bright amid the deep blue diodes. Mox and his charges vanished inside, sounds of breaking equipment, twisting metal, shattering glass signaling his progress.

Figuring he wouldn't survive a similar entrance, Davin began kicking back as he approached, tilting his feet to put a heel against the walls rather than his toes. A slow stall, one touch at a time so Davin wouldn't blow out his knees—both old and one wounded—with a hard press. Lasers at last started to follow him, the shots faltering in the dark and scoring the walls.

A little like the clubs he'd visited on Deimos, excesses and rewards for his early jobs on the *Jumper*'s crew. Too long ago, that, and way more fun than this.

The aft bay didn't have android body parts, for which Davin was deeply thankful, but it did have nutrient goop. Coffee grounds. A broad mix of freeze-dried foods and drinks. All of these lovely things greeted Davin in a bouncing swirl, set free along with their cooling gizmos by Mox's smash. A pack of frozen hotdogs glanced off Davin's shoulder, spinning away into some dark corner.

"What a waste," Davin muttered, kicking into the gloom.

Mox wasn't exactly hidden. He'd come to a broken rest at the bay's back, blue diodes illuminating his cradling arms and their occupants. Merc and Phyla, battered, nonetheless looked to be breathing when Davin caught up to them. Mox himself groaned, his exoskeleton sparking at several joints around Mox's hips. All that glorious black metal bore scrapes and dents, and a small hissing noise joined those sparks.

"All that hurt?" Davin asked, wincing at the damage.

"Not pleasant," Mox said. "I've lost most of it."

"Can you move?"

"No gravity. Fine."

Mox started to curl upright when a laser crashed into the room, burning a furrow over his head. Davin spun awkwardly, and he sent a few bolts back at the attacker. They ducked behind some shattered crates, an easy choice with reinforcements close at hand.

"Keep moving, buddy," Davin said, easing himself forward to lay down covering fire.

The metal man made ear-wincing noises as he moved, his exoskeleton grinding against the ground, the back wall. Davin felt Mox lurch behind him, kick off into another crate forest. As Mox went, Davin followed, walking in reverse.

A single through line on each level. Davin knew Heath's frigate by now, understood the cargo bay they were in had a single exit, one that'd be swarming with Heath's clean-up crew. An all-out charge by one man, admittedly a fearsome and incredibly skilled one, didn't pitch good odds.

"We need another way out," Mox said, voicing the obvious as they reached the bay's aft, starboard corner.

"Remember that prison break?"

"Which one?"

"Miner Prime," Davin said. "Though we did break out of Eden Prime too, didn't we? What's with Prime names and prisons? Seems a weird coincidence—"

"Focus, Davin."

"Sorry, adrenaline."

Davin's heart was bopping along to a fast beat right then, scurrying about as Davin chased shadows with the rifle's point. Eden's grunts were playing smart tactics, though. Advancing slow, easy. The sort of play you'd make with your marks trapped.

If only.

"How much do you trust our friends?" Davin asked. "Viola, Opal?"

"With my life."

"Good man, Mox. Me too. I say we give them a chance to prove it."

"Davin?"

"Time to see if these Eden soldiers have any spines. My guess is no."

"Don't get yourself killed, Davin."

The captain threw his man a wink, one shadowed by several wide orange lasers. Get himself killed?

Not a chance.

CHAPTER 23
FLAWED VICTORY

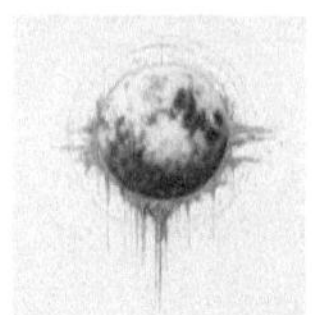

I f you wanted a spectacular light show, just get yourself attacked by a couple squads of feckless Eden soldiers. They seemed to think their best odds lay in blasting every swirling bit of food let loose in the frigate's back bay, the flashes well wide of Davin, Mox, and the still senseless Phyla and Merc.

Davin had his own rifle ready, angled back towards the approaching Eden soldiers, and found no curses coming to his lips. No sarcastic quips either. Mox had crashed in here thanks to gravity's momentum, and Davin had followed. No other exits meant they were trapped.

Meant he'd have to find a new gambit.

"Think I've still got it?" Davin asked his friend. Mox, wincing at the continued sparks coming off his busted hip and the exoskeleton attached to it, only gave a dire chuckle. "I'll take that as a yes."

"Sure, Davin."

Any further conversation, any reminiscing over past choices in their long intertwined lives wasn't going to happen here. Every breath came with burning bits as molten cargo and ash drifted by. The Eden killers were closing, and they wouldn't keep missing forever.

"Then wish me luck."

Davin threw the rifle as he took the first floating bound away from Mox. The weapon drifted free, floating up and away, a modern white flag. The soldiers shot at it, one getting lucky. Sheared in two with the shot, Davin's rifle popped like a tiny star, as good a signal as any for the captain to announce himself.

"We surrender," Davin called out into the laser-scarred bay. "We're unarmed."

His voice, like a light to insects, drew the Eden soldiers around him. Almost a dozen nozzles, some glowing hot from recent fire, angled towards Davin's face, his chest, his legs. Some soldiers drifted in the air, catching themselves on friends or battered shelving. It was, Davin considered, the most surrounded he'd ever been.

"Kill him," came the words before Davin could find a leader to address. Heath's voice poured from the frigate's intercom, with the bland certainty of someone bored with apparent victory. "He's a danger to me, to you, to this company."

"A little murder, Heath?" Davin stepped on the Eden captain's words, trying to get in front of any deadly instincts. "Still a crime this close to Earth, so far as I know, and there'd be a lot of witnesses."

When Heath didn't reply, Davin realized the speakers didn't go both ways. Not without Davin scooting himself closer to the mic, back near the bay's door.

"Orders are orders," one soldier said. "I say we off him."

"You know who this guy is? He stopped Bosser," said another, drawing Davin's nod and a single pointing finger. "It's been a while, but we'd be in trouble if this ever got out."

"Eden won't help you, either," Davin said. A good captain sensed the momentum shifting, shoved it right along.

"They're a big company. You're a few soldiers. They'll cast it as a bad lot, let you rot in that space prison I just left, and that place isn't any peach, let me tell you."

More nervous shifting. Too many fingers were too close to their rifles, though. Davin needed to end this, call it before someone did something stupid.

"Take me to Heath," Davin said. "The man wants me dead, let him do it. Then he's holding the risk."

Illustrate the danger and deliver a solution, the tried-and-true methods of a smart man like himself.

The Eden soldiers were all too happy to take him up on it.

The escort all the way to Heath was not done quietly. Mox, Phyla, and Merc were shepherded in behind Davin, while Heath narrated the floating procession with demand after demand to just shoot the Nines and get it over with.

If only he'd kept those androids around.

The Eden commander waited on the frigate's secondary bridge, the same small one Davin had visited earlier in his more reckless one-man assault. Back then, the frigate had been scurrying to deal with the shuttle crash. Now, most of the bridge was empty, and Davin was even more exhausted.

Heath wasn't alone, joined now by his right-hand lieutenant and another one of her android copies. Aya's robot version held a stiffer pose, lacked her biological counterpart's constant curiosity.

Those wide, studying eyes broke Aya into a head shake and a small smile as she took in the floating quartet, backed by Eden soldiers and their omnipresent rifles.

Behind her, the small bridge mimicked its bigger brother with a central platform and several desks dominated by terminals and their bright screens. To a one, left empty by Heath's evacuation efforts, they shone Eden's forest-green *E* logo.

Davin preferred the view outside the glassy viewport, stretching across the bridge's front-facing wall. The big ship faced Earth, always a beautiful sight.

"Always with the tricks," Heath said by way of a greeting. The man held a huge bandage to his side. "I didn't expect that shot to strike, Davin."

"Everyone seems to think I'm terrible in a fight, but hey, this old dog's still got it."

"I can attest to that," Aya murmured. "Ganymede will forever live in my nightmares, Davin."

"Aww, you're dreaming of me?"

Aya's smile only grew. "Soon, you'll be just dreams." Her eyes flicked back to the Eden soldiers. "You can leave us. Better if you're not witnesses."

This, at least, was one order the Eden soldiers were fine obeying. They kicked back, slipped through the doors, which whisked shut and left Davin, with a downed Mox and two wounded colleagues, at his back. Both Merc and Phyla were stirring, though, a fact that did not go unnoticed.

"Make it quick," Heath said, gesturing towards Aya's android. "This has gone on long enough."

"Not yet, it hasn't," Davin answered. "Still have some questions, Heath."

"Dead men don't need answers."

"You're not dead yet."

The reply drew glances back from both Aya and her bot, which had made one lethal stride towards Davin.

"I don't plan to be dead for some time," Heath said. "Unlike—"

"Look behind you, buddy."

See, Earth was always beautiful, but hanging against that big blue ball was something better still. The prettiest ship Davin had ever seen flew into view, a big dark shadow against the planet.

"See, the Jumper's loaded with weapons and more than a

few people who'd love to vaporize you, Heath," Davin said. "Which means you have one choice to make."

"And that is?"

"How you want to die. You can have your android kill me here, and you'll join me a minute later, or you can resign this whole thing now. Call it quits. I'm betting, if you kill the android project, Alissa might get you a comfy retirement package."

Hard to read a man's face from his back, but Heath's shoulders told enough of the story. Their gradual slump marked weighing options, heavy decisions, and—

"You're already dead, Heath," Aya said, quiet. "Davin killed you, remember? This was the plan."

"Not the real me," Heath mumbled, his hand pressing into the bandage. "The video undercuts Davin, you take the reins in public, and I—"

Heath turned his head, sharpened a look Aya's way. Whatever words he might've said next turned into a gurgle as Aya's android grabbed Heath's throat, tightened its grip, and broke the man's neck.

"Such a tragedy," Aya said. "Heath Swane was a visionary."

The android let Heath go, the man's body bobbing. Gravity really did make things better. Davin folded his arms.

"Well, not what I expected," Davin said. "Can't say I'm too torn up by it."

"Then your offer stands?" Aya asked, turning back to Davin.

"You walk into the sunset, Heath takes the blame?"

"The blame, the focus. You've already cost me enough." Aya spread her arms, as if to show off a body rendered scarred, though the Eden uniform covered it. All save her face and its plaskin repairs. "We were scientists, Davin. In search of perfection. Heath lost the way. I haven't."

Before Davin could reply, Aya gave another order, one

picked up by her android and acted on. The machine turned to the standing terminal, always a feature of these central platform bridges, and tapped away.

"What're you doing?" Davin asked, plenty relieved to get away from Aya's meandering.

"Showing you this isn't a trick."

A face appeared on the screen, a cityscape visible in the background. Alyssa, looking far from tortured. Bright, healthy, and wielding a placid smile.

"Davin," Alyssa said. "I've been waiting for this call."

The words warped the Nines captain. He thought Alyssa had been captured, killed, or, at best, escaped to a squalid hideaway in the remaining bits of the rainforest. Yet none of those things appeared true. She seemed to be fine, to be comfortable, to be in a place where . . .

"Why?" Davin asked, his voice almost breaking with the question. "What is all this, why is all this happening if you're there, if you're okay?"

"Aya told me," Alyssa answered without hesitation, as if Davin's question had been expected, planned for. "After you landed on their frigate the first time. She didn't think Heath would succeed, and wanted to find an exit."

Davin squinted at the screen, Aya and her android standing off to the side. Behind him, leaning against the wall, Mox cursed. Phyla and Merc remained senseless.

"How many androids did you destroy?" Aya asked. "Prisoners? You really believe a collection of prisoners could wipe out so many of our machines?"

"Aya sent the update, Davin. We've confirmed it here. She neutered their reflexes, their killer instincts. Not so much to be obvious, but enough to give you a chance."

"You're both assholes," Davin snarled. "People died for your game."

"More would have if Heath had won," Alyssa shot back. "I've watched so many die in this fighting, Davin. Aya's given us a way out. The end to all this. Proof that Eden's lost its way. That it needs new leadership, someone willing to make peace with us, and move the solar system forward."

"Doesn't do a damn thing for my crew."

"They'll live, Davin. You'll get paid, too. Your Nines will be taken care of. You'll never have to fight again." Alyssa tilted her head. "This is the only choice, now. The war's over. Say yes, Davin. And get yourself a drink."

The urge to raise his hand, send a signal to the Jumper to annihilate the bridge rose up, a tempting wraith twisting behind his eyes, but a whimper chased the thought away. Phyla, waking up, coming back into the pain.

He owed her. Owed his crew. Owed, if Davin was being perfectly honest, himself.

"What's going to happen?" Davin asked.

"I'll let Aya explain. There's a lot to do now. Thank you, Davin. Earth already owed you, and now so does Mars, Ganymede, and all of us."

Aya did explain, only after calling up the frigate's crew to stations. For medical staff to come to the bridge and tend to Phyla, Merc, and Mox.

Heath's recorded death would be broadcast, along with his many threats. Alyssa, with the backing of Earth's governments, would spin down Eden's military programs. The company would revert to building, expanding, and supporting human colonization of the solar system.

Aya herself, of course, would take over Heath's accounts. Android work, strictly peaceful, would continue. There would be no trials, no prison time, no dumping innocents out of airlocks. The last of Eden's warmongers would be discarded, and humanity would welcome a bright new dawn.

"She said that, really?" Phyla said, days later, with a fizzing silver cocktail in hand. She leaned on a table with Davin, who made short work of his own beverage.

Neal's looked as it always had, the tumbling psychedelic backdrop as good as any to welcome Phyla back to normal life.

"More than once," Davin said. "Alyssa repeated it too. It's like a chance at peace turns everyone into walking cliches."

"But not you."

"One of a kind," Davin said. "Just like our crew."

The Nines were there too, mucking up the dance floor. Opal and Merc swung each other around with precision while planets and stars whirled beneath their feet. Viola and Riley played budding romance's first beats, with Puk, rebuilt, hovering overhead. Mox would be showing up any minute, exoskeleton back in working order, with Latrice in tow.

"I don't believe them," Phyla said. "The war might end, but the fighting won't. There's too much money in it."

Davin nodded, swirled his empty glass on the table.

"One thing I can't quite place, you know?"

"What's that?"

"Alyssa dragged us all the way to Quito, only for us to get caught. She escapes, gets her little ducks in a row, then right when we're ready to blast it all to Hell, she shows up again. Not a damn scratch on her."

"Davin," Phyla warned, "You go digging too deep that direction, you might find things you don't want to know."

"Like maybe certain people aren't who, or what—"

Neal's door swung open, the metal man filling its bulk with a broad, beaming smile on his face. His exoskeleton gleamed, and Mox bellowed an order for another round, a request the bartenders took with unfazed aplomb.

"We got paid, we did the job," Phyla said. "Cassidy's good. You even kept your promise to Zoelie. We've earned a rest, Davin, and I need to get back on the bullets, or my ranking's going to drop."

"Leave it alone and enjoy life, is that what you're saying?"

"Yes, Davin." Phyla stretched a hand across the table, pulled towards her. "I'm saying we've got something good here. I plan on enjoying it." She kissed him something fierce. "You going to join me?"

How could he say no?

———

Get in fast. Rescue the VIP. Get out. Sever Squad is outnumbered, outgunned, and every second spent on Dynas ticks them closer to a fiery end.

When a strange rescue signal comes in, Sever Squad gets the call. They're tough, reckless, and one carries a giant hammer. Except this mission's different: the signal's calling for help, but the planet's deserted.

Oh, and Sever's home ship can't wait for them. If they want to get off-world with their rescue, they'll have to find their own way to fly.

Begin a new action-packed sci-fi adventure with *Drop Zone*:

ABOUT THE AUTHOR

A.R. Knight spins stories in a frosty house in Madison, WI, primarily owned by a pair of cats. After getting sucked into the working grind in the economic crash of the 2008, he found himself spending boring meetings soaring through space and going on grand adventures.

Eventually, spending time with podcasting, screenplays, short stories and other novels, he found a story he could fall into and a cast of characters both entertaining and full of heart.

A.R. Knight plans on jumping through to other worlds and finding new stories to tell in the limitless borders of our imagination.

Thanks, as always, for reading!

For Angela